Praise for

Promise of the Hills is a heartwarming tale of mature love and understanding. The characters, a devoted couple, Brax and Dae, and Ty, the young boy they take into their lives, all leap off the page and grab you by the heart. But some of the locals are not who they seem, and when Brax helps untangle a crime with dark undertones, their small town is turned upside down. A warm and satisfying read."
—LYNDA FITZGERALD, author of the
Sunshine State Mystery Series

Promise of the Hills is the love story of a couple in the autumn of their lives who find fulfillment by taking risks and making hard choices."
—MARY ANNA BRYAN, author of *Cardinal Hill,* winner of the 2015 Ferrol Sams Literary Award

Michael K. Brown has given us a winner—an intimate snapshot of the emotional journey of two lives challenged by adversity. Confronting the most horrific episodes of human-behavior, we're swept into the outcome of hope and finally, peace, in the lives of a southern family and a young boy desperately in need of the love he seeks. The true values of courage and commitment become palpable before leaving the reader with a smile of satisfaction and a tear of happiness
—STAN WAITS, Georgia Writers Association award winning author of *Another Long Hot Day*

Promise of the Hills is an absorbing modern novel of a beautifully-unveiled late-in-life love story, coupled with a subplot that becomes more bizarre. Set in the Georgia mountains, it also introduces a subject people don't want to talk about, especially in small towns, though such stories are all around us. It sends the protagonists to delve unexpectedly into solving a mystery, with plenty of twists-and turns that keep you alert. Michael K. Brown keeps the reader engaged with his effortless style of writing.

—**ELLIOTT BRACK**, veteran newspaperman, author, and current editor of *Gwinnett Forum*

Everybody loves a love story but when it's interwoven with mystery, drama, family angst and even a sinister presence, the reader gets hooked early on. Michael Brown's Promise of the Hills portrays the depths of a late in life relationship with a heart-touching story set against the picturesque backdrop of Low Country tides and mountainside green spaces. His poignant ending leaves you satisfied that the story has been richly told with lingering hope that it will be continued."

—**BARBARA JACKSON RYAN**, Low Country Publishing

PROMISE *of the* HILLS

PROMISE *of the* HILLS
Michael K. Brown

DEEDS PUBLISHING

Copyright © 2015—Michael K. Brown

ALL RIGHTS RESERVED - No part of this book may be reproduced in any form or by any electronic or mechanical means, including information storage and retrieval systems, without permission in writing from the author, except by a reviewer who may quote brief passages in a review.

Published by Deeds Publishing
Athens, Georgia
www.deedspublishing.com

Library of Congress Cataloging-in-Publications Data is available upon request.

ISBN 978-1-941165-83-6

Books are available in quantity for promotional or premium use. For information, write info@deedspublishing.com.

First Edition

10 9 8 7 6 5 4 3 2 1

ACKNOWLEDGEMENTS

I EXTEND MY SINCERE GRATITUDE TO MY LONG TIME WRITING partners Barbara Connor and Mary Anna Bryan for their help in developing this novel into its final form. Many thanks as well to members of the Atlanta Writers Club Collective critique group including Ken Schmanski, Linda Fitzgerald, Kerry Denney, Lorraine Norwood, Kristine Ward, Richard Bowman, and Glen Emery. Their input and suggestions were invaluable. And the proofreading by Mary Kirkland was thorough and very helpful. Finally, I could never accomplish any of my writing goals without the support and encouragement of my wife, Judy, who also happens to be an excellent proofreader and objective critic.

I am also indebted to Bob, Jan, and Mark Babcock at Deeds Publishing for providing me the opportunity for this story to be told.

The Appalachian region of our country holds a particular attraction to me; the beautiful landscape, the traditional music, the down to earth people. For that, I thank the Good Lord.

For Mitchell, Chandler, and Derek.

"You must live in the present, launch yourself on every wave, find your eternity in each moment. Fools stand on their island of opportunities and look toward another land. There is no other land; there is no other life but this."

—Henry David Thoreau

1

AT LAST, THE MAN IS DEAD.

That was the first thought that flashed into Brax Donovan's mind. He set the phone down on the side table and leaned back in the recliner. *I thought you would want to know*, the caller had said. Of course, he wanted to know. Though he tried to deny his feelings, Brax had waited for that day to come. The news wasn't surprising nor, in a way, even sad. The end of a life can be a blessing to those who suffer, he reasoned. The thought didn't assuage his guilt for finding a sense of satisfaction in John Whitehead's passing. Still, he didn't dwell on thoughts of the departed but rather on the widow. It had been three years since Brax had seen her and it seemed like an eternity. Yet he had never stopped loving Dae Whitehead.

He bent over and stroked the yellow Labrador retriever sitting at his feet. The dog lifted his head and Brax looked into Sunny's big brown eyes. "He's gone."

He grabbed his coffee cup and stepped onto the deck with Sunny at his side. The forest bore signs of springtime with a thin meshwork of new leaves and emerging green undergrowth. A good rain had fallen overnight and he could hear the faint gurgle of water rushing in the creek below. Two squirrels scurried up an oak tree, their claws making a familiar scratching noise on the bark. Far above, a hawk glided silently, its wings spread in graceful deception of killer instincts. Brax's skin tingled in the cool mountain air with the smell of a world turning green and he felt revived, as if returning to the fullness of life like the landscape around him. The sun peeked over a mountain in the distance, just above the fog.

The coffee had cooled to lukewarm but he savored the bitter-sharp taste of caffeine. As he drained the last drop from the cup, he tried to temper the exhilaration from learning of Dae's newly found freedom. The morning signaled the promise of a fine day and a walk in the woods offered a good way to calm his mind.

"C'mon, Sunny," he said, and headed for the steep path leading to the creek.

Wet leaves scattered in his wake as he shuffled with an unhurried gait. Sunny scampered ahead, stopping every few yards to sniff out animal scents among the plant life. The path leveled off in a hollow between two hills that captured the soothing gush of water and rustling sounds of woodsy creatures as if in a natural amphitheater. Brax stopped there when a redheaded woodpecker swooped down from behind and lit on the trunk of a poplar tree. As it pecked away at the soft bark, he admired the beautiful bird, resplendent with inky black wings tipped in white and a brilliant red head. Amidst the wild solitude, he felt a kinship to the land as if he belonged by nature in the mountains of North Georgia.

The woodpecker soon flew away and Brax began walking again, following the well-worn trail beside the creek. With Sunny tagging along, he made his way downstream for half a mile or so, past houses that clung to the hills high above both sides of the creek.

He came to a place where the water ran shallow over a bed of smooth sandstone. The hills tapered off behind him and the ground flattened out on both sides of the creek. There, he saw a young boy standing near a small circle of rocks that surrounded a pile of smoking embers.

"Hello," Brax said, from a distance.

The boy barely turned his head to reply, "Hello," and jabbed at the ashes with a stick.

Brax moved closer. "Looks like you've got it under control."

The boy continued to prod the remnants of the fire and glanced sideways at Brax.

"It's probably not a good idea to be burning around here," Brax said. "Might start a bigger fire." He raised his brows as if a gentle prod.

"Okay." The boy stopped poking the fire and turned to Brax with a guilty look.

He sensed an innocent shyness in the boy. "I'll help you make sure it's all out," he said, stepping closer. "What's your name?"

"Ty."

"That's a good name. How old are you, Ty?"

"I'm eight."

"Well, I'm a lot older than that. My name is Brax. That's short for Braxton. You ever heard of anybody named that?"

The boy looked at him curiously. "No."

"My full name is Braxton Bragg Donovan. I was named after a general in the Civil War."

The boy appeared to relax. "My whole name is Tyrus Raymond Benefield."

Brax smiled.

"I was named after Ty Cobb," the boy continued. "My daddy said he was the best player that ever lived. He's from Georgia."

"Yeah, they called him The Georgia Peach. How 'bout that? We're both named after famous people." Brax smiled again and a broad grin appeared on the boy's face. He casually took the stick from Ty's hand and poked the powdered remnants of the fire. "Where do you live?"

"On Eagle Bluff." Ty pointed behind him. "Over yonder." He lowered his head slightly but kept his eyes on Brax. "My mother said not to talk to strangers."

"Your mother's right, but I won't hurt you. I'll leave if you want me to."

"No, that's alright. You come here sometimes?"

"Yeah, sometimes."

Ty looked at Sunny nosing around the creek bed. "Is that your dog?"

"Yeah, his name is Sunny." Brax slapped his leg and made a sucking sound to call Sunny to him. "You can pet him. He's friendly."

Ty ran a hand over the Lab's back, barely touching the fur. Sunny lifted his head and licked the boy's hand. Ty pulled his hand away and turned to Brax. "My daddy won't let me have a dog."

"Maybe when you're older," Brax said.

Ty looked around, as if to see they were still alone. "Can I go?"

"Sure. I'll take care of the fire."

Ty began to walk away. He turned and spoke with his head down. "I wish I had a dog." He picked up his pace and quickly broke into a full run. "My daddy's mean," he said, loud enough for Brax to hear. He jumped a small ditch and disappeared down a weedy two-rut road.

Brax peered at the vacant road for a few seconds, wondering what to think of the boy's parting words. He bent down to the fire pit and tried to pick up some remnants of burnt paper on the outer edge of the ashes. They crumbled in his hands.

He stirred the ashes but couldn't identify anything in the pile. There were no wrappers, food container, or drink cans—things that usually wind up in a small fire in the woods. Maybe, he thought, it's just a secret place to play with fire as most boys like to do.

Brax gathered some wet, sandy dirt from the creek bank and tossed it on the ashes. Two more trips finished the job. He lingered for a while to see if anyone else showed up and then headed back to his house. After walking only twenty yards or so, he noticed a small pile of litter mixed among the underbrush beneath a wild holly bush. The sun penetrated the thin camouflage of holly leaves, revealing small tatters of paper. The shreds had unevenly ripped edges with burn marks and were obviously torn from larger sheets. It appeared as if the wind had blown them from the nearby fire circle. He bent down and stuck an arm through the prickly limbs to gather as much of the paper as he could hold in one hand.

When he retrieved a handful, the largest piece caught his eye. A fragment about the size of a dollar bill revealed a smoke-stained photograph. It took him a few seconds to put it in perspective and figure out what he was looking at. But he could make out enough human body parts to give him a shiver. He looked around again to make sure he was alone.

He stuffed the handful of paper into his pocket and reached into the holly once more, gathered all but the smallest of the remaining bits, and put them into the other pocket. As he continued home with solemn directness, he was oblivious to Sunny's whereabouts or the environment around him. Instead, he wrestled with thoughts of the dark side of humanity.

At home, he put his glasses on and spread the scraps of paper on the kitchen table. Meticulously fitting some of the tatters together like a jigsaw puzzle with missing pieces, he put together a crude mosaic. The picture became clear enough and he stared at it for a good minute.

The image of young girls, their breasts hardly developed, engaged in oral sex with white-haired men was clearly discernable. A sickening feeling came over him and he pressed his eyes closed with his hands.

After collecting himself, he got two sheets of paper from his desk, assembled the fragments of one picture on the first sheet and carefully taped them down. Repeating the process, he taped another picture on the second sheet. Acts of vaginal and anal intercourse between the men and young women were revealed in a patchwork fashion. He pulled a thin briefcase from a closet shelf and put the two sheets inside. A kaleidoscope of questions flashed through his mind as he sat down in his recliner.

Reports of child pornography often cropped up in the media, but his mind couldn't grasp why someone would be attracted by such vileness.

With visions of the pictures stuck in his head, Brax thought about the boy he had met earlier. He recalled Ty's self-conscious demeanor and his parting words: *My daddy's mean.* Maybe he was just expressing anger for not being allowed to have a dog. Or, maybe he didn't get along with his father for whatever reason. Brax remembered rebelling against his own father and had experienced the same from his youngest son. Even though he had only met the boy for a few minutes, he sensed a stronger passion in Ty—repugnance, or worse, fear.

Then it dawned on him what kind of man would enjoy looking at young girls being sexually exploited. A mean man.

2

HANDLING THE SICKENING PICTURES LEFT BRAX FEELING DIRTY. He washed up in the bathroom, changed shirts, and then headed to the kitchen for a glass of orange juice. As he passed through the main room, he glanced at the telephone still lying on the side table and the words seemed to come from the phone once again: *John Whitehead is dead.*

He needed to clear his mind. After grabbing the juice from the fridge, he settled into his recliner and began reading Henry David Thoreau's *Walden*. He read for an hour before his thoughts returned to Dae.

Closing his eyes, he recalled seeing Dae for the first time. Her pretty face and trim figure had caught his eye as she walked on the beach near Seaside Village, an "active adult community" on an island off the coast of Georgia. He smiled and remembered what his walking partner, Jim Hawkins, had said: "*She's a ten on the granny scale.*" Brax would learn that her name was Daedre, a family name handed down from English ancestors who had settled in the Georgia colony. But she went by Dae, as in "Day," and it somehow seemed to fit her and add to her attractiveness. She was sixty-seven at the time, but she looked much younger.

The smile faded as his thoughts flashed forward to the day they parted.

～

For almost a year they had been inseparable, even after Brax felt the sting of deception on learning of Dae's marriage. Over the Christmas holidays, they went their separate ways to spend time with their families and think about their future. The first morning back on the island, Brax waited for her in the clubhouse for their daily walk on the beach.

Dae looked radiant when she walked in wearing a bright blue sweater that accented her brunette hair and creamy complexion. But when he saw the look on her face he knew what was in her heart. He braced himself with a gulp of black coffee.

"I can't," she said.

A few tearful words, an embrace and moments later she was gone.

For the first time since they had met nine months earlier, Brax walked the beach alone that day. A stiff ocean breeze refreshed his senses and the shock of losing his lover settled into his mind. He wondered how something so good could have turned out so wrong.

When he arrived home after the walk, he heard a hard rap on the door.

Before he could respond, Jim Hawkins entered. "She's not with you."

Brax slumped into a chair. "It's over."

"Damn…" Jim dragged out the word, then stood in silence for a moment. "Well, I know you want to get drunk, so I'll leave. One smell of booze and I'd fall off the wagon like a greased pig."

"No, stay. I could use a little companionship."

Brax went to the kitchen and returned with a Coke for each of them. "Dae just can't do it. And I don't blame her. She's still married and I can't ignore that fact."

Jim fixed his eyes on Brax. "*She* ignored it for a long time. You know she lied to you and hooked you into this. Aren't you pissed about that?"

"You know I was at first. Hell, you're the one who told me she's married after finding out from that guy at the VFW. Yeah, she was wrong to hide it but she didn't know how to tell me." Brax paused with a faraway look in his eyes. "It doesn't change how I feel about her."

"I don't get it. You told me that her old man is totally out of it. He doesn't even know who she is, does he?"

"Jim, it doesn't matter what he knows. He's had Alzheimer's or some sort of dementia for years. And Dae told me their marriage was dead long before that. She said her husband was a shell of man even before he got sick. He was depressed and not all there." Brax paused and took a swig of Coke. "She's basically been a widow for a long time, but she would always feel guilty about breaking her wedding vows. I respect that and, in the long run, I'd feel guilty, too."

"Oh hell," Jim said, without a trace of empathy. "Okay, it's your life but I hate to see you give up on something that's good for both of y'all."

"Yeah, it's a kick in the ass but, hey, I can still kick back."

"So, will you two just be friends without the lovey-dovey? You're still going to see her aren't you?"

"No, I'm leaving Seaside. I told her I couldn't stay here. The temptation would be too much for both of us. It's best that we move on with our lives."

Jim set his Coke down and shook his head.

Brax forced a grin. "I'll miss you, you knucklehead."

A month later he moved from Seaside Village.

∼

Brax put the book down and went outside to refill the seed in a bird feeder. Afterward, he began pulling weeds from a flowerbed. Anything to take his mind away from the woman who taught him to love again after Jane, his wife of forty-three years, had died. Then Dae crushed his dream. But he couldn't deny it; he still loved her. Always would. He went inside to do what he knew he must.

To ignore John Whitehead's death would be disrespectful and he felt certain that Dae knew he had been notified. He took the phone from his pocket and scrolled to a number he hadn't called in three years. A rush of anxiety hit him, and he froze. What the hell was he going to say? If he were lucky, she wouldn't answer and he could just leave a voice mail. He laid the phone on the counter, grabbed a beer from the refrigerator, and took two big swigs. Fortified by a quick rush of alcohol, he picked up the phone again and walked into the den. Settled into the leather recliner with a hand firmly clasped to the arm of the chair, he stared at the highlighted name.

Then he pressed the key to call Dae.

She answered the phone on the third ring.

Brax tried to mask his apprehension with a deep voice. "Hello, stranger." He held his breath and two seconds of silence felt like an eternity.

"Brax," she said, barely above a whisper.

Hearing her say his name bridged the distance. "Yeah, it's me." The resonance returned to his voice.

"It's great to hear from you. How are you?"

"I'm still kicking." He paused. "Dae, Sally told me of John's passing and I wanted to express my sympathy."

"Thank you. It's a horrible thing to happen to anyone but he's in a better place now."

"Yeah…I think he is." He gathered his nerve and sat up in the chair as if she were there. "I feel awkward about calling you considering the way things ended between us."

"I know, but I'm glad you did. I've wanted to talk to you for a long time, but I didn't think you ever wanted to speak to me again."

"That's not true. I just didn't know what to say."

"Yes, I messed everything up. I'll never forgive myself for not telling you about my marriage. That was so selfish."

"It all worked out for the best." He covered his hurt with a lie. "It wasn't right for us to be together while John was still alive. You had more conscience about that than I did."

"I just couldn't live with myself. I'm sorry." Her voice cracked.

"No, no. Let's not relive all that."

Brax heaved his chest and exhaled a strong puff of air. "So, how are things at Seaside?"

"There are a lot of new buildings going up around us—I know you would hate that—but things haven't changed that much *so far*." She paused as if to ponder the question. "Of course, there's more traffic with all the construction. I'm sure you know that Jim moved to Warner Robins to live with his daughter."

Brax perked up at the mention of Jim Hawkins. "Yeah, we talk on the phone and he's been up here a couple of times. Says he's stayed off the booze and I believe him." He chuckled and added, "He even got set-up on e-mail and forwards me all this crap off the internet."

Her muffled laugh was audible. "I doubt he would have ever agreed to move if you were still here. He thought the world of you and he wasn't the same after you left." She delayed a second before adding in a serious tone, "A lot of people here miss you."

The implication didn't escape him. He leaned back in the chair and paused to clear the lump in his throat. "They're good folks. But life goes on and I like it up here. I live out in the boonies, but it's only a few miles from Rocky Ridge."

"I've been there. It's probably been at least ten years. It seemed like a nice little town."

"It's not bad as little towns go." He laughed.

"You left so quickly we never really had a chance to say goodbye." Her voice was warm, as if inviting him to make the first move.

He sensed her willingness yet he felt bound up in an emotional straightjacket. According to Sally Blankenship, Dae's husband had only been dead for three days and the specter of John Whitehead lying dead in a casket hovered over him. It wouldn't be right to rush things. "Well, you know," he said, "I was kind of messed up in the head. When Sally made a good offer on my place, I wanted to get out right away."

"I hated that you felt that way."

There was a moment of silence. He closed his eyes and gritted his teeth.

Dae changed the subject. "Sally's real nice. We walk together most days."

Brax felt the sting of irony and was tempted to joke about Sally replacing him in his house as well as on his daily walk on the beach. He held back. "I still walk every morning, too. Not with a pretty woman, though. Just with another old geezer like me."

"Oh, you're not an old geezer. I know how full of life you are.

I'll bet you're still playing your trumpet. I've listened to that CD you gave me more times than I should admit. I love those songs."

"I don't play much anymore. It takes a lot of energy and I'm getting too old for that. No one can accuse me of being a blowhard anymore 'cause now I can hardly blow. Can't even toot my own horn. Ha!"

"I'm glad to know you still have your sense of humor."

He could picture the smile on Dae's face and could almost feel her presence. Yet he couldn't make himself take that first step to reach out to her.

"It's been great talking to you," she said. "Please promise me you'll stay in touch."

"I will." Then Brax added the words that bridged a gap of three years. "I promise."

After leaving Seaside, Brax figured he'd live out his last days alone on the mountain outside Rocky Ridge. Now, with Dae a widow, he hoped he had been wrong about the living alone part.

～

Brax ate the microwave dinner with thoughts of Dae rolling about in his head. Their conversation that morning had gone well and he knew what would follow. It was just a matter of time, he assured himself. But what is the right amount of time? A month? Longer? Having never before felt the urge to pursue an ex-lover three days after her husband's death, he had no experience in the matter. Maybe he shouldn't worry about appearances. After all, times had changed and people looked at relationships a lot differently than they once did.

Dae had mentioned his trumpet and how much she enjoyed a CD he had given her. His enthusiasm for the instrument had tapered off since moving from Seaside and he had not blown a note in more than a year. Still, the horn was an old buddy and it had been with him in good times as well as bad. So he went into the bedroom and removed it from under the bed. He took it out of the case, ran his hands over the smooth brass, then fluttered the valves with his fingers. Raising the trumpet to his lips, he imagined he could still play with the power he once had. But instead of blowing, he hummed all the verses of *Stardust*, followed by *When I Fall in Love*. Those were the only songs on the CD he had given Dae.

Jane had loved those songs too, and she stared back at him from a bedside table. He picked up the photo and kissed the woman he had vowed to love forever. And he had been true to that vow, loving her for forty-three years and forever after that. He closed his eyes and he could see Dae, a woman he had known for less than a year before their paths separated. And he would love her forever, too. It sometimes felt strange to love two women as much as he did, but was that wrong? He didn't think so.

With the horn still in his hands, he went to the back deck. He stood there, staring trancelike into the forest, and thought back to his college days at the University of Georgia more than fifty years before. He could see Jane in the student section waving a red pom-pom. And he could see himself standing at midfield in Sanford Stadium as he raised the trumpet into position. When the Dixie Redcoat Band began the fight song, the crowd would go crazy.

He stepped to the edge of the deck and lifted the trumpet to his lips. With great effort, he managed to play an off-key chorus of, "Glory, glory to old Georgia." For just a moment, five decades disappeared and he was twenty-one again.

Sunny rose from his resting spot on the deck, looked at Brax, and let out a couple of *wuffs*. When he stopped playing, Brax was breathing heavily. A canopy of silvery-gray filled the early evening sky. The woods were thick with the shadow of night. He calmed down and heard the chirping of an unseen bird and faint sounds stirring in the woods. Soaking in the moment, he became absorbed in a feeling he often enjoyed—the companionship of solitude.

It would be even better if Dae were here.

3

A WEEK LATER, BRAX SAT IN HIS RECLINER READING HIS WELL-worn copy of *Walden*. But, for the first time, Thoreau's ruminations on solitude seemed out of tune with his own needs. He set the book in his lap, and the thought of being with Dae again stuck in his mind. *Stay in touch*, she had said, and he had promised to do that. But what did she mean? Would an attempt to rekindle their relationship be proper at this time? It took all of his willpower not to call her back and push the issue. She had been a widow for less than two weeks, and he suspected she was dealing with the same uncertainty.

A phone call from Jim Hawkins broke his reverie.

"Did you know Dae's old man passed away?" Jim asked.

"Yeah. Sally Blankenship called me."

"I just found out today. I was at my brother's place in Alabama for a week, and when I got home I had a boatload of messges on my recorder. So, what's going on? Have you talked to Dae?"

"I called her when I found out and expressed my sympathy. We chatted for a while."

"Are y'all going to get together?"

"Jim, the man's only been dead ten days. I'm not going to dance on his grave."

"Nah, you won't do that. But he hadn't really been alive for years."

"I can't look at it that way—and neither can Dae. We had a good conversation but it's been three years since I've seen or talked to her. I'll have to see how things go."

"She's waiting," Jim said. "I got to know her pretty well after you left, and I know how she feels about you."

"In due time," Brax said.

"It's time now. There's a time for spittin' and a time for gettin'. It says so right there in the Bible—Ecclesiastes, I think. And this is a time for gettin', so go for it."

"I didn't realize you were such a biblical scholar. I'm impressed. But it's a little too soon."

"Well, don't wait too long. Us old cocks can't crow forever, you know."

Jim hit home with that comment. Brax knew his friend was right. At his age, time wasn't on his side.

After Jim's call, Brax's mind was wrapped in a ball of indecision, and he needed to rid his thoughts of Dae for a while. He opened the book again and Thoreau's words spoke to him, not of solitude, but of vigor for life.

He put the book aside and left the house to begin the trek down the steep path to the creek. Sunny romped ahead in tail-wagging enthusiasm. At the bottom of the hill, Brax stopped at the creek bank and watched the water flow over the rocks. Nearby, a wild turkey crept through the underbrush. In the distance, two white-tail deer bounded up a high ridge with the grace of leaping ballet dancers. The soothing sound of the water cleared his mind of all other thoughts. Time hung in the air like gossamer as Brax stood mesmerized by what Thoreau called the genius of nature.

The spell was broken when he saw a figure in the distance

from the corner of his eye. Turning, he recognized Ty who had stopped on the path about fifty yards away. They eyed each other silently for a moment.

"Hi," Brax said, loud enough for the boy to hear.

Ty replied in a soft, inaudible voice.

Brax waved for the boy to come to him.

Sunny sniffed at Ty's pant legs, and the boy reached down to pat the dog. "Hi, Sunny." The reserve he had shown during their first meeting was no longer evident.

"How have you been?" Brax asked.

"Fine," Ty replied. "Is this where you live?" He pointed to the roof of the house barely exposed at the top of the hill.

"It sure is."

Brax thought he detected an admiring glimmer in the boy's eyes. "I was just going for a walk. Do you want to come with me?"

Ty smiled. "Okay," he said.

"C'mon, we'll go this way." Brax led the boy upstream with Sunny leading the way.

Before they had gone far, they came upon a tree that had fallen across the creek.

"Look, a bridge," Brax said.

"I can go across it," Ty said. He mounted the makeshift bridge and began walking over the creek. It would only take six or seven strides to reach the other side, and the water was no more than a foot or two deep, but the tree trunk suspended a good four feet in the air.

"Be careful." Brax moved to the edge of the creek, ready to catch Ty if he fell.

Ty teetered as he made his way across the tree bridge but reached the other side safely. "You do it." He motioned for Brax to follow.

Brax hesitated as he looked at the tree, knowing that his weight would make the balancing act shakier.

"Come on," Ty urged again.

Brax worried that he might lose his balance on the narrow footing. But he said to himself, *these are my woods,* and started across the bridge. He held out his arms to either side and, with slow deliberation, made tiny steps forward. Halfway across, the tree shifted under his weight and he stopped to steady himself. He remembered how easy it had been to walk a log as a young boy at home in the woods. Now, hovering over the creek, he felt like a rigid old tree instead of one of the nimble denizens that roam in the wild with sure-footed ease. But he reached the other side without mishap.

Sunny splashed through the creek and approached Brax as he stepped off the tree bridge.

"How 'bout that?" Brax said, stroking the dog's head. "Your old man did it."

Ty mounted the tree again and walked back across to the other side of the creek. Brax shuffled down the bank with Sunny alongside and found a narrow spot to step on rocks across the water. He joined Ty and they headed upstream again.

After a short walk, Brax stopped and bent down to pick up a fallen tree branch. Breaking off two pieces, he asked, "Do you want to have a boat race?"

Ty's eyes lit up as he let out an emphatic, "Yes."

Brax handed the straightest stick to Ty and kept a slightly bent one for himself. "We have to name our boats," he said. "What are you going to name yours?"

"I dunno."

"I think I'll name mine Uga," said Brax, thinking of his alma mater's bulldog mascot.

Ty studied his stick. "Mine is…" After a long pause, he said, "Buzz," an obvious homage to the Georgia Tech mascot.

Brax stepped to the edge of the creek, picked up a rock and placed it on top of a bigger one. "This is the finish line."

They walked upstream to a place where the water passed over a miniature dam of debris. Squatting on a large slab of stone, they placed their sticks side-by-side in the stream. Brax said, "Three, two, one, start!" He held his stick back slightly as they released them to begin the great boat race.

"Go Uga," Brax said, as his stick followed Ty's over the dam.

Ty took up the challenge. "Go Buzz!"

Moving along the creek bank, they kept their eyes on Uga and Buzz as the sticks floated lazily downstream. The sticks became caught in a little eddy and began bobbing and turning in circles. When they escaped into a stretch of foamy rapids, the sticks swapped places. Uga took the lead, which held until it crossed the stacked rock that marked the finish line.

"You win," Ty said, like a good sport. Then he added, "Let's do it again."

"All right," Brax agreed. "We'll call that the preliminary. This time will be the final."

They raced once more, and Brax held his stick back even more at the start. Buzz won the race when Uga became diverted into a still pool.

"Well, that makes you the champion," Brax said.

Ty grinned. "I'm going to keep Buzz." He slid the small piece of wood into his pocket.

Brax called to Sunny, who had wandered into the woods, and the three of them started back toward the place where they had met.

As he walked along with the boy and the dog, Brax thought

about what he had just experienced: simple, unabashed joy. That's how he remembered his childhood. He had thought those times no longer existed, that the world had become too complicated for him to understand. But he understood the boy because he saw himself in Ty. And he realized that no matter how much things had changed, he would never lose the boy inside of himself.

They continued downstream past Brax's house.

When they approached the clearing where they had met a week earlier, Ty began walking faster. "I have to go home," he said.

"Wait," said Brax.

The boy stopped and turned to Brax.

"Ty, have you ever seen anyone burning pictures in the pit?"

"Pictures?" Ty's eyes lit up like he had touched a live wire.

"Yeah, like maybe from a computer."

"I don't have a computer." Ty responded quickly, as if he were being accused of something.

"Does your dad have one?"

Ty lowered his head and shifted his eyes back and forth. "I don't know. Can I go now?"

"Sure."

Ty scampered away, and Brax gazed into the distance after the boy disappeared from view. Then he looked at Sunny and said, "He knows."

The joy he had experienced with Ty only a few minutes earlier faded, and he recalled the ugliness of the pictures he had found. *A young boy shouldn't see such things*, he told himself.

~

Brax racked his brain trying to remember Ty's last name. No

luck; his mind locked onto one of those blank spots that often occurred when he worked a crossword puzzle. As namesake of the great Ty Cobb, it was easy to remember the first part—Tyrus Raymond—*but what was his last name?* Then, while reading a magazine in the afternoon, it came to him as if sprung from a jack-in-the-box. *Benefield—that's it.*

Checking the local directory, he noted a listing for Thomas A. Benefield on 1456 Eagle Bluff Drive. He got in his truck and headed toward the neighborhood where Ty had said he lived. It wasn't far from his house but was off the main road, and he had never ventured into that neighborhood. He envisioned cheaply-built, decades-old frame houses with gravel driveways scattered among the woods like most others in the area.

The two-lane blacktop gained elevation as it wound around sharp curves past a dilapidated farmhouse, a mobile home set on concrete blocks, and dirt roads that led to houses barely visible through the trees. After three miles—probably no more than one in true distance—he turned onto a side road that led to a neatly landscaped entranceway. On either side of the entrance stood a stacked stonewall with the words "Eagle Bluff" etched within a concrete oval.

He entered the neighborhood and drove past houses set on lots of an acre or more, each constructed of stone and cement siding in the Craftsman style. All of the homes were fairly new and well maintained. The neighborhood appeared to be a cloister for country folk gone middle America. Or, maybe vice versa.

Nearing a cul-de-sac at the end of the road, he stopped just beyond the mailbox numbered 1456. The house sat on an upward sloping lot with a lush lawn of fescue grass, freshly mowed and trimmed. Azaleas blooming in beds of pine straw colored the yard with bright pink clusters. Yellow pansies accented the shrubbery near the front door. The tranquil, upscale environment wasn't what Brax had expected.

An empty driveway and closed garage doors gave the appearance that no one was home. Brax continued to the cul-de-sac, turned around, and headed home. As he passed back by the Benefield house, he caught a glimpse of a small figure running from the back of the house. The child ran toward the woods that dropped off sharply down the backside of Eagle Bluff. Even though he didn't get a good look, Brax knew it was Ty.

There is nothing unusual about a boy running into the woods on a Saturday afternoon. But, something didn't sit right with Brax. A boy should have playmates, not spend all his time alone in the woods. He couldn't forget Ty's self-conscious demeanor and his comment about his daddy being mean. And he was sure Ty knew about the pictures he had found. The look on the boy's face had answered that question. He was sure, too, that Ty knew about his daddy's computer. Even eight year-olds know about computers these days, he reasoned.

Brax drove away feeling sure about a lot of things. He looked at Sunny, who had his head stuck out the passenger window. "Something's not right around here."

4

THE NEXT MORNING, BRAX DROVE TO PATE COUNTY HIGH SCHOOL to meet his regular walking partner, Charlie Kramer. The air was fresh with the cool awakening of a spring day as the two men resumed their daily ritual following a bout with the flu that had put Charlie under.

"How're you feeling?" Brax asked, as they began circling the track around the football field.

"I've been raised from the dead," Charlie replied. "Really, I feel good as new now. Where's Sunny?"

"I left him at home. I'm going to town after I leave here and I didn't want to take him."

Kramer, a retired druggist and longtime resident of Rocky Ridge, meticulously checked the time of each lap with his watch and his pulse with a wrist monitor. "We're on a good pace," he said.

"Yeah, for a couple of old farts," Brax said. "Or turtles."

"Nah, we're doing better than most people our age."

They walked a few paces and Charlie asked, "You heard about Ken Childers, didn't you?"

"Yeah, I read his obituary. He had just turned seventy-three a couple of weeks ago."

"An old codger," Charlie said with a laugh, knowing Brax was a year older.

"Real funny. That's how people see us, you know—one foot in the grave. I remember when I was young I thought fifty was old. My dad lived to be eighty-six, though, and was still sharp up until the last few months."

"I don't worry about age," Charlie said. "I might not be able to work as hard as I used to but I'm as smart as I ever was and I don't plan on getting any dumber. Heck, this feels like the prime of life to me."

Brax laughed. "I wouldn't go that far but I agree with what a buddy of mine always says—you gotta keep spittin' and gettin'."

"That's right. Sometimes it's hard to look at it like that till you consider the alternative. I don't want to think about it. I just hope I outlive Liz. It's easier for a man to take care of himself than a woman."

"I'm not so sure about that," said Brax. "I've known some strong women." He took a couple of steps and added, "My wife was one of them."

"Liz is strong, too, in a lot of ways. But there're some things around the house she couldn't handle."

"Yeah, but I'll bet she does a lot of stuff you wouldn't want to do. I know because I have to and it's a hassle."

"I'll bet."

They walked without talking for half a lap. Then Charlie asked, "You ever get lonely, living by yourself?"

"I don't know if lonely is the right word but I wouldn't mind having someone around if they weren't too much of a pain in the ass."

"You mean like a woman?" Charlie laughed.

"I mean like *most* women. And most men, present company excepted, of course."

"Well," Charlie said, "most people our age, man or woman, are so set in their ways that they'll get on your last nerve."

"I know what you mean."

"I've learned to live with Liz and some of her ways that aggravate me to no end. We used to get in some real knock-down-drag-outs about the dumbest things, but I finally decided it wasn't worth it. I guess she did, too, 'cause we don't argue much anymore and I do some things that I know bug the hell out of her."

"I was married for forty-three years so I know all about that."

Brax recalled living with Jane and how they would sometimes argue over trivial matters. And he thought about Dae, wondering what it might be like living with her. She probably had some annoying habits he wasn't aware of since they had never cohabited. And he figured he did, too, knowing that eccentricities tend to harden with age. Then reality slapped him in the face. *Don't get ahead of yourself, old man.*

The two men walked eight laps—two miles—at a faster clip than they had in several weeks. Afterward, they each took a swig from their water bottles, then stretched for a few minutes.

"You're a native around here, aren't you?" Brax asked.

"Not really a native but I've lived here almost forty years."

"That's close enough. Do you know a guy named Thomas Benefield that lives up at Eagle Bluff?"

"Tom Benefield? Yeah, he's the principal at the elementary school. He goes to my church. Is he a friend of yours?"

"Not really. What do you know about him?"

"He's a nice guy." Charlie looked puzzled. "Why do you ask?"

Brax shrugged. "Just curious. I've met his son who seems like a good kid. He lives in a neighborhood not too far from me. Thought I might go over and introduce myself to his folks."

"You met Tom's son?"

"Yeah." Brax looked at Charlie, hoping to hear more about Ty.

"Kind of an odd kid," Charlie said. "I can't remember his name, but he seems a little...I don't know...undeveloped socially or something. He comes to church with his parents but I don't see him mixing with the other kids."

"He was pretty shy but he seemed okay to me. His name's Ty. He said he was named after Ty Cobb."

"That fits—his father's a big baseball fan. Loves the Braves. And Ty Cobb was a helluva player. Came from over at Royston, you know."

"Yeah, I know all about Ty Cobb. Some people say he was tough, others call him something else." Brax paused and raised an eyebrow. "They say he was *mean* as hell."

"Hmm," Charlie mused in agreement. "No doubt about it. He was a real SOB."

Brax stretched his arms behind him. "Anyhow, tell me more about Ty's dad."

Charlie thought for a second. "Tom runs a good school, and from what I hear, all the kids really like him. My grandkids go there and my daughter says the teachers are excellent."

"You said he was a nice guy."

"He seems to be. Liz and I sat with him and his wife at the church picnic last summer. His wife was kind of quiet, like the boy, but they were friendly enough. He and I talked off and on for an hour or so." Charlie took off his heart monitor and stuck it in his pocket. "You ready to go?"

When they walked to the parking lot, Charlie stopped as they approached their vehicles. "Maybe it's none one of my business, but I was wondering how you met this kid and why you're interested in meeting his parents."

"I ran into him down by the creek near my house, and we got to talking." Brax thought quickly to come up with a logical reason to visit Ty. "He's a baseball fan like his dad. He wanted me to see his card collection and show me his trophies." Brax felt uncomfortable about the lie. He knew it sounded odd for an elderly man to take up interest in a young stranger's baseball card collection, but it was the best story he could come up with on the spot.

"You sure you're not lonely?" Charlie asked with a laugh.

"Hmmph," Brax grunted, a grimace squeezed on his face.

Charlie laughed again, like a kid with a gotcha. Then he turned more serious. "Hey, do you have plans tonight?" he asked.

"Uh, I was thinking about cleaning the toilet and ironing my underwear. That's what I do to ward off the loneliness."

"No, I'm serious. How about having dinner with us? Liz likes to have people over and she's a pretty decent cook."

"Thanks, I appreciate it. But…I don't know. Maybe some other time."

"Come on—we'd love to have you."

Brax politely agreed to have dinner with the Kramers, but his mind was on the pictures in the briefcase he had put in his car. After Charlie left, he toweled off, changed into a clean polo shirt, pulled jeans over his athletic shorts, and headed for the Pate County courthouse.

He parked at the town square, entered the courthouse with his briefcase in hand, and followed the signs to the sheriff's office.

"May I help you?" a woman asked from behind a desk.

"I'd like to speak to someone about a crime," Brax blurted out.

"Do you want to file a report?"

"No. I'd like to *speak* to someone," Brax repeated. "It's about…

child pornography." He cleared his throat and felt as if his face was on fire.

The woman stared at him for a moment. "I'll see if the Lieutenant is available."

"Thank you."

She left her desk and disappeared into a hallway. A minute later, she returned, followed by a man wearing a red tie and a white dress shirt that glistened like fresh snow against his cinnamon skin. He was younger than Brax had expected, mid-thirties maybe, and built like an athlete, with broad shoulders and trim waist.

"Hi, I'm Lieutenant Johnson."

"Nice to meet you. I'm Brax Donovan." He reached out and shook the officer's hand. "Can we speak in private?"

"Sure, come on in."

Brax followed the Lieutenant into an office with two desks, but no one else present. The officer grabbed a side chair and pulled it to the front of one of the desks. "Have a seat," he said, settling into a swivel chair on the other side.

Brax sat down and set the briefcase on the floor beside him. "I found something that I thought I needed to report. It's some pornographic pictures of young girls having sex with adult men. I think somebody ought to find out who took them."

Johnson squinted. "You said you *found* these pictures?"

"Yes, in the woods not far from where I live. They're really just scraps, but you can tell what they are."

Brax opened the briefcase, pulled out the two taped-together pictures and laid them on the desk.

Johnson took the sheets and looked at them briefly. "That's quite a job on your part," he said, looking up.

Brax explained about finding them in the bushes near the fire circle. "I think I know who put them there."

Johnson raised his brows. "You do?"

Brax nodded. "Probably somebody that lives on Eagle Bluff."

"What makes you think that?"

"Just an educated guess. It's nearby." Brax realized he had overreached. "Maybe I should have just ignored them. Somebody was trying to get rid of them."

"No, you did the right thing."

"It's sick," Brax said.

"Yeah. This is more than child porn. It's child abuse."

Johnson asked Brax more questions about where he had found the pictures and the circumstances surrounding their discovery. Brax was tempted to mention his encounter with Ty but felt there was no basis to implicate him. He gave the officer the two pictures, along with his address and phone number.

"I appreciate you bringing this in. People who are involved with this sort of stuff don't stop with looking at pictures."

"That's what I've heard." Brax paused. "The girls don't look like Americans ... I mean ..."

"I know what you mean," Johnson said. "It's hard to tell but they might be Hispanic or even Asian."

"Yeah. Those kind of Americans." Brax held back a grin.

Johnson raised a brow as if to acknowledge Brax's back step. "I'll speak with the captain about it, but I'm sure you understand that there's not a lot to go on here."

"Yes, I know."

Brax left the courthouse with mixed feelings. He thought he had done the right thing but worried that the pictures could wind up gathering dust in a dormant file. He wished he had told the officer of his firm belief that the principal of Sequoia Elementary School was a sexual predator.

5

THE SUN BEGAN TO BREAK THROUGH THE MORNING HAZE AS BRAX joined Charlie Kramer on the track the following Monday.

"I don't feel real frisky," Brax said, twisting his body with his arms outstretched. "Let's not worry about the time."

Beyond the bleachers, snow-white blossoms from cherry trees dotted the school grounds and clusters of brilliant yellow forsythia radiated against the brick façade of the building. A breeze stirred the sweet scent of clover and dewy grass.

"You'll get cranked up," said Charlie. "It's going to be a great day."

"Yeah, but it'll be the same day no matter how fast we walk."

"Ah, come on, old man." Charlie set his watch and started walking at a brisk pace.

Brax urged his legs to keep up.

As they rounded the first turn, Charlie said, "I talked to Tom Benefield at church yesterday."

Brax felt his pulse quicken. "Oh yeah?"

"Yeah. I told him you had met his son."

Brax didn't respond.

"He said he wanted to meet you."

"So, you told him my name?"

"Uh huh. That's okay isn't it? You said you thought about meeting the boy's family."

"Sure, it's all right." Brax focused straight ahead at the white lines on the track, hoping that his comment about meeting Ty's family would fade away.

They walked several paces before Charlie added, "Funny thing, though, Tom told me his son isn't really into sports—doesn't have any baseball cards or trophies."

Brax felt the noose of a lie tighten around his throat. "Hmmph," he grunted.

"Isn't that what you told me the boy said?"

"Maybe he was just putting me on."

"Could be."

Brax thought he heard a hint of doubt in his friend's voice. "He's just a kid," he said, trying to put the subject to rest.

Charlie checked the time as they finished the first lap. "Four-thirty-two. We need to pick it up."

"I'm following you."

They began walking a little faster.

"Like I told you," Charlie said, "there's something not quite right about that boy. I wouldn't get too involved with him if I were you."

"Come on—I'm not involved at all. I'll probably never see the kid again. There's really no reason for me to meet his family. I don't know why I said that." Changing the subject, he asked, "Did you watch the Braves last night? They looked like crap."

They finished the morning walk with no more mention of Ty. Still, Brax felt uncomfortable knowing that Tom Benefield was aware he had met his son, and he cursed himself for having ever mentioned it to Charlie.

Four days had passed since his visit to the Sheriff's office, and Brax thought he might never hear anything again about his discovery of the pictures. So he was surprised when, soon after returning home from his morning walk, he received a call from Lieutenant Johnson.

"I'm following up on our meeting last Friday," Johnson said. "I'd like to take a look at the place where you found the pictures. Can you take me there this afternoon about four o'clock?"

"Sure," replied Brax. "You have my address. I'm on Highway 41, about a mile and half past The Blue Hen. We can walk from my house."

Brax was encouraged by the Lieutenant's interest in his discovery. Yet he couldn't imagine how that random piece of evidence could actually be used to track down a pedophile.

His mind was filled with dark thoughts that clouded a beautiful day, but he hoped some good might come from finding something so vile.

As the time approached, he took a seat on the bench on his front porch and anxiously awaited the officer's arrival. A few minutes past four, Johnson pulled in front of the house in an unmarked blue sedan.

Brax stepped from the porch with Sunny close behind. "Good afternoon," he said, as the officer exited the vehicle.

"Afternoon," Johnson responded. Wearing khaki pants, a white polo with a Sheriff Department logo, and soft sole lace-ups, the lieutenant appeared more casual than he had in the office. But, the badge on his belt and the gun strapped snugly inside his holster was a not-so-subtle reminder of the nature of his job.

"Nice place," Johnson said, looking at the house.

"It works for me."

"Good looking dog, too."

"His name's Sunny. He's a good dog." Brax patted the Lab. "Aren't you, Sunny boy?"

Sunny panted with his tongue hanging out and looked at Brax as if to agree.

"C'mon in," Brax said. "Would you like a Coke or something else to drink?"

"No thanks," Johnson replied. "I'd like to get started if you're ready to go. I just need to put on my boots."

"All right. I'll lock up."

Brax locked the front door, then walked to the officer's car.

"How long have you lived here?" Johnson asked as he pulled a pair of ankle length hiking boots from the trunk.

"Three years. I had it rented out before that."

"Are you from around here?" Johnson asked.

"Not really. But I was born in north Georgia—outside Dahlonega—and lived there till I was nine. We moved to Marietta after that and I grew up a city boy. I still like the mountains, though."

"Yeah, me too. I grew up in Blairsville. I worked in the Atlanta Police Department for fifteen years before I moved back here six years ago. I had to get out of that urban hell hole."

"You've been a cop for twenty-one years? You don't look that old."

"I'll be forty-five in July."

"You look in damn good shape for your age."

"I still work out, but I can't run anymore. Bad knees." Johnson stood, his boots laced. He raised his right hand to Brax and made a fist, exposing a large ring with a blue inset.

Brax looked closely at the ring and read the inscription aloud.

"Georgia Southern, Division 1-AA 1990 National Champions. That's nice—I figured you were an athlete. What position did you play?"

"Linebacker, a little tight end."

Johnson locked his vehicle and said, "Ready?"

"Yeah, we'll go this way." Brax pointed to the side of his house. Johnson followed Brax and Sunny trotted along. They walked the path down the steep hillside until they reached the creek.

"This is my property line," Brax said, and swept his hand in both directions. "I've got seven acres."

"It's good land," said Johnson. "I'll bet you see lots of deer and other game."

"Yeah, I do. You a hunter?"

"I hunt a little in deer season. A friend and I go quail hunting every January. How about you?"

"I don't do any of that," Brax said. "I never did and I'm too old to start now. Don't really see the point to…killing things."

Johnson smiled but kept his eyes fixed on Brax as if trying to decide what to think about the comment.

Brax pointed downstream. "The creek leads to where I found the stuff. It'll take a few minutes to get there."

Conversation was sparse as they made their way along the trail, winding through a maze of oak, chestnut, and hickory trees beginning to bear new leaves. With a younger man at his heels, Brax moved faster than he normally did. They passed a house that was visible over the treetops where several people gathered on a deck that clung to the hillside and smoke billowed from a grill.

Further on, they saw a woman with a dog walking the opposite direction on the other side of the creek. Sunny exchanged barks with the other dog but Brax held him back with a commanding, "No, Sunny!"

Nearing the break in the forest, Brax said. "We're almost there." When they reached the clearing, he was surprised to see Ty standing over the fire pit.

The boy moved away from the circle of rocks as Brax and the officer approached.

"Hey," Brax said.

"Hey," the boy replied. His eyes grew big as he looked at Johnson. The badge and gun on the officer's hip glinted in the afternoon sun. "I haven't been burning," Ty said, as if to plead his innocence.

"Good," Brax said.

"I've gotta go," Ty blurted. He began running away.

"Son…" Johnson called to him. "Wait a minute." He hustled after the boy.

Brax watched as the officer tried to catch up with Ty, but the boy never stopped or turned around. Johnson gave up the chase and returned to the clearing.

"I could have caught him," Johnson said, "but he hadn't done anything wrong. I just wanted to talk to him." He looked at Brax and raised his eyebrows. "Do you know him?"

"Not well. I've seen him a couple of times."

Johnson looked around. "This must be the place you told me about. Is this the fire pit where you think someone tried to burn the pictures?"

"Yeah."

"Show me where you found them."

"It was over there." Brax tilted his head to one side.

He led the officer to the area where he had found the scattered scraps of paper. It took him a moment to get his bearings before he bent down to the holly bush that had obscured the pictures. "They were right there," he said pointing to the ground behind the bush. "Just scattered in little pieces like you saw."

"Hmm." Johnson murmured. He dropped to his knees to look closer. A few seconds later, he stood and asked, "Did you look around to see if you could find anything else near here?"

"A little bit," said Brax. "Not very thoroughly."

"It might be a waste of time, but let's give it a try."

The two men began to comb the area, looking for any sign of additional scraps of paper. Sunny nosed around in the brush and leaves along with them. After several minutes with nothing to show for their efforts, they headed back to Brax's house.

Following the path home, they said very little. Brax wondered what Lieutenant Johnson was thinking. The officer hadn't mentioned Ty since their short-lived encounter, and a question seemed to hang in the air between them. When they finished the climb up the path to Brax's cabin, Johnson broke the suspense.

"That boy we met..." Johnson's voice trailed off. "He said he hadn't been burning. That's an interesting thing for him to say." He glared at Brax. "You never mentioned him before. I've seen him around—can't remember where."

Brax felt the blood run to his face. "As I told you, I've only seen him a couple of times. His name is Ty. He lives up at the top of Eagle Bluff."

"Where did you meet him?"

"Right there where we were." Brax took a deep breath and his chest heaved as he exhaled. "Standing around that circle of rocks."

"Was he tending a fire?"

"Yeah, I asked him to stop."

Johnson squinted. "Mr. Donovan, this is the kind of information I need. The pictures you discovered had most likely been burned in that very place." Johnson's tone conveyed his irritation.

"And you never told me about finding that boy tending a fire there."

"I know." Brax gritted his teeth. "I should have said something."

"Yes, you should have."

"There's something else," Brax said.

"Yes?"

"When I met him he acted a little strange—maybe just shy—but he said something that bothered me."

"I want you to tell me *everything*." The last word spewed from Johnson's mouth with the weight of authority.

"He ran away from me and said, 'My daddy's mean.'"

"What else?"

"That's all."

Brax sensed the officer's skepticism. Then something else came to mind and he felt another surge of embarrassment. "Oh yeah, his name is Ty Benefield. His dad is the principal at Seqouyah Elementary." He realized that sounded as if he knew a lot more about the boy than he had admitted.

"Tom Benefield?" Johnson paused as if to ponder the name. "Yeah, now I remember. I've seen the kid with him. Have you talked to Tom about the pictures and seeing his son down here?"

"No." Brax felt as if he were standing in quicksand. "I've never met the man. A friend of mine told me who he is."

The lieutenant fixed his eyes on Brax, and he felt as if he were under the intense light of an interrogation room.

"I'll follow up with Mr. Benefield," Johnson said. "I don't think he's what you would call a mean man, but you know how kids are." The officer's countenance seemed to relax, though Brax sensed that a veil of doubt remained in his mind.

"Yeah, I know," said Brax. "That's why I didn't mention it before." The words spilled from his mouth and he wished he could take them back, knowing that they only emphasized his foolish mistake of not mentioning Ty in his original report. "I wasn't trying to hide anything. Sorry if it appears that way."

"No." The officer shook his head, but there was a solemn look on his face. "Guess we've done all we can right now. I sent the pictures off to the GBI Crime Lab in Atlanta for forensics. We should have the results back in a week or so. Meanwhile, let me know if you find anything else. Or any *other* information about this."

"I will." As the officer walked away, Brax added, "By the way—you can just call me Brax."

Johnson stopped and turned around. "My name's Lance." He paused for a moment before adding, "I'd really like to catch this slime ball we're looking for. I have a ten year old daughter." He turned back and walked to his car.

Brax stood with his hands folded on his chest as Johnson got into his car. "Damn it!" he said, as the vehicle disappeared down the main road. He felt stupid for having put himself in a position to have his credibility questioned. And he wished he had never seen those miserable pictures.

~

After Lieutenant Johnson's visit, Brax continued to agonize over the way he had handled things. He felt guilty as if he had lied by not being completely forthcoming. That night he slept fitfully, and the next morning still wondered why he hadn't told everything from the start.

Five days later, he pulled a letter written on fine stationary from his mailbox, and his thoughts turned in a completely different direction. The return address told him all he needed to know, and his heart thumped. He walked inside, carefully sliced open the beige envelope with a kitchen knife and settled into his favorite recliner. The cursive handwriting was neat and swirly, distinctly feminine.

Dear Brax,

I don't think people write letters anymore, but e-mails seem so impersonal and I couldn't think clearly when we talked on the phone. So, this is the only way I know to express how I feel.

Though I have never regretted my loyalty to John and never wished for his death, I truly believe he would want me to pursue my own life to the fullest. And since the last time I saw you, there hasn't a day gone by that I haven't thought of you. I know your love for Jane will never die, and I understand that, just as I believe you understand my love for John. However, we have to live in the NOW, and we can't deny that.

Brax, I don't know how to say it other than to bare my soul and admit that I still love you. I will understand if you have moved on with your life, but my love will be with you—as the song says—

Forever,
Dae

Brax set the letter in his lap and gazed blankly into space. His eyes welled with moisture and he wiped them with his fingers. He raised the letter and read it again slowly, absorbing the graceful loops and curves of each word. Then he folded it, put it back in the envelope, and carried it with him into the kitchen.

He pulled a bottle of scotch from the cabinet and poured a stiff drink to settle his nerves. With the envelope in his left hand, the glass shook in his right as he took a big swallow. His legs felt weak and he set the drink down to brace himself with his hands on the counter.

He regained his balance and looked down at Sunny, who had sauntered into the kitchen. "We're going to have company."

6

BRAX THOUGHT ABOUT DAE'S LETTER ALL AFTERNOON. BEFORE HE called her, he needed to let the emotional charge cool off. Romantic excitement is unbecoming of a mature man, he thought at first. Yet, she had been completely forthright about her feelings, so he decided he needn't hold back on his.

He scrolled to Dae's name on his cell phone and pressed the call button. Gazing through a window, he felt as calm as the evening shadows that stretched across the deck. He knew what he wanted to say and it wouldn't take long.

"Hi, it's me," he said.

"Brax," she said, a wistful tone in her voice. "I'm so glad you called."

"I got your letter," he said. "It means a lot to me. In fact…it means everything in the world to me, because I love you and I always have."

From her letter, he knew she felt the same way. Yet expressing the truth after trying to suppress it for three years was like standing naked in a crowded room.

"That's wonderful," she said as her voice cracked. "You know I love you."

Her words stirred him in a way he hadn't felt in years. "I want to see you," he said.

"I want that, too."

"Do you have any plans, tomorrow?"

"Nothing important. You know, just another day on the beach." She let out a subdued laugh. "Can you come here?"

"Is that an invitation?"

"Brax Donovan—didn't I spill my heart out in that letter?"

"Yes, you did and I can't explain how good it made me feel. I can leave early in the morning and be there about twelve-thirty or one if I don't get hung up in Atlanta traffic."

"I'll be waiting."

They said their goodbyes and that was it. The call went exactly as he had hoped.

He called Charlie to tell him he wouldn't be walking in the morning. After he took Sunny to the kennel, he got his truck washed and filled-up with gas. That evening, he tidied the house, packed a light bag and went to bed earlier than usual, planning to be on the road by five in the morning.

Sleep didn't come easily. The thought of seeing Dae again and rekindling their relationship tossed in his head. His spirit welled with anticipation, an urgency to face a new day that he hadn't felt in a long time.

At 5:15AM, Brax pulled out of his driveway. The sky was as dark as the coffee in the insulated mug sitting in the console of his truck. Aiming to get to the island by noon, he figured it would take him seven hours or so to make the four-hundred mile trip, counting traffic delays around Atlanta. He stopped at the end of his driveway, pulled a disc from the case on the passenger seat and stuck a Patsy Cline CD in the player. Since moving to the foothills of Appalachia and retiring his trumpet, his musical taste had turned from big band oldies to traditional country and bluegrass. The infectious beat of *Walkin after Midnight* stirred the drowsiness from him, and he began singing along with Patsy. As the song ended, he wailed, "...thinkin' of y-o-o-o-u." A mental image of Dae stared back at him, like a beckoning mirage.

The CD had finished playing by the time he reached the four-lane highway. He stopped at Hardee's, refilled his coffee cup and bought a ham biscuit. Back in the truck, he settled in for breakfast on the move as drizzling rain began to fall. Passenger vehicles, campers, and semi-trucks moved swiftly, pulling him along as if he were in the trailing pack at Talladega Speedway.

An hour later, daylight broke and he reached the interstate, twenty miles outside of Atlanta. In the midst of morning rush hour, traffic backed up to a near standstill, and there was no way to avoid it. He put a Chet Atkins guitar instrumental in the CD player and relaxed to the soothing sound of the music as the wave of vehicles inched forward. His temperament was different now from what it had been when he fought the traffic wars in his working years. Now, he needn't rush to the office for a meeting, ringing phone, or inbox full of mail. Recalling those days, he felt thankful that retirement had rescued him from the sea of commuter lemmings.

Beyond Atlanta, the rain stopped and, fueled by the anticipation of seeing Dae, he stretched the speed limit. He pulled a CD from the case without looking and suddenly rock music from the 60s filled the car. The pulsating sound urged him on and the speedometer dialed up as if it were a noise meter. He checked in front and behind for patrol vehicles, then eased off on the gas as he approached ninety. Five minutes before eleven o'clock, Chuck Berry sang the last chords of *Johnny Be Good,* and Brax was at the outskirts of Savannah. He called Dae and told her he would be there by a little past noon.

"I'll see you then. Drive carefully."

He thought he heard a hint of excitement in her voice. "Ten-four, good buddy," he said in an exaggerated drawl. He laughed out loud, imagining the absurd look on her face.

~

Brax followed the road over the causeway to the island and directly toward the ocean. Before he reached the beach, he saw a large white building gleaming in the sun above the tree line. Having moved from the island before the onset of major development and the completion of the hotel, his worst fear loomed in front of him—an obscene structure of concrete and glass.

"Son-of-a bitch," he muttered.

Approaching the ocean, he turned left at the T intersection and passed by the hotel, towering six stories high on the beach side of the road. An elaborate water feature and an array of colorful plants adorned the entranceway of The Breakwater Hotel. Across the road, a condominium development was under construction. A sign read: "Luxury Living at Serenity Shores. Units Starting at $500,000."

Minutes later, Brax passed through the gate at Seaside Village, using the code Dae had given him.

When he stepped out of the car, Dae walked straight from her front door and into his arms without uttering a word. They embraced warmly and kissed. Burying himself in the sweet taste of her lips and the womanly fragrance of her skin, he felt weak-kneed.

"That was worth the trip," he said, gathering his composure. "It's been a long time since I've done that."

"Too long," she said. Her eyes glistened and the look on her face said *I've missed you.*

He gazed at her and said, "You look great."

But, in fact, he coud see a difference in her. She was seventy now and, though no less beautiful in his eyes, her face was thinner, a little less firm. Or was he simply looking at her in a different light than he once had? But the strands of gray in her hair were more noticeable now, the realization of what he had once seen as the promise of silver. The promise of their future together.

"And you're still as handsome as ever."

He knew better, but hearing her say it was like drinking a sweet elixir.

With a wry smile, he asked, "Well, woman, what do we do now?"

Smiling back, she said, "Now we eat lunch. Are you hungry?"

"Yeah, it's been four hundred miles since my last biscuit."

"I think I can do better than that."

"You always did."

She took his hand and they went into her house where she had the table set for a meal.

"Smells good," he said.

"Do you remember what we ate the first time we had dinner together?"

"Yes, we ate right here." He thought for a moment and she waited silently while the wheels turned in his head. Then it came to him. "We had pork chops."

"Oh good, you remembered. I cooked the same meal, just for this occasion."

"Gee," he said wide-eyed, "that's what I like—a moveable feast." He smiled. "Seriously, what can I do to help?"

"You can pour us a glass of cheer." She handed him a bottle of Zinfandel.

He uncorked the wine and filled two goblets as she set the food on the table. Before they sat, he handed her one of the glasses and raised his to hers. "Here's to us."

"To us." She grinned and touched her glass to his.

Brax took his seat, put the napkin in his lap, and said, "Kind of like starting all over again, isn't it?"

"Yes."

"I like that."

"Me, too."

Brax savored the meal as if it were manna. Dae served cheesecake for dessert and they each had another glass of wine. Afterward, filled with food and alcohol, his eyes sagged with drowsiness. "Sorry," he said, after covering a yawn with his hand.

"I'll bet you're tired," Dae said. "Why don't you lie on my bed for a while?"

"I'll just sit on the couch."

"No, come in here." She took his hand and led him to her bedroom.

He sat on the edge of the bed and took off his shoes. Completely drained of energy, he rolled onto his back.

She covered him with a thin blanket as he closed his eyes.

∼

When he awoke, Dae lay beside him. Brax looked at her through the narrow slits of his eyelids.

"Am I in heaven?" he asked.

"Yes," she said.

"That's good." He sat up and the cobwebs began to clear from his mind. Checking his watch, he saw it was almost two-thirty.

"Boy, I was out like a light."

"You needed the rest."

"Have you been here the whole time?"

"No, just a little while."

"It's hard for me to believe I'm here."

"Yes—pretty amazing, isn't it?" She hugged him and kissed him on the cheek.

He returned the kiss, then asked, "You know what I want to do?"

"What?"

"Walk on the beach. You know, like we used to."

"That'll be fun."

He pulled the blanket aside and they rose from the bed.

Brax went to his car, got his bag and returned to change into a T-shirt and shorts. After Dae changed, they left her house for the short stroll to the beach.

Passing the clubhouse, Dae said, "I remember walking in there the first morning after I moved here. You were working a crossword puzzle."

"Yeah. That was my daily routine," he said through a suppressed laugh. "Nothing was routine after that day. I knew right then you were someone special, and I'd be glad I met you. I'm not sure how, but I knew."

"I wasn't sure at first. But by the time we left the beach that morning, I felt the same way."

They passed through the gate, across the road, and onto the short path through the dunes.

Walking beside Dae for the first time in three years, Brax felt as if those years had evaporated, and he had simply become older without ever having left the island.

When they emerged from the dunes, he was struck by the number of people on the beach. Several groups of young people huddled on blankets nearby, jabbering away or preoccupied with hand-held devices. A stream of people of all ages strolled along the waters edge. Dozens of young kids played in the surf. He looked southward at the big hotel, clearly visible in the distance.

"Things have changed," he said, a hint of disgust in his voice.

"It's a little different," Dae responded.

"A lot different. It's more obvious to me because I've been away." He spread his arms in a conciliatory gesture. "But, I'm not going to get on a rant about development."

Dae smiled and took his hand. "Good. Let's go this way." She led him in the direction opposite the hotel.

As they retraced the steps of their original walk on the beach, Brax vividly recalled that morning. "Déjà vu," he said.

"Yes, it seems like only yesterday when we were here for the first time. I remember we came to a pile of driftwood and you tripped while trying to help me step over." She laughed.

"Yeah, I tried to be Mr. Cool."

"You made a joke of it, and I thought you were so funny. I think your sense of humor was what attracted me the most."

He feigned a look of disbelief. "Not my good looks?"

"Oh yes, that, too." She smiled again.

They passed a few people lying on the beach and others walking in the opposite direction.

Brax felt like he had stepped into a world that he had almost forgotten about. The white sand shone brilliantly in the full sun, sea gulls squawked as they glided overhead, and the briny smell of the ocean filled the air.

"I always liked the beach in the morning because we had it all to ourselves," he said.

"Sally and I still walk in the morning. We don't get started as early as you and I used to, though. She's not an early bird like you."

"Well, she lives in my old house and she walks with you, so she can't be all bad."

Dae laughed. "No, she's nice."

"Like me?"

"Yes, like you."

"Jim told me that Jaws doesn't live here anymore." He referred to a friend and former neighbor who had changed his name from Willie Simmons to Momadou Jawara in honor of his African ancestry.

"That's right. He married Brenda—you remember, the young lady he took to the Christmas party —and took back his real name."

"Good for him."

"Yeah, I think Willie fits him better."

"I meant good for him for getting away from all this development." He grinned.

"You said you weren't going to—"

"I'm just kidding." He patted her rear and added, "Darlin'." Then he bent over with laughter.

Dae rolled her eyes. "You're such a doofus."

His playful smile slowly disappeared, and he regained his composure as they approached a group of Seaside residents huddled together in a cluster of beach chairs. Several of his ex-neighbors waved with greetings, and he stopped to chat. He felt odd, considering the newness of Dae's widowhood, and he didn't prolong the conversation.

When they resumed walking, Dae asked the question both of them had ignored. "How long are you going to be here?"

"I don't know. I brought some extra clothes, and I don't really have a schedule. We need to talk about…our future."

"Do you want to move in with me?"

A few seconds passed before he responded. "Let's not get into it right now." He pulled her to him as they maintained their pace. "We can talk it over when we get back to your house."

"Okay," she said, leaning into him.

Several minutes later, they stopped and took off their shoes to wade in the calm sea.

"Brrrr, it's cold," Dae said.

"It feels good," he replied. "This is the first time I've been in the ocean since I left." He moved out a few yards, still only knee deep and tiny bubbles lapped on his shorts. Then he bent over, and splashed some briny water on his face. He waded back to Dae who stood near the shore with the surf only halfway to her knees.

"You'll like the mountains," he said.

The smile on her face glowed in the afternoon sun.

~

After returning from the beach, Brax picked up his cell phone from where he had left it on Dae's bedside table. There was a voice mail and the caller I.D. indicated the Pate County Sheriff's Office. He listened to the message from Lance Johnson, asking him to return the call. He depressed the highlighted number and the Lieutenant promptly answered.

"Are you at home?" Johnson asked.

"No," Brax replied. "I'm out of town."

"When will you be back?"

"I'm not sure. In a day or two."

"Alright, call me then. I'd like to talk to you again."

"I can talk now," Brax said.

"It'll be better to wait until you get back."

"Is it urgent?"

"No, just some business we need to take care of. Don't interrupt your trip."

"That's fine. I'll let you know as soon as my plans are firmed up." Brax ended the call and squeezed his face in thought.

Dae couldn't avoid hearing his side of the conversation. "Do you need to leave?"

"No. I'll tell you about it later."

Evening shadows covered the patio as Brax turned the hot dogs on the grill. "I don't think I can handle more than one of these. That was more lunch than I usually eat all day. It was great, though," he quickly added.

Dae looked up from setting the table. "I'm glad you enjoyed it. I don't get to cook a real meal very often."

"We can fix that. You know—just so you don't get out of practice."

She walked over and patted his stomach. "Yeah, I'm sure that won't be a problem."

They ate on the patio, washing down a light meal with iced tea as the warmth of approaching summer ebbed and daylight turned to dusk. Afterward, Brax took the empty plates to the kitchen, returning with a beer for himself and a glass of wine for her.

"I only brought enough clothes to stay a couple of days," he said." Do you want to talk about our living arrangement now?"

"Yes, I'd like to know what you want to do."

"It's not just up to me. It's a mutual thing, you know."

"I didn't mean it like that," she said. "I meant we needed to talk about it."

"What do you want to do?" he asked.

"I want to be with you."

"I do too, but we're four hundred miles apart. Do you want me to move back here?"

"If you'd like to, that's fine with me." She took a sip of wine. "Had you rather I move to Rocky Ridge?"

He rested his beer on his chest. "Let's think about this." He paused. "You have a nice house at the beach and I have a peaceful home in the mountains. That's the best of all worlds isn't it?"

"You mean keep both houses?"

"Why not? If we get tired of one, we can go to the other. We'll be like those rich bastards that buy those half-million dollar condos down the road." He laughed at the irony.

"We can do that."

"Well, you haven't seen the place in Rocky Ridge. Can you go back with me when I leave?"

Dae scrunched her shoulders and wrinkled her forehead. "Yes," she said.

"Can you stay a month?"

"I'm with you forever—remember? You can't get rid of me now."

He smiled, then brought up the subject they had ignored. "Do you want to get married?"

She looked startled. "Oh gosh...I don't know."

"That answers my question."

"No, that's not what I meant."

"That's all right. I just wanted to get it out in the open."

"I think we should give ourselves a little time."

He took a gulp of beer. "You're right, there's no need to rush."

"No." She said with a glazed look in her eyes. "No need at all."

Brax could read her mind. She'd been a widow for less than two months. It wouldn't look right. Moving on, he said, "So, I'll stay here tomorrow and we'll leave the next morning. Is that our plan?"

"That's our plan." She raised her glass.

He raised his beer bottle and exclaimed, "To our plan."

~

In the quiet darkness, Brax wrapped Dae in his arms, and she pressed close to him. He felt the warm softness of her flesh against his as the overhead fan stirred the air. He kissed her neck and shoulders, then nuzzled his cheek to hers. She smelled sweet and fresh, like a gardenia in bloom after a summer rain. He exhaled in rhythm to her deep breaths as though their bodies were one.

"Love me forever," she whispered, then buried her head in his bare chest.

"I will. I promise."

She didn't have to say it; he knew she would always love him.

He closed his eyes, and the promise of forever beckoned him.

7

BRAX SHUFFLED ALONG BESIDE DAE AND SALLY BLANKENSHIP ON the moist, hard-packed sand beyond the receding tide. The rising sun bathed the shore in the amber glow of a beautiful morning, yet his thoughts were on some disturbing pictures. The images of naked young girls being abused were etched in his mind. He remembered Lance Johnson's call and wondered what the officer wanted to speak to him about. When his companions spoke, the dark thoughts faded and he was back in the moment.

"So, you'll be leaving in the morning?" asked Sally. "How long will you be gone?"

"I'm not sure," Dae replied. "Maybe a couple of weeks."

"Longer," said Brax.

"Well," Sally said, "don't forget about me while you're there. Maybe you'll meet a nice man who's looking for a young-at-heart widow." She giggled. "I haven't had any luck here."

Dae wrinkled her brow. "Oh, you'll meet someone. I know you will."

"Then I would be as lucky as you," said Sally. "Of course, I'm not as pretty as you but, even at my age, I might catch a guy's eye. Like the last woman at closing time." She laughed.

"Sally!" Dae frowned at her friend.

"Hey, c'mon," Brax said. "You'd be a prize for some man. And he'd be the lucky one, not you." In truth, Sally's short, plump body displayed age-defying skin tone and her full cheeks appeared to be in a constant smile. Brax found her attractive in a way totally opposite to the beauty of Dae.

"Thanks. Really, I was kidding. I'm just jealous of you two. You're such a perfect couple."

"Well," Brax said, "neither one of us is perfect, but we *are* a couple." He turned to Dae. "I guess."

She took his hand. "Yes, we're a couple."

As they neared the imposing new hotel, Brax spoke in a serious tone. "It's started now. And there will be more of this to come. In a few years, you won't see the turtles anymore."

"Yeah," Sally said. "I'm afraid they're going to build more hotels. But why does that keep the turtles away?"

"The lights. The females won't nest near artificial lighting. Or, if they do, when the hatchlings emerge, they think it's the reflection of the ocean and go inland toward the light. They die of heat exposure."

"That's sad," said Dae.

Sally agreed. "Darn, I didn't know that."

"They're an endangered species." Brax resisted the temptation to add, *like us.*

The sobering comment dampened the conversation for a while. When they reached the section of beach behind the hotel, they turned around and started back.

A few minutes later, Brax stopped and bent over to take off his sneakers.

"What are you doing?" Dae asked.

"I'm going in." He pulled off his T-shirt. "Anybody else?"

"No." Dae didn't sound amused.

"I'll pass," said Sally.

Brax jogged to the water's edge and waded out waist deep. He continued into deeper water and then plunged headfirst into the calm sea. When he stood, the water was up to his chin. He turned to his walking partners on the beach and yelled, "It feels fantastic. I think I just saw Jacques Cousteau."

"Brax," Dae shouted, "we're ready to go back. Come on."

A kid—that's what he was. A young boy trapped in an old man's body. He began swimming toward the beach, then stood in the shallow water and walked to shore. His shorts clung to him as he toweled off with his tee before stretching it back on over his head. Picking up his shoes, he said, "Y'all ready to go?"

Rolling her eyes, Dae replied with an impatient, "Yes."

Brax rejoined the ladies and they walked a few yards before the stern look on Dae's face melted. She turned to Brax and said, "You look like a big loggerhead turtle." Then she roared with laughter and Sally joined in.

"Well, at least I'm not extinct," Brax said. "*Yet.*"

They laughed again and the conversation remained light-hearted until they reached the path through the dunes to Seaside.

"Would you please keep an eye on my place while I'm gone?" Dae asked Sally.

"Sure."

"I'll leave you a key and the code to the alarm. I'm sure everything will be all right, but don't hesitate to call me if you need to."

"Don't worry, honey—you have a great trip. You're in good hands." Sally looked at Brax and winked. "Right, Brax?"

"Oh yeah—good hands."

The salty crust began to dry on Brax's body. He wasn't sure when he would see the ocean again, but he'd had his fill for the time being. Soon he would return to his house in the mountains and Dae would be with him. He would be home.

~

Brax rose early on the morning of their departure. He brewed a pot of coffee and waited for Dae to stir from bed. An hour later, she spoke to him through the open bathroom doorway.

"Do you want to walk the beach one more time before we leave?"

He stopped shaving and looked at her reflection in the mirror "No, I'd like to get started. I told Jim we'd stop by to see him in Warner Robins. It's not too far out of the way. Is that okay?"

"Yes, I'd love to see him again."

After a light breakfast, Dae made her final swing through the house, putting things away as if preparing her home for inspection.

Brax grabbed Dae's two bags from the bedroom while she touched up her face in the dresser mirror. "I hope you don't mind riding in a pick-up. I took out the spit cup and the gun rack just for you," he joked.

She turned to look at him. "Your truck is fine, but I don't think it's going to snow so do we really need the four-wheel drive? Why don't we take my car? It might be more comfortable."

"Yeah, you're probably right. It'll take a while to make a hillbilly girl outta' you." He laughed.

"Don't be so sure about that. I'm a Georgia girl and I've got red clay and peach fuzz in my blood." With an exaggerated twang and a wry look on her face, she added. "So tarnation, Jethro, hitch up the wagon and let's git. Times a wastin'."

"Yes'm," he mimicked.

Ten minutes later, Brax locked his truck in the garage. He

pulled away in Dae's car and through the exit gate of Seaside Village. They were finally on their way to a life together.

~

Brax flipped the turn signals as he approached a rest area. "We're only an hour from Warner Robins. I'm going to stop here and call Jim."

"Good, I have to go to the ladies room."

Before calling Jim, Brax made the call to Lance Johnson. It went to voice mail, and he left a message that he would be home the following day. Knowing he would be meeting with Johnson, he planned to tell Dae about the pictures when they got home. He waited for her to return from the restroom and then called Jim.

"We'll be there in an hour," Brax said.

"Dae's with you?" Jim asked.

"Yeah, I told you she was coming home with me."

"Well, she's had time to change her mind. She's not bound and gagged in the trunk is she?"

"Yeah, but she was making too much noise kicking the trunk lid so I let her out." He handed the phone to Dae. "Say hello to Jim."

"Hi, Jim—it's Dae. Can't wait to see you again."

"Likewise."

"Be there in a bit," she said.

"My tail's a waggin'."

She laughed and handed the phone back to Brax. "He's still the same old Jim."

"Yeah," Brax said, as he headed back onto the interstate. "He's that all right."

"Sally liked him a lot. They had a little thing going for a while."

"Really? I've never heard about that."

"He didn't tell you about it?"

"No. What happened?"

"It just kind of…evolved. You know—bridge at the clubhouse, walking with us on the beach a few times, dinner at my house. Stuff like that with other people around. Then they went on a few dates by themselves. He even took her to play Bingo at the VFW a couple of times. She loved it."

"I would give a million dollars to have been a fly on the wall during one of those *dates*. I'm sure that's not what Jim called them." He took a sip from a water bottle in the console. "But, the more I think about it, the more it makes sense. I think they would be a fun couple."

"So do I and Sally felt that way, too. She wouldn't admit it, but she was a little down after he left."

"Do they stay in touch? He's only three or four hours away."

"Not really. You know how Jim is—he won't be serious about anything."

"You're right—I do know how he is. But you're wrong to think he's never serious. He's not how other people see him. He helped me a lot when you and I were…you know…"

"Working out our problems," she said, finishing the thought with a grin.

"Yeah."

Dae shook her head and got back on track. "I don't know what happened between Jim and Sally. I like her, though. And I'll tell you one thing—she's a good person."

"She seems to be." Brax kept his eyes on the road ahead. "I'll find out what happened."

"Don't tell him I mentioned it to you. I don't want him to think she sent me here as some kind of matchmaker."

"Don't worry, leave it to me. I know how to handle Jim."

Brax smiled at the irony. With their roles reversed, he now felt motivated to help Jim find a new partner in his senior years.

∼

Brax followed the GPS directions to Jim's daughter's house where Jim had lived since moving from Seaside. The brick, ranch-style home was set back from the street a good hundred feet in a quiet neighborhood densely wooded with tall pine trees.

Jim stood with a welcoming hand raised outside the front door when Brax and Dae pulled into the driveway. "Well, look who's here," he said as they got out of the car. He met them on the walkway, put an arm around Dae and extended the other to Brax. "Good to see you, old man." He turned to his daughter, who had walked up behind them. "You remember Kathy, don't you?"

"Sure." Brax leaned to Kathy with a perfunctory hug.

Dae and Kathy exchanged greetings, reminding themselves of their prior meeting at a Brunswick hospital. Three years earlier Jim had suffered a heart attack while living at Seaside.

"Yeah, that was when my heart decided it needed a tune-up," Jim interjected. Then he bellowed, "C'mon in," and waved an arm toward the house.

Jim led everyone through the home and onto the screened porch in the back. An overhead fan droned with a whirring noise as Jim offered Brax and Dae a seat in a cushioned metal-framed loveseat. Settled down, they had a three-sided view of a small back yard with neatly trimmed St. Augustine grass surrounded by a pine thicket. A small table in front of them was set with empty glasses and a large bowl of chips.

Kathy left and returned with a pitcher of iced tea. She filled the glasses, then sat in a side chair that matched the one Jim had taken.

Brax took a swig of sugary sweet tea. "This is real nice."

"Yeah, Kathy's a good daughter to put up with me."

"Don't listen to him," Kathy said. "Dad helps out a lot around the house. He mows the grass and keeps the yard looking nice." She looked at Jim affectionately. "He's a good handyman, too."

"Oh, hell. Don't get carried away," Jim said. "I got a hammer, a pair of pliers, and a screwdriver. And I know how to get to Home Depot."

"And to the park," Kathy added. "Dad takes Ethan to all of his games and practices. Ethan loves his Grandpa."

"I remember your son," Dae said. "We met him at the hospital when we visited Jim. He is so cute."

"Those sawbones fixed me," Jim said. "They put me back together like a broken Timex and I just keep on tickin'."

"Dad's doing fine," Kathy said, looking at her father.

Brax interjected. "How old is Ethan now?"

"He's ten," said Kathy. "It's hard to believe—he's in the fifth grade now."

A big smile swelled on Jim's face. "Ethan's an athlete."

After serving her guests a light lunch, Kathy led Brax and Dae to Ethan's room. A doting mother, she commented on each of her son's trophies and pictures.

As he listened, Brax thought of another young boy about the same age. The haunting words echoed in his mind—"*My daddy's mean*"—and he wondered how Ty was treated in his home.

Leaving Ethan's room, the ladies began talking of their Georgia ancestries. Kathy then led Dae to the living room to show her family scrapbooks.

Jim motioned to Brax. "Come on, we'll catch up with them later."

Brax followed Jim to the screened porch. As they hashed out their thoughts on sports and politics, he tried to think of a way to bring up Sally's name. In a brief lull, he just let it roll. "Dae and I walked on the beach with Sally yesterday."

"That sounds familiar," Jim said.

"I understand you and Sally went out a few times."

"I can't imagine who told you that."

"Maybe Sally told me. Maybe that's how I know she likes you but she hasn't heard from you in over a year."

"Is that a crime? Am I under arrest?"

Brax ignored the sarcasm. "She seems like a nice woman. Cute, too."

"Okay," Jim said. "Let's cut the crap. You want to know what happened between us. Well, not everyone gets starry-eyed like you and Dae. Just because two people are old and alone doesn't mean they're a good fit."

"I understand. Hey, it's none of my business. I was just curious." Brax stared out at the backyard for a moment. He sensed his friend was hedging. "So, there was no…chemistry?"

Jim slumped in the chair with his head down. "I'm just an old drunk with a bad ticker. I can't wish that on anybody."

"Did you fall off the wagon again?"

"Not yet."

"How's your heart?"

"Like I said before, it's still beating."

Brax felt Jim's emptiness. He had known it himself before meeting Dae. "You deserve more, Jim." He leaned forward.

"Life—that's what you deserve. There's only so much of it and you've got to take it while you can. You always said we gotta keep on spittin' and gettin' and here you are giving up."

Jim looked directly into Brax's eyes. "Thank you, Dr. Phil." Neither man smiled. "I'm not giving up. It's not bad living here with Kathy and the boy. I could be a lot worse off."

"That's not the point. Yes, Kathy's a terrific daughter and I know you love Ethan. That's all good. And I don't know squat about Sally or if she's right for you. What I *do* know is you're not just an old drunk with a bad ticker, so cut out that horseshit thinking."

"You can't deny it's the truth."

"No, it's not the truth. The truth is what you make of it. I'm a cynical person just like you and I'm no shining example, but I want you to get out of this cloud of self-doubt." Brax pursed his lips in frustration. "People *like* you. You need to like yourself."

Jim stared beyond Brax, and they sat without speaking for a long time. Only the low whish-whish-whish of the overhead fan stirred the silence.

Then Jim spoke. "It's not easy to change."

"I know." Brax hoped that somehow his words had helped. He stood up and said, "We need to get going."

It felt good to say "we."

~

Brax maintained a steady speed and the traffic flowed smoothly on the interstate as he and Dae passed through Atlanta before the start of rush hour.

"We've got about an hour and a half to go," he said.

Dae turned from the side window. "Do you really think we should get married?"

Brax jerked his head around, and gripped the steering wheel tightly. "I just asked you that question a couple of days ago and you said you didn't know."

"I've been thinking about it all day," she said.

"That's fine but, geez, this is a weird time to bring it up."

"It can wait until we get to your house."

"It's *our* house." He felt a rush of panic. Was she having second thoughts? What the hell brought this up? It was a rash, impulsive side of Dae he had never seen and it was unsettling.

"I'm going to pull off at the next exit and we'll talk about it."

"No, it can wait," she insisted.

"No, it can't."

Brax's mind raced with a myriad of conflicting thoughts. The few minutes it took to get to the next exit seemed like hours. Beyond the off ramp, he drove a short way to a large convenience store and parked under the cover of the fuel island.

His pulse surged as he looked at Dae. "I love you."

"I love you, too." She leaned into his shoulders. "Will you marry me?"

He opened his mouth but words didn't come out. Then he laughed. "That's what I'm supposed to say. Yes, yes, I'll marry you." He pulled her to him and kissed her.

"I just want to know that it will happen," she said. "We can wait awhile."

"You know I'll do whatever you want. I hoped we would get married, but I didn't want to push you."

"I don't need to be pushed. I want it more than anything."

"Good." He sighed with relief. "Wow, this is something. You sure know how to keep things interesting."

Dae settled back in her seat and laughed. "I was going to wait until we got to Rocky Ridge to say something but it just burst out of me."

"I'm glad you feel like that because I feel the same way."

The fuel gage on the car was below the quarter mark, so Brax got out and filled the tank. When he pulled away and headed back to the interstate, he said, "That was real romantic, wasn't it? You can tell your family that I proposed to you when I stopped to get gas."

"Except I proposed to you." Dae laughed.

A minute later, Brax neared the end of the entrance ramp and accelerated to merge into traffic. He exhaled a deep breath, then said, "This should be fun."

"What?" she asked.

"Living with you." He couldn't hold back a grin.

8

BRAX FOLLOWED THE TRAFFIC CIRCLE AROUND THE PATE COUNTY courthouse in the heart of downtown Rocky Ridge. On the courthouse lawn, a large sign publicized the 23rd Annual Lake Gansagi Bluegrass Festival. A man playing a banjo sat on a bench under an oak tree.

"That's Banjo Bob." Brax lowered his window and the plunky notes drifted into the car. "He plays at that same spot most days. Kind of a local icon."

"This looks like a scene right out of Deliverance," said Dae.

"Don't mention that around here. A lot of people in this part of Georgia hate the redneck stereotypes in that movie."

"I didn't mean it like that."

"I know. Anyhow, old Bob can play about any song in bluegrass style. I love that kind of music."

"It's a lot different than what I've heard you play on your trumpet."

"Yeah, it is. Guess I'm just getting back to my roots."

She peered through her window and read aloud the name of a local restaurant as they passed it. "The Hungry Bear."

"Great home cooking," he said.

"This is a pretty little town."

"I think so, too." He picked up speed as they passed beyond the business district. "The house is only a few miles from here."

The hills in the distance were covered with trees, a lush landscape bathed in green. The road began a steep incline with sharp curves winding around the side of a mountain. A river ran through the valley below, coursing through land dotted with pastures and farm fields.

"That's the Saugoochie," Brax said.

Dae leaned toward her window. "This is so scenic. It's like another world."

"Yeah, it's about as different as it can be from Seaside."

Buildings were scattered along the way as if by chance rather than choice. In one place, a dingy white clapboard home perched atop a hill only yards from the road. Further on, a dilapidated house trailer sat in a depression at the end of a rutty dirt road. Halfway up a steep grade, a modest-sized brick Baptist church and a small country store with two gas pumps occupied a level spot.

Dae remained quiet and Brax wondered what she was thinking. In the euphoria of discovering love again, he had not given much thought to how she would adjust to living in a rural environment.

Several signs along the way led them to the Blue Hen, an antique store and gift shop. The large white metal building had a blue roof and perched on a plateau overlooking the river. The parking lot was more than half full.

"I want to go there sometime," Dae said.

"You'll have plenty of opportunities. We're almost home."

"How far are we from town? It seems like we've gone quite a way."

"Ten miles from the courthouse."

A minute later, he turned onto a side road. They passed only one house before he slowed down at his mailbox, then pulled onto his driveway. The long blacktop drive led through a corridor of trees before reaching an open space with a small patch of grass in front of the house. Made of honey-colored split logs, the house had a second floor dormer and green metal roof. Brax sometimes called it a cabin, but its substantial size defied that description.

"Ooh," Dae said as they got closer. After a long pause, she added, "What a perfect setting." Another pause. "And the house is charming."

He heard in her voice the polite praise that one has when a gift is not quite up to expectations.

"I wouldn't go that far but I think it has…character." He parked under the carport and helped Dae out of the car. "Let's go in first. I'll come back and get the bags." He unlocked the door and led her inside.

She stood in the center of the main room and looked around. A large stone fireplace with bookshelves on either side occupied most of one wall. Brax's leather recliner from his villa in Seaside looked almost contemporary among the hodge-podge of dated furniture. The dark paneled walls and low lighting contributed to an ambience of timeworn casualness.

Seconds ticked away on the mantel clock as he tensely awaited her reaction. Only a few hours earlier they had left Seaside and her almost new home, bright with lots of natural light and tastefully decorated in vibrant colors. Now, they stood in the midst of an entirely different scene.

"It's cozy," she said.

"Yeah. It needs a woman's touch. I'm not much of a decorator."

She grabbed his arm and snuggled against him. "I like it."

The room seemed to brighten.

"I've got to see this view," Dae said, moving to a back window. Brax unlocked the door and followed her onto the deck. She stepped to the railing and peered out at the surrounding woods and the mountains beyond. "So wild," she said.

"I sit out here every morning and drink my coffee. It's my favorite part of the cabin."

"Brax, this is not a *cabin*."

"Well, it's made of split logs and it's pretty rustic."

"It's a nice home in the mountains."

He realized that she didn't like the thought of making her home in a *cabin*. "Yeah, I think so. There's a creek down at the bottom of this hill. I've got seven acres of land." He thought for a second and said, "It'll be yours, too—someday."

"And you'll have a house in Seaside Village. I mean *we* will, as soon as we get on with this marriage." She smiled.

He leaned on the railing and wanted to set a date right then; firm up the commitment to their future. Instead, he said, "The sooner the better. Let me show you the rest of the *house*."

"Where's your dog?"

The dog. *Damn it.* He meant to tell her about Sunny before then. He knew Dae didn't allow pets in her house in Seaside.

"I can smell it," she said before he could answer.

"Uh, yeah, he's a yellow Lab." He tried to shake off the need to be defensive. "He's at the kennel. His name is Sunny—like the color of the sun—S-U-N-N-Y."

"That's cute."

Brax couldn't read her expression. "I can keep him out of the house."

"How long have you had him?"

He took her non-answer to mean that it might be better to keep the dog outside.

"Pretty much the whole time I've lived here. I bought him from a breeder in Dawsonville. He's a good companion." He paused. "But not as good as you."

She laughed. "Well, I hope not."

It felt good to hear her laugh. *She'll like Sunny.*

They walked through the kitchen and down a hall to two small bedrooms with an adjoining bath on the main floor. Brax's computer and desk were in the front bedroom; otherwise the furnishings appeared caught in a 1970s time capsule.

A set of stairs led up to the master suite where a large window encased in a dormer provided a view in front of the house. Another window faced the woods in the rear.

Dae walked past the sturdy oak chest and dresser to the edge of the king-size bed and silently surveyed the room. She sat down on the brown bedspread and looked around at the stark sheetrock walls that had aged milky white.

"Maybe we could use a little color," she said.

"You don't like drab?"

"Everything is fine with the house." She looked at him with a gleam in her eyes. "I love it. But you know how I am about décor. I think with a few changes we can bring a little touch of life into it."

He knew that she didn't truly love the house, but it felt good to hear it.

"Tell me what you want done and I'll get on it."

"There's no need to do anything right now. Let's just get settled in."

"So, I can bring the bags in? You're going to stay?"

"Oh, shut up. You know you can't get rid of me."

She looked in the bathroom and walk-in closet before returning to the bedroom. "I can't wait to spend the first night in my new home."

"Good, I'll get our things out of the car."

The steps creaked as Brax clomped down the stairway but he felt like he was walking on air.

~

The next morning, Brax brought Sunny home from the kennel. After he let Sunny out of the car, he removed the towel he had placed on the seat to keep the dog hair off. Then he used a hand vac to clean the floorboard and checked to make sure there were no signs of the dog left in Dae's car.

He led Sunny to the back of the house and onto the deck. Through the window, he saw Dae in the main room and motioned for her to come outside. She stepped onto the deck in her robe.

"Hello Sunny," she said with a smile.

At the sound of his name, Sunny thrust forward with enthusiastic abandon, shoving his head upward into Dae's midsection. She recoiled from the sudden force of his weight and then steadied herself with her hands on the dog's head. Brax held his breath for a moment until Sunny settled down and nuzzled against Dae's housecoat.

"You're a handsome boy," she said, stroking the Lab's back.

Brax pulled Sunny away with a sense of relief. "This is Dae, the lady of the house. C'mon, you've been cooped up for three days. You need to get your legs back." He clapped his hands, nudged Sunny on the rear, and said, "Go." The dog scrambled off the deck and ran to the edge of the woods, poking his nose to the ground every few feet.

Brax followed Dae as she went inside.

"I think he likes you," he said to her back. "He likes everybody."

She turned and said, "We'll get along just fine." Then she smiled.

Brax put an arm around her shoulder and gave a squeeze.

∼

Brax held the door for Dae as they left the Hungry Bear Restaurant.

"I'm stuffed," he said.

"Me, too," she said. "That was really good."

He pulled back his shoulders and took a deep breath. "You can't beat this weather."

She crossed her arms and hugged herself in the cool air. "It's wonderful. I'm glad I brought this sweater."

It was after eight o'clock and the moon shared the sky with the setting sun. Across the street, the grass on the town square glowed with a deep green luster and approaching twilight cloaked the granite courthouse in a veil of satin gray. Brax stood transfixed by the vision. He recalled the only time he had been inside the building; the day he showed those repulsive pictures to Lance Johnson. Then he remembered that the lieutenant wanted to talk to him again.

"What are you staring at?" Dae asked.

Brax turned away from the courthouse. "Nothing." He took her hand. "Let's walk around a little." *I'll tell her about it when we get home.*

Vehicles trickled past in both directions, occasionally breaking the quiet with voices and music that spilled from open windows.

The sidewalks were almost empty. Beyond a brightly lit Stop N Go market, they stopped to look in several storefronts of businesses closed for the night. Outside a former movie theater, now a music hall catering to a young audience, they perused the advertisements.

Brax studied a poster with figures in Gothic garb. "The Apostles of Hell. Why would anybody like this crap?"

"They're a new generation," she replied. "Always looking for something different."

"It's scary what passes for music these days. That's why I like bluegrass—it's bound by tradition. It comes out of the earth, just like the trees and the mountains, simple and pure like—" He stopped and pulled her to him. "Sorry, I was babbling."

"No, I admire your passion."

They left the music hall and began strolling the four blocks back to the car. "There's a bluegrass festival coming here in two weeks and the Kruger Brothers will be there. They're great instrumentalists. One plays the banjo and the other plays the guitar. You might not like old-timey bluegrass with cat-scratch singing, but you would love these guys. I've got a CD I can play for you."

"You don't have to convince me. I like different kinds of music, and I'd love to experience some local culture." She grinned.

"Or lack thereof," he said, and laughed.

Brax knew she was hedging the truth. A bluegrass festival was about the last event he could imagine Dae attending of her own choice. And he knew she would cringe at some of the less talented performers. He owed her one.

"I knew there was a reason I wanted to marry you," he said.

"Well, you'll have to take me to Atlanta to see the Nutcracker Ballet at the Fox for Christmas."

"Ugh."

On the ride home, a light rain began and Dae fell silent, her eyes focused on the mountainous countryside laden with leafy oak trees.

Brax glanced at her. "This is a lot different from South Georgia."

She continued looking out the window.

"How do you feel about living up here?" he asked.

"It's pretty remote."

"I should have warned you."

"I'll get used to it." A pause. "But remember—we agreed to keep both houses."

"Yeah," he said. "I remember."

How could he forget? His truck was locked in the garage at her house in Seaside, and he knew her heart was still there, too. But when he thought of that place, he often recalled moving from there with the specter of her dementia plagued husband hovering over him.

By nine o'clock, the rain picked up and the outside world turned black under a starless sky. They watched TV for a while, sitting in the dimly lit den like bears in a cave. Then, tired from the trip, they went to bed early.

When he kissed her goodnight, she said, "I'm happy as long as we're together."

"Me, too."

He rolled over and stared into the darkness. Even though he was content that she was being truthful about her love, he knew she was compromising to please him. Living in Rocky Ridge was not the perfect solution he had thought it would be. And he realized that, even in love, perfection is never achieved. He closed his eyes to find that elusive ideal in the shadows of a dream.

~

Brax sat up with his pillow against the headboard and studied Dae's face. When she opened her eyes, he said, "Good morning."

She yawned and mumbled something he took for "morning."

"I think you slept well. You were out like a light."

"Oh, I love the sound of rain hitting the metal roof. And this bed is so comfortable."

"Good. Maybe a new bedspread with a little color will save it."

"When did you say we were going to The Blue Hen?" She raised her brows.

He got up from bed and leaned down to nuzzle her cheek. "*Hen* pecking me already?" He laughed as he headed for the shower.

Later, Brax took a cup of coffee to the deck and settled into his rocking chair. He turned to see Dae walk from the house with a glass of juice in her hand. "Have a seat," he said.

She sat in the rocking chair beside him. A bright red streak flashed in front of them as a cardinal fluttered from the ground onto the limb of a maple tree. Squirrels scurried among the tree branches, jumping from one limb to another.

"I could sit here all morning," she said. "Everything is so green."

Her cheery voice and the upbeat look on her face were as refreshing to him as the cool morning breeze. He looked up at the white clouds floating in a sky that seemed to turn bluer by the minute. "Looks like the rain's over."

She walked to the railing and took a sip of juice. "You said there was a creek at the bottom of this hill. I think I can hear the water running from here. Can we go see it?"

"Sure. The path is steep though, and after the rain, it'll be pretty slick. Let's wait till this afternoon when it's dryer."

"All right." Dae walked to the other end of the deck and stood quietly looking out at the woods. She seemed to savor the juice as she swallowed the last drop. "Would you like a little breakfast?"

"That would be great but I don't have much to choose from. I'm not exactly Chef Ramsey even though I *have* been called a nasty sumbitch like him more than once. But there are some frozen waffles and sausage patties in the freezer."

"That'll do."

They ate a leisurely breakfast including grits Dae had found stuffed away in the pantry. Afterward, she set up her laptop on the kitchen table and busied herself for a half hour, checking her e-mail and Facebook site.

Brax sat at the other end of the table working a crossword puzzle. When the doorbell rang, he muttered, "Who in the hell could that be?" Glancing at his watch, he saw it was nearly nine-thirty—later than he had realized. He opened the door and felt a guilty rush as he looked into the eyes of Lieutenant Johnson.

"Lance, come in."

"Thanks." Johnson stepped inside. Wearing a white shirt stitched with a Pate County Sheriff Department insignia and a pistol snug on his hip, his presence changed the mood in the room. "Sorry to disturb you so early, but I thought I would catch you while you were home."

Brax led him into the living room and motioned toward Dae who looked back through the kitchen doorway. "This is my... friend, Dae Whitehead."

Johnson gave a quick nod to Dae. "Hello, ma'am."

"Hi," she said, a puzzled look on her face.

Johnson turned back to Brax. "I'd like to speak to you in private."

Brax looked at Dae and cursed himself for not telling her about finding the pictures.

"I can go upstairs," she said.

"No." Brax motioned toward the deck. "We can talk out there."

Johnson followed him outside and got right to the point. "I'd like your consent to search your computer."

"Why?" Brax asked through a grimace.

"Just checking everything out. It's part of the investigation."

Brax huffed. "Why in the world would I bring the pictures to you if I had anything to do with them?"

Johnson stared at Brax coldly. "People do crazy stuff. Not saying you do, but some things I've checked out don't add up."

"Like what?"

"I can't go into it. I just don't take anything for granted."

Brax walked to the edge of the deck and looked down with his arms folded before turning back to the officer. "You don't have a warrant, do you?"

"No." Johnson stood firmly, his eyes still locked on Brax.

Brax unfolded his arms and paused for a moment. "I have nothing to hide. You won't find anything of interest on that old relic."

He led Johnson back inside, past Dae at the kitchen table, and to his desk in the front bedroom.

Johnson eyed the computer monitor on the desk with the power light off. "Is there anything you need to look at before I take it?"

"No, I can use hers if I need to." Brax tilted his head toward Dae.

Brax bent down, unplugged the computer, all the accessories, and set it on top of the desk.

Johnson pointed to some CDs on a rack. "I'd like to look at those also."

"Sure. Here, take this too." Brax pulled a flash drive out of a drawer and handed it to the lieutenant. "You can look through the rest of the desk if you like."

Johnson didn't hesitate to search the desk drawers as if compelled by duty. Then he picked up the computer and carried it to his car. Brax followed with the CDs and flash drive in a plastic bag.

The officer handed Brax a sheet of paper. "You need to sign this."

Brax quickly read the statement authorizing temporary release of the items and signed it.

"I should have them back to you in a week or so," Johnson said.

After the officer left, Brax went inside and found Dae sitting on the sofa in the main room. He took a seat in his recliner. "I guess you're wondering what this is all about."

"Of course I am." Her voice carried the sharp edge of irritation.

"Look…" he stammered, "I'm sorry." He put a hand to his chin. "I should have told you about it before now. I kept meaning to, but with everything going on the last of couple of days…I don't know…I just kept putting it off. Besides, it's not a feel-good story."

"I'd like to hear it."

Brax put his hands on the arms of the chair and leaned his head back. "I found some pictures in the woods. They were tattered and partially burned. When I brought them home and pieced them together, I realized they were of grown men having sex with young girls."

He stopped with a blank stare on his face as the images appeared in his mind. Then he continued in a solemn tone, reliving the events as he spoke. He told her of meeting Ty, taking the pictures to Lance Johnson at the Sheriff's office, returning to the site with the officer, and meeting Ty again at the fire pit.

"There's something about that boy. He knows where those pictures came from. When he was running away, he said, 'My daddy's mean.' It was a cry for help."

"Why would they want *your* computer?"

"Like I said, it's just a part of the investigation, and I'm glad they're taking this seriously. That officer didn't have a warrant—no legal right to take it. But I let him have it. They won't find anything incriminating. I hardly ever use it except to work crossword puzzles."

Dae had a painful look on her face. "It's horrible to think about young girls being abused like that. Or, young boys, for that matter."

"They're the scum of the earth," Brax said.

"But I wish you had told me about it. I had no idea what was happening. That policeman came to the door, had a private conversation with you, and then took your computer away. What was I supposed to think?"

"I know it looked bad. I'm sorry I didn't tell you about it."

"Now the police have your computer. This whole situation might be more serious than you realize. It could tie you down here in Rocky Ridge until things are cleared up. Brax, you need to consider how that affects *me* as well as you."

"C'mon…" He was beginning to get riled, but had no defense. "Yeah, you're right."

"It would have been considerate of you to tell me about the dog, too."

"Oh, crap, I told you I'd keep him out of the house. You said you were okay with Sunny."

"And I really am, but that's beside the point. You shouldn't keep things like this from me. I don't like those kind of surprises."

He stood from the chair. "Okay, okay. I guess I need to tell you about my secret wife." He laughed.

She winced. "That's a *horrible* thing to say." Then her face turned to stone. "You'll never let me forget that, will you?" She snapped around and stormed off.

The comment slipped out of his mouth, and he realized too late that it had reopened the wound of her past deception about being widowed. "I didn't mean it. I was just being an idiot." He tried to grab her arm but she jerked it away.

She didn't turn around. Instead she tramped up the stairs, into the bedroom and slammed the door.

He went to the top of the stairs and stopped outside the door. "Dae, I'm sorry. You know I wasn't thinking."

She didn't answer.

Brax clinched his jaw and scolded himself. "Damn. Damn. Damn it."

Leaving her to anguish in private, he returned downstairs. He felt like the jerk he had told her he could be at times. And he didn't know any words that would erase the hurt he had caused her. Starting a new life with Dae had washed the grime of weariness from his spirit, but now the bar of soap in his hands felt mighty slippery.

9

BRAX WATCHED TELEVISION FOR A FEW MINUTES BEFORE PICKING up a magazine and thumbing through it. He tossed the magazine aside and ambled to the back window and stared vacantly into the woods. Then he went to the bottom of the stairs and saw the bedroom door still closed. He crept up the steps, trying to suppress the squeaks, and stopped at the landing. The faint sound of Dae's voice drifted from inside the room. He leaned closer and turned his ear to the door.

Straining to make out what she was saying, he clearly heard, "It's awful."

Awful. The word pierced through the door like a sharp dagger. He didn't know if she were referring to the house, Rocky Ridge, or maybe him.

He knocked on the door. "Dae."

"I'm talking to Julie," she said.

"Shit," he whispered. He felt his future slipping away and couldn't decide whether to barge in or go back down the steps. He just stood there.

Dae's voice was low, inaudible. Then she spoke louder. "You can come in."

She sat on the edge of the bed, her back to Brax. "Love you," she said and laid the phone on the nightstand.

Turning to Brax, she asked, "How far is Charlotte from here?" Her eyes were moist.

"I'm not sure—five or six hours I guess. Look, Dae—"

"Julie and Ben and the girls are dying to meet you. They want us to come visit them soon."

His eyes widened. "You're not still mad at me?"

She sighed. "What you said was cruel and it struck a nerve. Please don't ever joke about that again."

Brax leaned back against the chest of drawers. "I won't. But I might say something else stupid. I'm human."

She sniffled and turned to look out the window. Then she looked back at him. "I know you didn't say it out of meanness, but it still hurt."

"I realized that as soon as I said it. It was just me being a dumbass." He sat down beside her on the bed. "You know that movie where the guy said, 'Love means never having to say you're sorry?'" He took her hand. "He was wrong about that—I'm sorry."

She raised their entwined hands to her cheek.

"Well, maybe the guy was right after all, but I said it anyhow." He grinned. "I still love you, though."

She leaned to him and snuggled to his arm. "That's all I need. And I'm sorry, too."

He buried a cheek in her hair and they sat quietly for a moment.

Brax spoke first. "I guess we survived our first quarrel. Only took one day." He snuffled the hint of a laugh.

Dae rose from the bed, took a tissue from the nightstand, and wiped her eyes. "I realize I'm too sensitive. It's awful the way I overreacted." Then, as if flipping a switch, she added, "About that trip to Charlotte?"

"We'll go soon, but let's settle in here for a few days. How about next weekend?"

"Okay, great. I'll send Julie an email and see if that will work for them."

Dae looked in the dresser mirror and dabbed her eyes once more before turning around. "Right now, I'd like to go to the Blue Hen. I might see something there to brighten up this room."

"Alright. I think we could use a little break."

The Blue Hen had one large room with a high ceiling, and areas divided by furniture and accessories. Brax followed Dae as she strolled through dining room sets and seating arrangements for dens and living rooms, occasionally stopping to comment on a price or compatibility with their home. After making her way into the section with bedroom furniture, she was drawn to a display of linens.

She stood in front of an array of bedspreads with coordinating sheets, pillowcases, and shams. A burgundy spread with green and gold floral accents caught her eye and she moved closer to feel the fabric. "This one is real pretty. Do you like it?"

"Yeah, it looks good. I didn't know they cost that much though. There are other stores in town that sell this stuff, you know."

"I like this one."

"That's it then."

"The walls in the bedroom could use an update, too."

"You mean like wallpaper?"

"No, just a fresh coat of paint. But that can wait."

Brax envisioned a makeover of the whole house. That might

be just the trick to win her approval. So after buying the bedspread and linen, along with some towels for the master bath, he drove to the paint store in Rocky Ridge.

"Do you want me to bring in the bedding set so we can match the color?" he asked.

"There's no need to—I want Sienna Sand. That's what I have at Seaside and it will be perfect."

He bought a gallon of paint and all the supplies he needed to paint the bedroom.

"I shouldn't have mentioned it," she said, as they left the store. "It doesn't have to be done right now. And you don't need to do it yourself. We can hire a painter."

"No, I'm all primed up. I may be getting old, but I'm not dead. It'll only take a few hours."

"I'll help."

"Mmm," he murmured, "don't take this wrong, but I'm very meticulous about painting and I want to do it myself. Besides, I might lose my religion once or twice, and I don't want to set your ears on fire."

"I've heard it all, but have it your way."

"Good. We can spruce up the house and make it more up-to-date," he said as he put the materials in the truck.

"Yes. As you said—it has character."

It was faint praise. But for the first time he thought he heard the slightest hint of enthusiasm for the house.

On the way back, Dae said, "It hasn't rained any more and the ground has dried. I want to go to the creek when we get home."

He perked up when she said *home*. "Great. I'm ready for a walk myself."

At the house, Dae went straight to the master bedroom, opened the package of bedding, changed the linens, and covered them with the new spread. She stood back and looked at the bed. "Doesn't that look nice?"

"Yeah, it makes a difference."

She placed the new towels in the bathroom and asked, "Are you ready to go to the creek?"

"Sure, but we need to put on some grubby clothes."

After changing into well-worn shirts and jeans, they began the hike with Sunny leading the way down the path behind the house. The leaves and pine needles that carpeted the steep slope were still wet from the evening rain. The narrow trail was sheltered from sunlight by a canopy of trees, and the two hikers were swabbed with dampness as they brushed against limbs and underbrush.

When they reached the creek, Brax put his hand out. "This is it—my property line."

Dae stepped to the edge of the creek. She looked down and seemed spellbound as the water ran swifty with a soothing babble. "How peaceful. Everything is so…unspoiled."

"That's why I like it." He stooped to pick up a soggy candy wrapper trapped in debris on the side of the creek and put it in his pocket. "It's only spoiled by man." He turned his head and gazed at the woods around them.

Dae said, "You mean like those pictures you found?"

"Yeah."

"Were they near here?"

"Not too far away, maybe a mile. Do you feel like walking that far?"

"Sure."

"It's this way." He started downstream and whistled for Sunny, who had wandered into the woods.

When they reached the clearing, Brax stepped to the fire pit.

"This is where I saw the boy. You know—Ty. He ran off in that direction." He pointed to a scraggly dirt road behind them. Then, as he had done with Lance Johnson, he showed her the place where he had found the pictures. "I wish I had never picked them up. Getting involved with something like this could be a real pain. And it may never lead to anything."

"Why do you think they were here?"

"I think someone was burning them in the pit. Pictures like this can get you put in jail. I think whoever did it was interrupted by somebody else and ran away before everything completely burned up."

"Do you think it was Ty?"

"I really do," Brax replied. "A kid his age shouldn't see that kind of garbage."

"Yes." Dae frowned. "Youthful innocence. It's sad to lose that."

"Or have it taken away." Brax paused for a moment with a blank gaze. "Ready to go back?"

"Uh huh."

They followed the creek upstream and stopped at the foot of the path to their house.

"It's a lot harder going up than coming down," he said.

Halfway up, Dae stopped to catch her breath. She bent over with her hands on her knees and then straightened to lean on a tree.

"You want to sit down a minute?" Brax asked.

She shook her head.

"This is a lot tougher than walking on the beach," he said. "I usually walk on the track at the high school not far away. A buddy and I meet there every morning except Sunday. You can go with me tomorrow if you feel like it."

"I'd love to. I like walking on level ground." She started up the hill again.

Emerging from the trail, they were greeted with a burst of sunshine in the small treeless space behind the house. Once inside, they finished off a bottle of Gatorade.

After checking the refrigerator and pantry, Dae said, "I need to go to the grocery store. I saw a Publix in town last night."

"Good. That can be your first trip to town on your own."

She poured a glass of water and plopped down on the sofa in the living room. "I'm sweaty—I need to take a shower. But I want to talk about something first."

Brax walked from the kitchen with an energy bar in his hand. "Talk about what?"

"The trip to Charlotte we discussed."

"You said you'd email your daughter. I thought we agreed on Saturday if that's okay with her and her husband."

"His name's Ben." She put the glass of water to her cheek. "I want to tell them we're getting married."

He took a bite of the energy bar and then said, "O…kay."

Brax had no reservation, yet he felt the vise grip of finality that comes with a lifetime commitment as he squeezed the word from his mouth.

"We need to decide when and where."

He walked across the room and slouched into the recliner. "You tell me and I'll be there."

"You have family, too. Don't you want to let your sons know?"

"Sure, but I can't do that until we decide when."

"Brax, that's not the way it works. People have to make plans."

"So, you want a big church wedding? I was thinking of something simpler."

"That's what we need to decide before we go to Charlotte. And before you talk to your family."

"I just said I'll do whatever you want."

She heaved a sigh. "You're no help."

Brax ran his fingers through his hair.

"Location is the question," she said. "My family is in Charlotte, not to mention Germany, and yours is scattered around the country."

Brax knew that Dae's son, Justin, was in the Army and stationed in Germany with his wife and daughter. And his own three sons were separated by different time zones. "Atlanta…Dallas…Seattle." His eyes got big as he mentioned the cities where his sons lived. "Do you want everybody involved or just a small, private ceremony?"

"I doubt Justin can come, but I want all of our immediate family members invited. I want a simple ceremony and I want it soon."

So much for my input, he thought. "Where?"

She smiled. "The place where we met—on the island at Seaside."

The idea caught Brax by surprise. He had bittersweet memories of Seaside and thought of it as a part of his past rather than his future. Although he and Dae had agreed to keep her house there, he envisioned Rocky Ridge as their primary home. Now it was clear that they had not discussed their living arrangement thoroughly, and her thoughts were different from his.

Dae kept her eyes glued on him as he contemplated the idea.

Finally, he said, "That's perfect." In his mind, he had just agreed to more than the wedding locale.

"Isn't it exciting?"

He just smiled.

"We'll tell both of our families next Saturday. I can't wait to see the look on Julie's face. You can call your sons, and I can talk to them on the phone. We can set up a face-time call."

He shrugged. "Whatever."

"I want to set the date for four weeks after we announce. That's June the third."

"I'll mark it on my calendar." He realized she had it all figured out, but he didn't mind. *You tell me and I'll be there.* His words were never truer.

"Perfect," she said, ignoring his josh. She stood up from the sofa with a big smile on her face. "I'm going to take a shower."

Brax needed some time to absorb what had just happened. He walked to the deck, poured some dog food in a bowl, and watched Sunny lap it up. On the corner of the deck, he noticed a sheet of paper anchored to the floor by a flower pot. He knew that neither he nor Dae had put it there, and somehow it had escaped their attention when they returned from their walk. He bent down and lifted the paper from under the pot. The letter-sized sheet was folded in half, clean and undamaged.

He opened the sheet, stared at it briefly, then folded it again. His hands trembled and he felt as if he might be infected by mere contact with the evilness his eyes had seen. Naked young girls. Grown men satisfying their most depraved urges.

10

BRAX STARED OUT AT THE WOODS FROM HIS CHAIR ON THE DECK. He didn't see the trees or the sky that glistened through the open spaces, nor did he hear the water rushing in the creek. Instead, his mind was filled with the vile images on the sheet that lay in his lap, images that seemed to be seared into his eyes.

Amidst the serene setting, he felt the pull of a dangerous unseen force tugging at him, like a strong undertow in an otherwise calm sea. He was caught up in something very dark and, for a brief moment, wished the force would simply go away and leave him alone. It was a guilty feeling, and he felt ashamed to place his own discomfort above the torment suffered by young girls. He had known his own suffering and for all his adult years had tried to block out the painful memories. Now the embers of those once fiery thoughts flamed back up like they had been ignited by a puff from the devil.

As he rocked in the chair, it became clear to him what he should do. It was as if Moses had handed him a commandment written on a tablet of stone. Seeking retribution upon the person who found pleasure in abusing young girls was the only thing that mattered now—more important than where he and Dae would live, the time and place of their marriage, or what color the damn bedspread was.

"I'll get the bastard," he said aloud.

Sunny roused to his feet and sidled up beside the rocker. Brax patted the dog's hindquarter and stood from the chair. "We'll get him, won't we?" He folded the sheet, went into the living room and sat in his recliner waiting for Dae to join him.

"Feeling better?" he asked when she came downstairs after her shower.

"Yes. Are you going to clean up?"

"In a minute. I need to talk to you about something first." He raised the sheet in his hand. "I found this on the deck."

"What is it?"

"Another picture like the ones I found before."

Dae moved forward and reached her hand out, but Brax pulled the sheet away.

"You can look if you want to, but it's really nasty." He laid the sheet on the side table and spread it open.

She walked to the table and looked down briefly before turning her head and stepping back. "That's disgusting. How did it get on the deck?"

"Well, it didn't blow in with the wind. Somebody stuck it partly under a flower pot so that we were sure to see it." He re-folded the sheet to hide the images.

"Someone came onto our deck," she said, as if the thought had just registered.

"That's right. And you and Lance Johnson are the only people that I've told about finding the other pictures. I think I know somebody who wants me to see more of them."

Dae stood silent with a far-away look in her eyes. Then she said, "The boy?"

"Yeah, Ty."

"What are you going to do?"

"I need to talk to Johnson again."

"Yes, let the officials handle it."

Brax took the sheet from the table and stood up. "If they don't, I will."

"No, let *them* handle it."

Brax didn't respond. He walked into the front bedroom, removed a manila folder from the desk, and placed the sheet in it. Then he called Lance Johnson and left a message that he needed to meet with him.

"I'm going to take my shower now." From the hall, he caught a glimpse of Dae at the kitchen table, peering at her laptop.

She turned and spoke in a loud voice. "Julie says Saturday is good for them. We can go, can't we?"

"Uh huh." He responded out of reflex. His mind was only on one thing: his next meeting with Lieutenant Johnson.

Thirty minutes later, Brax was in the living room, working on a crossword puzzle in a magazine, when Lance Johnson returned the call.

"I'd like to meet with you again," Brax said, setting the magazine aside. "I've found another picture."

"Was it in the same place in the woods?" asked Johnson.

"No. Someone put it on my deck."

"Put it on your deck? That's crazy. Can you bring it to me this afternoon, say...about four o'clock?"

"I'll be there."

Brax ended the call and turned to Dae on the sofa. "I'm meeting with Johnson at four."

She put her electronic tablet in her lap. "I want to go with you."

"I don't think you should. This could get ugly."

"That's why I'm going. They have already taken your computer, and I don't want any more suspicion aimed at you. I'm your best character witness." She stood. "Besides, you can take me to the supermarket afterward."

Brax shook his head and smiled.

～

Brax led Dae down the hall in the lower level of the courthouse to the Sheriff's office. At the front desk, he recognized the woman he had met on his first visit. He spoke to her through the portal of the glass window while she flailed away on a keyboard.

"I'm Braxton Donovan and I have an appointment with Lieutenant Johnson."

She looked up from the monitor and eyed them for a moment as if making a judgment. "You can go in," she said, and resumed typing.

They entered the office where Brax had met with Johnson before. A heavyset man wearing a white uniform shirt sat behind the second desk that had been empty during the first meeting. The man remained tilted back in his padded chair, appearing smugly in charge of the small domain.

Johnson stood and moved from his desk to greet Brax with a handshake.

"You remember Dae, don't you?" Brax asked.

"Yes, nice to see you again." Johnson shook Dae's hand, then pulled up chairs for her and Brax. "Have a seat."

Johnson turned his head toward the other man. "This is Captain Hembree."

Hembree rocked in his chair slightly, his elbows resting on the arms. "How y'all doin'?" His voice was deep and his drawl as thick as milk gravy.

Brax and Dae each responded with a polite "Hi." They sat down and Johnson returned behind his desk.

"We're getting married soon," Brax said, and looked at Dae. Saying that at his age felt strange, but he thought it would give her more credibility as an interested party.

Johnson arched his brows. "Congratulations."

"Thank you," Dae said, returning his smile.

Johnson looked at the folder in Brax's hand. "Is the picture in there?"

"Yeah." Brax placed the manila folder on the desk and opened it.

Johnson studied the picture for a few seconds. "It looks like it was printed from a computer."

"Or photocopied from something else," Dae said.

Johnson closed the folder without touching the sheet, and handed it to Hembree. The Captain opened the folder, took a brief glance at the picture, then closed the folder and set it on the corner of his desk.

"That boy—Ty—put it there," Brax blurted out.

"What makes you think that?" asked Johnson.

"He's the only person that could have. I think he put the other ones in the fire pit and he's seen me there more than once. The first time we talked, I could sense that he wanted to tell me something. But he was too scared. He knows where I live though."

"That's a lot of loose ends to tie together," Johnson said.

"You need to search his father's computer. That's where this came from."

"Mr. Benefield?" Johnson looked at Brax with disbelief written on his face.

"Don't look at me like that." Brax shifted to the edge of his chair and raised his voice. "He wouldn't be the first person that works with young kids to take advantage of the situation. Don't assume the man's a saint, for Christ's sake." Brax lowered his voice and scowled at Johnson. "Some people who seem *normal* on the outside are actually screwed up on the inside."

"You're jumping to conclusions." Johnson paused and a stern look grew on his face. "I appreciate that you brought in this evidence, but I'll handle the investigation."

"Just check out his *damn* computer." Brax said.

"Brax," Dae said, nudging him.

"How hard could that be?" Brax continued. "I let you have mine and there was no reason for it. You didn't find a thing, did you?"

"I said I would handle it." Johnson's voice was firm and his eyes met Brax's stare. "Why don't you take a deep breath and cool off?"

Brax shifted in his chair and looked at Dae.

Taking his own advice, Johnson blew a puff of air and seemed to relax. "We had cause to look at your computer and we don't have a report back yet."

"What cause?"

"I spoke with Mr. Benefield and told him of your encounter with his son. He said that he had heard through a mutual friend that you had expressed an interest in meeting Ty. Said that you wanted to look at his baseball cards. Tom assured me that Ty has no baseball cards and he was concerned that you might have other intentions regarding his son. He wanted me to warn you to stay away from the boy."

His conversation with Charlie Kramer flashed in Brax's mind and now his own words were coming back to haunt him. Feeling the anger building inside, he stood up. "So, you wanted to look at my computer because of some bullshit allegations. And you thought I might have an interest in a young boy even though I voluntarily brought you pornographic pictures with young girls. Talk about *loose ends*," he said, raising his voice a couple of notches. He felt the blood run to his face.

Dae stood and clutched Brax's arm. "Calm down."

Johnson rose from his chair and gripped the desk like he wanted to throw it at Brax.

Brax continued. "You need to quit pussyfooting around with this…pervert."

Johnson's left eye began to twitch and the veins bulged from his neck. "Listen—"

Hembree popped out of his chair. "Look here," he bellowed, "Lieutenant Johnson will handle this matter. He has lots of experience in working criminal cases. Fact is, he could do my job if I didn't have squatter's rights. So don't get all fired up like some vigilante. You'll just screw things up."

Brax felt Dae tug hard on his arm and they both sat down. The two officers returned to their seats and the room became quiet.

Johnson looked at Brax and broke the silence. "Have you had an experience with child pornography or child abuse before?"

Brax paused before he replied, "No." A lie, he thought, was the best bandage for an old wound.

Johnson glared at Brax before continuing. "Well, you obviously have strong opinions about this case, and there's nothing wrong with that. But I need you to work with me. I don't want you to speak to anyone—even close friends—about the pictures. We don't want whoever is responsible for this to know that we are looking for him. We'll find out who that person is."

Brax sighed and rubbed his eyes. "Okay." He looked at Johnson for a second and then rose from his chair. "Let's go," he said to Dae.

As the couple reached the doorway, Brax turned and looked at Johnson, then Hembree. "I know who it is."

Hembree stood again, sucked in his big belly and tugged at his belt. "Just do like Lieutenant Johnson said and keep that opinion to yourself. Impedin' an investigation is a serious matter."

Outside the courthouse, Brax and Dae walked past Banjo Bob plucking away on his instrument.

Banjo Bob looked at Brax and said, "Join in," between lines of *American Pie*.

Brax raised his hand with a halt sign. "Not today." Once, he had sung along with Bob, recalling most of the lyrics of Don McLean's classic song, but this day his spirit wasn't in it.

"I see what you mean about him playing different kinds of songs," Dae said.

Brax continued walking and didn't respond. He felt strangely removed from everything around him as if he were suspended above the earth.

When they reached the car, Dae asked, "What's wrong? Are you still angry?"

"No." He stared through the windshield into the distance. "I want to take you somewhere."

"I need to go to the grocery store."

"We can go there later." He started the car and pulled from the curb. "It's a place called Athy." He pronounced it *A-Ty*. "It's about forty miles from here."

"What's there?"

"You'll see."

They spoke very little as Brax drove through the rural countryside on a lightly traveled road. Nearing his destination he spoke up.

"Athy is not on any map. It's just a little community and not much of it is left anymore. It's spelled A-T-H-Y and old-timers called it A-ty, with a silent H. That's how it's pronounced in the town in Ireland it was named after. A lot of Scots and Irish settled around here after the Cherokees were rounded up and sent away."

"The Trail of Tears," she said.

"Yeah, a sad part of history. But you would know about that." He referred to her career as a teacher and author of a textbook on early Georgia history.

The road snaked down a mountainside before it flattened out at an apple orchard.

"It's not far from here." Brax turned onto a desolate road with overgrown underbrush on both sides of the poorly maintained blacktop. Two miles beyond, a church stood in a clearing just off the road, and he turned onto the dirt driveway.

A faded crust of peeling white paint covered the wood plank building. A set of four wide steps led to the front door, which was sheltered by a small gable roof. Directly above rose a steeple with an empty belfry. An expanse of gravel and scattered weeds formed a parking area in front. The church had been obviously abandoned.

Brax parked directly in front of the church. They got out of the car and approached the front door. On the left side of the door, a weathered sign read:

ATHY BAPTIST CHURCH

ESTAB. JAN. 15, 1873

"This is where I was baptized" he said. "The original church was on this same site. It burned to the ground in 1920 something. This building lasted almost a hundred years. The new church is farther down the highway, past where we turned off."

"Did you grow up in this area?" Dae asked.

"Not really, but I was born in my grandparents' house not far away. It's not there anymore."

Dae took Brax's arm. "Why did you come here?"

"To visit my parents. I haven't been here in a good while." He looked to the side of the church toward a graveyard surrounded by a rusty iron fence. "They're over there."

He led her through the arched gateway. They wound through rows of headstones, most of them aged and slightly atilt with family surnames and carved images of angels and lambs. Some had faded artificial flowers stuck in metal vases. Several inscriptions listed birthdates in the early 1800's. He pointed out burial plots of relatives as he passed by. "That's my grandmother and grandfather." Next to them were the graves of his aunt and uncle—his father's brother. In another place, two cousins and their spouses were buried.

Near the back of the cemetery, he stopped in front of two graves that shared one headstone with DONOVAN chiseled into the granite. On the slab atop one of the graves, the inscription read:

JOSEPHINE MOSLEY DONOVAN

SEP 12, 1910—MAY 15, 1988

The other slab read:

MARTIN JASPER DONOVAN

AUG 17, 1903—NOV 21, 1990

Brax stood silently staring at the graves. Then he took Dae's hand, led her to a weathered concrete bench nearby, and they sat down.

"Mother was a saint," he said.

"Did people call her Josephine?"

"Only Dad. Everyone else called her Josie."

"Did he go by Martin?"

"Yeah." Brax lowered his head and stared at the ground. "My daddy was mean."

She gasped, then whispered, "Oh my God." She turned to the side, looked at him, and put her hand on his arm. After a long pause, she said, "Brax, look at me."

He turned to her.

"Did your father harm little girls?"

"No. He preferred boys." He looked at her calmly and felt the virtue of truth.

Dae cupped her hands over her mouth and closed her eyes.

Brax picked up a handful of small rocks from the ground and walked back into the maze of burial sites. Standing at the foot of his father's grave, he juggled the rocks in his hands.

It wouldn't do any good, he realized. It never had in the past. He threw the rocks into the air and they landed scattershot in the distance. Then he returned to the bench and reached his hand to Dae.

She stood and they embraced, clinging to the promise of tomorrow, surrounded by memories of yesterday.

They walked to the car and soon Athy was behind them.

11

BRAX CURSED AND LET OUT A GROAN AS HE GOT DOWN ON HIS knees to wipe a drop of paint off the hardwood floor. A bead of sweat dripped from his nose and splashed beside his hand. The oversized furniture shoved to the middle of the master bedroom left only a tight space around the walls. The sheetrock was so dry it soaked up the paint like a sponge, making it necessary to use two coats.

Dae nudged the door against him and he stood up to let her in. "How's it coming?" she asked.

"I got most of it on the walls," he replied.

"I wondered about that when I heard all the colorful language."

She stepped past a roller lying in a tray and looked around. All four walls were covered with a fresh coat of her favorite color, Sienna Sand, and the smell of paint filled the room.

"Looks like you're about finished."

"Getting there. I just have to detail around the ceiling."

Brax grabbed a brush and bucket of paint and climbed halfway up a stepladder. When he made a stroke at the top of the wall, a glob of tan paint hit the white ceiling. A stream of obscenities spewed from his mouth as he took a wet rag to his mistake.

"You got some right here, too." Dae pointed to a spot of paint on the doorjamb.

"I *know*," he blurted. "I'll get it off. I wish you'd leave until I'm through."

"Well, if you're going to be an ass…" She left the room, closing the door firmly behind her.

Brax began trimming next to the ceiling and suddenly he sensed his father looking at him with critical eyes.

~

Before he was in his teens, Brax had begun tagging along with his father as a helper on week-end odd jobs: hanging drywall, patching roofs, laying brick, or painting houses. Everyone knew about Martin Donovan; he was not only a hard worker who could do about anything, but he also did things right. He was a perfectionist. That work ethic was ingrained in Brax and, by the age of fifteen, he was doing some of the work himself. The first time he painted a room on his own, the detail work was sloppy and he was made to repaint all the trim.

"That's better," his father said after the redo. "Take pride in your work and do it right."

His father was not only demanding but also short tempered, a proclivity that Brax unfortunately inherited. Still, there were admirable traits: a strong work ethic, generosity to his friends, even a sense of humor.

But Brax knew the dark side that was hidden from view, and lived in that darkness until the shame became unbearable. He was fourteen when, in the shadows of his bedroom one night, Brax said, "No more." His father was bigger and stronger, but Brax had hidden the .22 rifle under his sheet and was prepared to do whatever it took to end it.

"It's a man's world," his father said. "Don't ever forget that, boy." His eyes were hidden in the dark and his black silhouette hovered over Brax like a bear ready to attack. Then he walked away and there was no more.

∼

When he finished the trim at the ceiling, Brax could almost hear the words he had always longed for: "Good job, son."

He put the materials away and replaced the furniture. Then he returned downstairs to the kitchen, poured a scotch on the rocks and took a big swig. The whiskey had a mellowing effect and he regretted having lost his temper earlier. He led Dae upstairs to look at the finished job and reset the mood.

"Looks great," she said. "But, I didn't know it would stress you out so much."

"Sorry about that. I warned you I might lose my religion. I had forgotten how much fun it is to paint a room. Whose idea was this, anyhow?" The hint of a smile creased his face.

"I told you we should hire a painter." Dae huffed. "Stubborn."

Brax raised his arms with a melodramatic thrust. "It was a labor of love."

"Those words coming out of your mouth didn't sound like love to me."

He moved to kiss her but she laughed and pulled away. "You've got paint on your nose."

He set the glass on a side table and ran the sleeve of his T-shirt across his nose. "*But I have love in my heart, mon cheri,*" he said in a lousy French accent. He pulled her to him and kissed her.

"You smell like scotch."

"You're so full of compliments."

"I'm glad you're feeling better. You're not nice to be around when you're mad." She leaned into him. "Thanks for your hard work, though."

Later in the shower, the warm water soothed some of the stiffness from Brax's body. Feeling clean and refreshed, he walked into the bedroom and smiled as he admired his work.

She likes it. More rooms, more work. Jeez, I've got to find a painter.

~

After dinner, Brax poured another drink. He slumped into his recliner across the room from Dae, who was absorbed in a historical novel. In the quiet room the blank television screen stared back at him.

Dae looked up from the book and asked, "Are you tired?"

"A little," he replied.

Fatigue began to set in and an overwhelming sense of melancholy, fueled by the alcohol, welled up inside him. Recollections of old demons stirred in his head. Their visit to Athy the day before was still stuck in his mind. He wasn't sure why he had been compelled to take her there. They hadn't spoken about the trip since returning; she seemed reluctant to bring it up. The darkness of his revelation regarding his father hovered over them like a rain cloud. His throat felt as if he was choking, and he could feel his heart pounding.

He gazed at the glass of scotch resting on the arm of the chair.

Dae set the book aside and their eyes met. "What are you thinking about?" she asked.

"Mom never knew." She didn't respond and he let the thought sink in. "At Dad's funeral I stood at the foot of his grave and said I loved him. Mom had already passed away, so it wasn't for her benefit. I'm not sure why I said it or if I even meant it."

He took a sip of his drink and began speaking again as if talking to himself. "There's a fine line between love and hate, and I never knew where that line was between him and me. He could be mean—maybe hard is a better word—but he had a good side, too, and before he died he asked me to forgive him. I told him I did, but there are times when I feel like I lied, not only to him, but to myself as well. At the cemetery yesterday, I thought of those pictures of young girls being abused and I wasn't in a forgiving mood. I guess true forgiveness is in the hands of God."

She moved from the sofa and knelt in front of his chair. "I'm glad you told me. Now I understand how you feel about Ty."

"I doubt his experience is like mine. I think this is about young girls. But, you don't have to be physically involved to be victimized. Just knowing about this stuff at an early age can change your whole outlook on life."

Brax lowered his head and closed his eyes. Then he looked up and said, "Having sex with a child is repulsive to normal people. It makes no sense to us. You can imagine how confusing and scary it is to a child."

Dae rose from her knees and sat in his lap with her arms around him. "I love you." She kissed him on the cheek.

They sat silently, her head on his chest. Seconds later, she raised her head and asked, "Am I squashing you?"

"No." His mood lightened as he exaggerated a gasp for air.

"Oh, you." She gave his arm a playful slap and stood up.

The dark thoughts of his childhood disappeared. Everything felt good again—the taste of the scotch, the comfort of the recliner, the kiss on his cheek, the affirmation of her affection. He was reminded how simple the pleasures of life can be when you're with someone you love and know they love you. Even when you sometimes act like an ass.

The smell of paint lingered in the master bedroom, so they slept downstairs in the room that included his desk. When he looked at the vacant space that his computer normally occupied, he was reminded of the void he had felt in his life. But now, lying next to Dae, he no longer felt that emptiness.

At that moment, he understood why he had taken her to Athy.

～

Brax parked near Charlie Kramer's car behind the visitors' bleachers at the high school stadium. As he and Dae approached the track, they saw Charlie stretching a leg on top of a trashcan.

"Good morning," Brax said.

"Hey," Charlie replied, as he let his foot down.

Brax looked at Dae and back to his friend. "Charlie, this is Dae Whitehead. She's going to walk with us this morning."

"Good." Charlie extended a hand to Dae without smiling. "My pleasure."

"Thank you. Brax has spoken highly of you. I've looked forward to walking with you fellows. I try to get in a walk every morning myself."

"We've been tied up for a few days," Brax said. "Just getting settled in."

"I understand."

Brax noticed right off that Charlie seemed oddly reserved,

considering they hadn't seen each other in a couple of weeks. Even in greeting Dae, he didn't display his typical exuberance.

Once they began walking, it struck Brax as to what might be bothering Charlie. Before they had completed the first lap, he asked him a pointed question. "Have you talked to Tom Benefield lately?"

Dae nudged Brax. He turned to her and she shook her head, signaling to him with squinted eyes not to pursue the matter.

"I saw him at church Sunday," Charlie said.

"Did he say anything about me?"

"Brax," Dae whispered.

"Why would he do that?" asked Charlie.

"I thought you might know why," replied Brax.

"Look," Charlie said, "I don't want to get involved with whatever is going on between you two."

Brax was convinced that Benefield had given Charlie reasons to question his interest in Ty. He felt tempted to tell Charlie about the pictures he had found and his own conviction of Benefield's guilt, but he didn't want to embarrass Dae. Nor had he forgotten Lance Johnson's admonition to keep quiet about the matter. Still, the unspoken suspicion he felt from Charlie gnawed at him.

"We've never met," Brax said. "He doesn't know a thing about me."

"It's nice this morning," Dae said, putting a chill on the talk about Benefield.

The three walkers scuffled along for several minutes, speaking only in brief spurts. Then, with no segue, Brax said matter-of-factly, "Dae and I are getting married in a few weeks."

"Really?" Charlie looked at Dae and slowed a bit. "Congratulations."

"Thanks," she replied.

The conversation tapered off and the men struggled to keep up with Dae's brisk pace.

Brax figured that telling Charlie of their marriage plans might ease his suspicion. Maybe he would assume that a man committed to marriage in his twilight years wouldn't have sexual interest in a young boy like Ty. Ironically, it was just that kind of thinking that could provide cover for someone who enjoyed respect within the community while leading the secret life of a pedophile. Someone like a school principal.

When they finished eight laps the trio walked to their cars, and Charlie had a last word with Dae. "Nice meeting you. Will you be moving to Rocky Ridge?"

"I think so," she said, turning to Brax.

"Yeah," Brax said, "she'll be with me for the next couple of days. We're going to Charlotte on Saturday to see her family. We'll tell them we're getting married." He laughed.

Charlie looked surprised. "Was I the first one to hear about it?"

"Almost," Brax said, recalling his announcement to Lieutenant Johnson. His face turned serious. "I thought as a friend you might want to know."

"Absolutely. I'm glad you did." Charlie stuck his hand out and the two men shook. "Congratulations again."

"We'll see you in the morning," Brax said.

"I might not make it. Liz wants to go to the mall in Buford. Start without me if I'm not here."

On the way home, Brax spoke to Dae about Charlie's aloofness. "He acted like a different person. He's usually real friendly but I could tell he's bought into whatever Tom Benefield said about me."

"I was afraid you were going to stir things up. The sheriff's officer told you not to say anything about that man."

"I can say whatever I want to."

"No, you can't—not as long as I'm around."

He had nearly forgotten one of the rules of marriage—the one that says the wife is always right. He shifted his eyes from the road for a second and looked at her. "I guess that settles it."

When Brax pulled into the driveway, Sunny trotted from behind the house. Out of the car Brax greeted him with a playful rub.

Dae went to the front door and Sunny slowly walked toward her. "You can come in," she said.

Brax looked on in amazement as Dae let Sunny inside for the first time since her arrival.

She led Sunny to the foot of the sofa. "You can sit here," she said, with a pat on the dog's back. "But you're not allowed upstairs," she added, looking at Brax.

"Yeah," Brax said, speaking to the friendly Lab as if he were a child. "That's off limits now."

He turned to Dae. "That was a surprise."

"We're family now." She smiled.

"Well I'll be damn. How 'bout that."

～

That afternoon, Brax and Dae relaxed on the deck, drinking iced tea and reading their books. When his phone rang, Brax hoped it was the handyman he had hired to finish painting the inside of the house. Instead, the caller display read PATE CTY SHER and Lance Johnson was on the line.

"I have your computer back from the GBI. Can you come to my office to pick it up? I'd like to meet with you again."

"Meet with me?"

"Yes, I have some questions about what was in the computer."

"Well, I'm leaving in the morning for Charlotte." Brax looked at Dae sitting in the rocker beside him. "But I don't want anything hanging over my head. I can be there in an hour or so."

"I'll see you then," Johnson said.

Brax stood up and put the phone in his pocket. "That was Lance Johnson. He wants to meet with me again."

Dae placed a bookmark between the pages and closed her book. "About what?"

"I'm not sure," he said, shaking his head. "This is strange. He said he wanted me to stay out of this and now he wants to talk to me again."

"It sounds urgent." Dae stood from her chair. "I'll go with you."

"You don't have to go. I won't get mad like I did last time."

She looked him in the eyes and said firmly, "I'm going with you."

He pursed his lips. *I guess that settles it.*

Brax was uneasy about talking to Johnson in Dae's presence. He had unwittingly put himself in a corner and couldn't figure a way to squirm out. Not being computer savvy, the contents of the hard drive were a mystery to him, and he worried what might still be hidden away in some secret cyber vault. He wondered if they could track the Internet sites he had visited. And why in the heck hadn't he thought about that before he agreed to let Johnson take his computer?

12

BRAX AND DAE ARRIVED AT THE SHERIFF'S DEPARTMENT LESS THAN an hour after the call from Lance Johnson. They found him sitting at the front desk behind the glass partition.

Johnson let them into the reception area and spoke directly to Brax. "I'd like to meet with you in private."

Brax jerked his head back. "What's going on?"

"I'd like to ask you some questions of a personal nature." Johnson looked at Dae. "No offense, but a third party might inhibit the discussion."

"She's not a *third party*," Brax said. "I told you we are going to be married soon. I don't have to talk to you—I've got my Miranda rights."

"You're not in custody. I'd like your cooperation but you can leave any time you want."

Brax pulled Dae aside and spoke in a low tone with his back to Johnson. "I don't have anything to hide from you, but I'll have to talk to him sooner or later."

She grasped his arm. "I know—it's okay with me. I want you to have your meeting. But please don't lose your temper."

Brax turned back to Johnson. "I could just get my computer

and leave, but I don't want to get in a pissing contest or get a grease-ball lawyer involved. I'll answer your questions."

"Good." Looking at Dae, Johnson said, "You're welcome to wait out here."

"Thanks, but I'll leave." She turned to Brax, "I'm going to the bookstore across the street and maybe walk around town for a while. Call me when you're through."

Johnson opened the door and Dae began to leave, then turned to face the two men. "I want you both to stay calm—no shouting."

"There won't be any shouting," said Johnson.

As Dae walked down the corridor toward the outside, Brax said from behind her, "Tell everybody to look for me on America's Most Wanted."

Following Johnson into his office, Brax noted that the second desk was unoccupied as it had been the first time they met. He tensed for a tete-a-tete when the officer closed the door.

"Would you like coffee or a Coke?" Johnson began.

Brax shook his head. "No, I'm fine. Am I under suspicion of something?"

Johnson pursed his lips and then replied, "As I said, you're not in custody. Let's call it curiosity, not suspicion. I just want to ask you a few questions."

Brax was sure he had nothing to hide from a legal standpoint. But recalling Johnson's comments about questions "of a personal nature," he wasn't as confident about potential embarrassment. Despite his initial protest, he was glad that Dae had been excluded from the meeting. Leaning back in his chair, he crossed his arms as if he was about to be mentally strip-searched.

"Fire away," he said.

Johnson sat erect with his hands on the desk. "This is not a fight." Then he settled back and appeared relaxed. "There were a lot of internet searches in your computer about pedophilia, sex crimes, and deviant behavior. Do you have a particular interest in that type of activity?"

The realization that his internet searches could be traced made Brax uneasy. "I wanted to know more about that kind of thing after I found the pictures. Try to figure out how these sick bastards think. How they operate without getting caught."

Johnson squinted as if he wasn't buying it. "A lot of the searches were dated prior to the incident you reported."

Brax unfolded his arms and rested his elbows on the sides of the chair. He tried to think of an excuse for why he had searched those sites but drew a blank. "There's tons of crazy stuff on the internet. You can find all kinds of filth. Is it a crime to be curious?"

Johnson clasped his hand and intertwined his fingers. "I asked you the last time we met if you had any experiences involving sexual crimes and you said no. You weren't being truthful, were you?"

Brax looked at the officer defiantly. "I wasn't under oath."

"I'm pretty good at reading people," Johnson said, "and I knew when you got so emotional that you had a personal interest. Do you have a daughter who was abused?"

The question shocked Brax and he felt like a fox with a hound on his trail. Johnson was off base but he was getting close. "I don't have a daughter."

"We also found a website you visited several times that promotes sex between men and young boys." Johnson didn't say more but the question was obvious.

"Hey, I don't have any interest in Ty Benefield or any other boy and I never have."

"I believe you."

Despite the reassurance, Brax sensed that Johnson wasn't satisfied with the explanation.

"I saw something on television about an organization that promotes *love*," Brax made quote marks with his fingers, "between men and boys. I couldn't believe it was legal. Those guys ought to be strung up and castrated."

"I agree. Freedom of speech…" Johnson seemed to search for words and his face contorted in obvious disgust. "Some people don't deserve that freedom." Then he locked his eyes on Brax. "You looked at one site that features sex between men and their children." Stroking his chin, he asked, "Were you abused by your father?"

Brax turned his head away and then back to the officer. His hands twitched and he felt his whole body tense up. He knew that the look on his face answered the question and the room fell silent.

Johnson broke the tension. "I could use a cup of coffee. How about you—want something to drink now?"

"Yeah, I'll have a cup."

Johnson grabbed a mug from the edge of his desk and stood up. "Come on, let's take a little breather."

They went into a small break room. Johnson made a fresh pot of coffee and rinsed a ceramic cup from a cabinet for Brax. Leaving the dark subject of sexual perversion behind, the conversation centered on their mutual interest in college football. They talked for about fifteen minutes before heading back to the office.

After a stiff dose of caffeine and a spirited discussion about the upcoming football season, Brax felt more relaxed.

Johnson settled behind his desk and drained the last sip of coffee from his mug. "I think you're right about Ty—he knows something."

Brax couldn't resist a smirk.

"When I met with Tom at his house," Johnson continued, "his son was present and I asked the boy if he knew anything about burning pictures at the fire pit near the creek. He said 'no,' but I could tell he was lying."

The smirk on Brax's face turned to a smile. "You're good about knowing when someone is lying."

"You get a lot of practice in this job."

Brax nodded. "I've told you from the beginning his dad is the one you need to focus on."

"I can't go on gut feel. I have to have evidence, or at least probable cause, to get a warrant."

"You didn't have either one when you took my computer."

"I knew you would let me have it if you weren't involved, and I wanted to eliminate you as a suspect. Now, with the report of your computer from the GBI, I'm on the spot. My superiors want me to interrogate you as a suspect. Like I said, though, I'm pretty good at reading people, and I thought you would level with me."

"I lied to you before because I didn't want to talk about it," Brax said. "Especially with my wife-to-be sitting right next to me. At the time, she didn't know about my past. Now she does."

"I understand." Johnson took a pen from his shirt pocket and wiggled it in his fingers. "I have an idea of how to check out your theory about Tom Benefield. However, it won't be easy to convince Captain Hembree and Sheriff Wainright to agree. And, if you're wrong, I could be stepping into quicksand."

"Well, I'm convinced I'm right, but you don't have to jeopardize your career."

"I want to catch this guy as much as you do. I told you I have a daughter." Johnson paused. "She's in the fifth grade at Sequoyah Elementary."

"Ah." Brax grimaced, realizing that Johnson had a personal concern. "What's your idea?"

"I can't tell you. It's best you stay out of it altogether."

"That suits me, but I can't ignore stuff that's left right at my back door."

Johnson raised an eyebrow. "Yeah. That gives me a little more confidence in my plan."

Brax left the Sheriff's office with his computer in hand and mixed emotions in his head. He realized Johnson was sharp and he had grown to like the officer. He was curious about Johnson's plan, but thought he was headed in the right direction. Yet he feared that the plan might lead to the identity of innocent young girls who would grow up with a stain they could never wash away. He hoped Johnson's daughter wasn't one of them.

On the ride home, Brax told Dae about the meeting. He swallowed a gulp of pride before admitting to the questions that Johnson raised about the websites he had visited. When he mentioned the site that advocates man-boy relations, the blood ran to his face.

"Why would you want to look at those disgusting things?" she asked.

"Because I'm trying to figure out what kind of creep I'm dealing with. Why a man would want to have sex with a child. What kind of sickness came over my father."

"It's all horrible but I wish you would back away and let the police handle it. And, please—don't mention anything about this when we get to Julie's house."

"No, I won't." He thought for a moment before boiling over. "I've got that much common sense. And don't you *judge* my motivation."

"I didn't mean it like that."

In a flash, Dae's voice turned upbeat. "Let's get this off our minds. We've got a wedding to think about. Isn't that exciting?"

"Oh, yeah." He tried to sound convincing but it wasn't that easy for him to make an emotional u-turn.

The wedding was a mere formality to Brax. Though he loved Dae as much as he had ever loved anyone, rather than excitement he felt a deep, solid devotion. Marriage would legitimize that feeling but it wouldn't make it any truer.

∼

The next morning they left for Charlotte to meet Dae's daughter and her family.

"Maybe it's a good time to get away," Brax said, as he pulled from the driveway. "I've stirred up enough excitement in Rocky Ridge. I can't believe how a simple walk in the woods has gotten me into such a screwed up situation."

During the drive, Dae spoke fondly of her daughter, two granddaughters, and son-in-law. "Julie and Ben lead busy lives. She had a good job in corporate management before she took a part-time position to spend more time with the girls. Jenny is twelve and Emma is nine and they are the brightest little things. Gosh, Jenny's not so little anymore. I can't believe she's almost a teenager."

"I never had any girls," said Brax. "Three sons were fine with me. Jane never said it but I always knew she wanted a daughter."

"Having a daughter is wonderful. I love Justin to death, but Julie and I are like best friends."

"She's got your looks, too. I feel like I've already met her family after seeing all those pictures on your computer."

Dae smiled. "Ben is in finance and he does well. You'll like him—he's into sports as much as you are. I couldn't ask for a better son-in-law."

"Sounds like the All-American family. Their name is McAfee, isn't it?"

"Yes. They moved into a new house last year." Dae reached for a bottle in the console and took a sip of water. "I can't wait to tell them we're getting married. It won't be a shock but they'll still be excited."

There was a spark in Dae's voice when she spoke of her family. It reminded Brax of something he had lost sight of: being around people was her sustenance of life. He realized what a change it had been for her to leave Seaside where she was surrounded by an active community of people her age. Now, she lived with him and a dog in a house surrounded by nothing but trees. He drove in silence for several minutes before he broached the subject.

"I don't think Rocky Ridge is the best place for us to live," he said.

"I thought you *loved* it here."

He knew he had surprised her. "It was alright as long as I was by myself. But the house is not a good setup for old people. Too many steps. Too many things to take care of with a big house, especially one that's about as old as we are. And it's out in the middle of the sticks."

"Are you saying that because you believe that's what I think or do you really feel that way?"

"Both. I know that's how you feel and I can see it now. It won't be too long before I'll have a tough time climbing that hill behind the house. As long as I can come back every now and then and listen to the water in the creek, I'll be fine."

She didn't respond at first as if to digest what she had just heard.

"Are you *sure* that's what you want?" she asked, sounding like a judge considering a plea bargain.

"Yes, but it's not about me—it's about us. You still have the house in Seaside, and we always said we'd keep both places. I think we should live there full time and visit Rocky Ridge every now and then until we get too old to enjoy it. Is that what *you* want?" He knew what her answer would be, and as he spoke, had convinced himself he felt the same way.

"Yes."

There was a question left hanging that he knew would have to be answered. "I'll have to part ways with Sunny," he said. "It won't work with him at Seaside. He needs room to roam, and I know you don't want him in the house. I've seen this coming and Charlie said he would like to have him for his grandkids."

"Oh—I know you love that dog. But he'll be taken good care of, won't he?"

"Yeah, he'll be fine."

"I'll miss him, too, you know."

He believed her but he also sensed her relief. Covering his own mixed feelings, he changed the subject. "I want to go to the bluegrass festival next weekend. After that, I'll pack my things up and we can go back to Seaside."

"All right. We'd have to be there for the wedding anyhow."

"Wedding?" He faked a puzzled look.

"You know—that little thing we agreed to."

"Oh yeah, now I remember. I stopped at the Quick Trip and you proposed to me at the gas pumps." He laughed hard.

"Don't you dare mention that to Julie and Ben." The serious look on her face melted and she began to laugh with him.

After the laughter died, he drove for several miles in a light mood, still amused about Dae's "proposal." Then he thought back to his meeting with Lance Johnson. What the heck was the Lieutenant's plan? That thought soon faded and another, more troubling one, popped up. Moving from Rocky Ridge would not only mean giving up Sunny, but he might also never see Ty again.

13

SHORTLY AFTER NOON, BRAX TURNED INTO THE CHARLOTTE SUBdivision where Dae's daughter lived. The main street led through a neighborhood of large homes with well-kept landscapes. A side street ended in a cul-de-sac where Julie stood at the front steps of a two-story brick house.

She met Brax and Dae on the front walk and greeted her mother with an affectionate embrace. Turning to him with a polite hug, she said, "Brax, I'm so glad to finally meet you."

"It's my pleasure," he replied.

Inside, they were met by Julie's husband, Ben, and their two daughters.

A few minutes later, Brax sat at the kitchen table eating lunch with the McAfees. As Dae and her family caught up on the mundane details of their daily lives, he tried to act interested. In truth, he was sizing them up as his soon-to-be relatives. And he assumed the same of them since he knew that Dae had been open with them about their relationship.

After the meal, the conversation moved into the den. Brax sat beside Dae on the sofa and the McAfees gathered around in a circle of chairs like they were viewing a performance.

As soon as everyone settled into their seats, Dae spoke with a lilt in her voice. "We have something we'd like to tell you," she said. She took Brax's hand and looked at Julie. "We're getting married."

"Oh, my *gosh!*" Julie rushed to the sofa with her arms open.

Dae rose with a big smile on her face and embraced her daughter. Brax got to his feet and stood awkwardly beside the two giddy women.

"Mom, that's awesome," Julie said as she released her mother. Then she hugged Brax while jabbering away excitedly as if the news was unexpected.

Ben and the two girls followed with more hugs. Then everyone stood in the middle of the room trying to carry on a six-way conversation.

"When is the big day?" asked Julie.

"I'm thinking four weeks from now," her mother said. "June the third. I want to have it at Seaside. Can y'all make it that weekend?"

"Are you kidding? We'll work around whatever is on our calendar. There's no way we would miss it." Julie looked at Ben who gave a '*why not*' shrug. "Let's go in here and talk about this." She led Dae into the living room.

The two young girls hurried from the den, leaving Brax and Ben to get acquainted. Ben sat erect, his body poised as if uneasy at rest. Brax felt oddly out of place as he and Ben talked about their professions and upbringings. When he excused himself for a bathroom break, Ben directed him to the powder room off the foyer. As he washed up, he heard voices through the wall.

"He has a funny name," the youngest voice said. "Is he going to be our new grandpa?"

"Yes," Julie said. "Call him Mr. Donovan for now."

"I don't think Uncle Frank will like him," said the older girl.

"Yes, he will. We'll all like him," Julie said. "Y'all go on out."

Brax heard the front door close and waited a few moments before returning to the den. He wondered how he was perceived by Dae's family. What had she told them? Did they know he had been her constant companion at Seaside for almost a year before he found out she was married? It was a bad time to realize he'd never questioned Dae about that and he felt the discomfort of unspoken judgment.

Resuming their conversation, Ben mentioned a CD that Brax had recorded and given to Dae a few years earlier.

"I've heard you play the trumpet. Julie made a copy of the CD you gave to her mom. You're very talented."

"Ah, that was a long time ago," Brax said. "About forty years, in fact. The CD was made from a cassette I recorded when I was playing regularly. I still have my horn, but I had to give up playing. Ran out of wind." He tilted his head back with a half laugh.

"Well, it sounds good."

The two men sat without talking for a moment.

"Since I moved to North Georgia I've gotten back to my roots," Brax said. "I grew up in the Atlanta suburbs, but a lot of my relatives were country people. I used to visit them and learned to like old-time country music. You know—songs about hard times and yellow-haired girls. Gospel harmonies and acoustical instruments. Everything simple and down-to-earth."

"I went to Appalachian State," Ben said, "and one of my roommates was in a bluegrass band. That's *real* traditional country music."

"Yes it is," Brax agreed. "Dae and I are going to a bluegrass festival in Rocky Ridge next weekend."

Ben stood up. "Here, I want to show you something." He led Brax to the basement stairs. Several pictures hung on the walls beside the steps. One of the pictures was a photograph of Ben standing next to a man in dark glasses sitting on a stool with a guitar in his lap.

Brax instantly recognized the iconic blind musician. "Doc Watson. Did you know him?"

"A little bit. My roommate introduced us and he was easy to talk to. A nice man. An incredible talent, too."

Ben's fondness for bluegrass was a 'welcome to the family' moment for Brax. The men returned to the den and, over the course of an hour, Brax warmed to his soon-to-be relative.

Their conversation was interrupted when Dae and Julie reentered the room.

"We've got it all worked out," Dae said. "I have the clubhouse reserved for four hours. And I called Horace Hassel. He's going to do the ceremony."

"I guess I better call my sons then," Brax said.

"Ooh—did I get too far ahead?"

"No, I'm just along for the ride."

"Don't say that. I want it to work for everybody."

"It will work for us—that's the main thing. This isn't the Royal Wedding."

Dae pursed her lips, apparently not amused by his flippancy. Julie and Ben were silent. The room felt stuffy.

Brax stood up. "I'm *just* kidding." He put a gentle hand on Dae's back. "I'll make some calls now."

Brax's first call was to his oldest son, Mason, a lawyer in Dallas. Mason stayed in frequent contact, so he wasn't surprised by the news.

"That's great, Dad. I'm happy for you. I'll see what kind of schedule I can put together."

"You don't need to do that. It'll be a low-key affair in the clubhouse. The preacher is a puddin' headed old geezer, and it won't take more than fifteen minutes."

"It's not just about the wedding—I want to meet my new stepmother. Not to mention, I haven't seen you in over six months. It'll be a good vacation for us if I can swing it at the office."

Until then, it hadn't registered with Brax that he was about to introduce into the family a maternal figure whom none of his sons had ever met. It was an obvious fact, yet one he had ignored as if they knew Dae through telepathy.

"Looks like I'll be moving back to Seaside after the wedding," Brax said.

"I thought you liked it in Rocky Ridge."

"I do but, even though she won't admit it, Dae doesn't like the house or living in the boonies. And it's not a good setup for a couple of *senile* citizens."

"You're a long way from being senile, but I think it's a good move. Seaside is a perfect place for you. I'm glad you're moving back."

"It'll work out. You know I wouldn't be happy if I didn't have something to bitch about."

When the call ended, Brax reflected on what Mason had said; *It's a perfect place for you.* His son was right. For three years he had lived alone and had become inwardly focused, even more so than he had been at Seaside before Dae moved there. He wasn't sure what might happen with Sunny, not to mention Ty, but the wheels were in motion, and he wasn't about to stop the train now. *Yeah, everything will work out.*

There were two more sons to call, and he expected they would also want to meet his new wife. Brax looked forward to seeing his family and having them meet Dae, but the island wasn't the easiest place to get to. It would be a lot simpler if she had picked a more convenient location for the wedding. Like the lobby of the Atlanta airport.

As he had told Mason, there was always something to bitch about.

"Did you talk to your sons?" Dae asked, as they prepared for bed.

"Yeah, they were all surprised. Mason knew we were back together—he and I talk about once a week—but he didn't think it would happen this fast. Neither Logan nor Dylan had a clue but they were happy for me."

"Are they coming to the wedding?"

"I'm not sure."

His voice carried a little tone of concern and his mind was somewhere else. "Tell me something—who's Uncle Frank?"

She winced. "He's John's brother. Who brought up his name?"

"I heard the young girls mention him."

"They don't understand," she said. "He hates me."

"Why?"

"For being with you while John was still alive. Somehow, one of John's Army buddies found out and told Frank. He was furious."

"You never told me about that."

"I didn't want you to worry about it or get involved."

"Well, I'm sure as the devil involved now." He thought—*another secret*—but he knew better than to say it.

"You shouldn't be concerned about him. We've done nothing wrong."

Brax sat down in the chair beside the bed. Despite Dae's comment, he suspected that he hadn't heard the last of Uncle Frank.

"Julie will be a big help with the wedding," Dae said, returning to the original subject. "She's so organized. It's funny—I remember spending hours and hours planning for her wedding, and now she's helping me with mine."

He tried to forget about Frank. "Well, let's not make this too complicated."

"No, it will be a simple ceremony."

"I'm not just talking about the ceremony. I mean getting everyone together before and after. Making a big production out of it and receiving a bunch of gifts we don't need."

"We're getting married." Dae sounded impatient. "It's not a *production;* it's a commitment of two lives and a celebration. We've both gone through a lot and don't know how much time we have left. We *deserve* a celebration."

"You're right. Go ahead and plan whatever you want and I'll be perfectly happy."

He knew she would anyhow.

~

The family gathered in the foyer the next morning before piling into the McAfee's van for the ride to church.

The service was familiar to Brax. He recited the Apostles Creed and the Gloria Patri with only a slight falter. After the sermon, the congregation filed down the aisles for the communion ceremony. He had partaken in the ritual many times in the past but often simply went through the motions. Now, with Dae at his side, he felt a genuine connection to The Holy Spirit. Back in their seats, he placed his hand in hers. It was as though they had just been united in unspoken sacrament.

After lunch at a busy restaurant, it was almost two o'clock when they arrived back at the McAfee's house.

"We'd better be on our way," Brax said. "It's a five hour drive home." He looked at Dae. "The one in Rocky Ridge."

"I told them we were moving to Seaside after next week," she said.

"I think that's wonderful," said Julie.

"Yeah, it's great," said Ben.

"It'll be convenient living there," Brax said. "We can just walk across the street to the beach. You know how we honeymooners are."

He winked at Julie and she laughed.

Dae rolled her eyes.

∼

A few miles from Julie's house, Brax reached the interstate and settled in for the return trip to Rocky Ridge. The traffic on Sunday afternoon was moderate and he nursed a black coffee to stay alert.

"Did you like the service?" Dae asked.

"Yeah, I did."

"The church is beautiful. It's a little farther from Julie and Ben's new house than where they lived before, but I'm glad they still go there." She opened her mouth as if to speak, then cleared her throat. "Something happened there one night that I need to tell you about."

"One night?"

"Yes, it was Christmas Eve just before we broke-up."

"Hmm. *We* broke up? As I recall, you're the one who said it was over."

"Oh," she sighed.

"At the time," he continued, "it tore me up but it didn't change the way I felt about you."

"That's what I need to explain. Julie knew about our relationship from the beginning and was aware that you didn't know I was married. She didn't judge me for deceiving you, and after you found out about John, she supported me in wanting to live with you. But all along I knew it was wrong."

Dae paused. Brax took a sip of coffee and waited for her to continue.

"I went to church with Julie and her family for the candlelight service. It was a beautiful program and when I looked at the altar, I remembered the vows I took at my wedding. Vows to John, to myself, and to God. And I realized that to forsake those vows would haunt me for the rest of my life. I couldn't do it. The service ended at midnight and when we went out into the cold air, the church bell rang in Christmas Day. A peaceful feeling came over me, and I felt the presence of God."

He set the cup in the console and took a deep breath, recalling his own epiphany during the communion ceremony that very morning.

"The next day I told Julie that even though John was no longer himself, he was still my husband, and I couldn't be with you anymore. Brax, it was the hardest thing I've ever done and it broke my heart to hurt you."

He pulled the car to the emergency lane and turned off the engine. "I'm glad you told me. Yes, it hurt at first but deep down I knew you were right."

She stared through the windshield and didn't respond. Then

she turned back to him. "I never stopped loving the man that I married."

"I've never doubted that. And I still love Jane. I always will. I fell in love with her forever, just like you did with John." He started the engine. "Forever never dies."

He let a car pass and then pulled onto the highway.

They were forty-five miles from Rocky Ridge when Dae's phone chimed with a message alert. She reached into her purse, pulled out the phone and looked at the screen.

"Oh no," she said, in a pained voice.

"What is it?" Brax asked.

"It's an email from John's brother."

"The one that hates you—Frank?"

"Yeah. He's always causing problems."

"What do you mean?"

She sighed. "He's violent and he's been in a lot of trouble with the law." Shifting her weight in the seat, she said, "He was in prison for twenty years or so."

Brax was beginning to realize that John's brother might be more than just a disgruntled relative. "What does the email say?"

"You can read it when we get home."

"No, tell me now."

"He's such a jerk. It's ugly." She leaned forward in her seat and looked at her phone for several seconds. Then she read the message aloud.

"Hey whore, I heard you're getting married. I can't wait to meet you and lover boy at the wedding. I hope you two douchebags don't have a long life together."

Brax looked at Dae, a rush of anger building inside of him.

"What a first class…" He started to say something gross but he held his tongue. "How does he know we're getting married?"

"Watch the road," she said, as the car drifted toward the oncoming traffic. Then she inhaled a deep breath and blew it out. "I posted it on Facebook last night. I'm sure he didn't see it but he must know someone who did. I'm sorry."

He shook his head and felt the anger subside. "It's not your fault. We're not trying to keep anything a secret. Hey, this guy's just looking for trouble. I know how to handle him."

"I told you he's dangerous."

"You said he is an ex-con. What was he in for?"

"Uh…he almost beat a man to death with some sort of tool—a wrench I think."

"Huh, should be a fun wedding."

Brax laughed, but inside his gut was churning.

14

AFTER THE TRIP TO CHARLOTTE, BRAX LOOKED FORWARD TO THE bluegrass festival. It was a chance to get his mind off all the changes in his life that were swirling around him like gusts of wind. He glanced at Dae as the long line of traffic approaching Lake Gansagi came to a stop. "Most of these people are headed for the same place we are."

The vehicles started moving again, and soon the lake appeared in the distance. "The festival is near the campgrounds on the other side of the bridge," he said.

A few minutes later, he drove onto a large open field bordered on one side by a line of trees that led to the edge of the lake. A man in a straw hat directed him down a tire-track path past rows of vehicles lined up like dominoes. Tall grass scraped the bottom of the car as he pulled in beside a camper with a Virginia tag and littered with stickers of bluegrass festivals. He and Dae got out and began walking toward the gate of a chain link fence a good 200 yards away.

"Good grief," she said, "it looks like everyone in North Georgia is here."

"Some of these people travel around the country to attend

events like this," Brax said. "They're like college football fans without the booze and craziness."

Inside the fenced area, a large tent was set up with a stage and hundreds of folding chairs. The program hadn't begun but a group was warming up on stage. The high-pitched notes of a mandolin resonated through the speakers with a sharp plinkedy-plink cadence.

"I've heard bluegrass music," she said. "I like the instruments, but sometimes the singing is off key."

"Yeah, it can sound pretty primitive. Hill people don't *hear* the voices, they *feel* them. It reminds them of their granddaddies and grandmamas singing to them on the front porch of the old country home."

They walked past smaller tents with food stands, souvenirs, and crafts. Clusters of musicians were scattered about, jamming in makeshift groups. In one spot, people were gathered around Banjo Bob who sat in a cane-bottom chair with his instrument in his lap. Brax raised a hand to greet Bob and the banjo player flashed a toothy smile, framed by a white beard and mustache. A younger man sat beside him with a guitar as they played a duet of *Wildwood Flower*.

"Ole Bob's like a pig in slop," said Brax.

"He plays pretty well, doesn't he?" Dae asked.

"Yeah, when he's sober. He goes on a drinking spell every now and then for a couple of days. Otherwise, he's sharp as can be."

The crowd continued to stream in, and the chairs under the big tent began to fill. Brax and Dae settled into their seats as the first act, a group of five fiddlers, began. Three more bands followed before a break at noon. They bought hot dogs and Cokes from a concession stand and mingled with other festival goers sitting at picnic tables under a pavilion.

After the intermission, a troupe of young people introduced as the Apple Cider Cloggers appeared on stage. The clickedy clack of tap shoes rang out as the dancers—four boys and four girls in matching red and white outfits—tapped in furious rhythm to the recorded music.

Brax looked closely at a small boy who was dwarfed by his older mates. "I can't believe it. That's Ty—the little one on the left end."

"Are you sure?" asked Dae.

"Of course, I am."

Brax kept his eyes on Ty while the cloggers moved from the first song directly into another. The boy's face radiated with joy and brought a smile to Brax's face. He was glad to know that Ty could dance and smile and have fun. Maybe the knowledge of a dark secret hadn't robbed him of the innocence of youth.

When the music stopped, the dancers moved offstage to a round of applause.

"They're cute," Dae said. "So full of energy."

"Yeah," Brax agreed, "it makes me sweat just to watch them."

During a break, they left their seats and found an ice cream vendor. After finishing their cones while moving among the concession stands, they stopped at a table with a display of T-shirts. Brax picked up one stitched with *Bluegrass at Lake Gansagi* on the front and, on the back, a picture of bluegrass instruments floating on a lake.

He grinned and held the shirt up to Dae. "You'd look good in this."

Her eyes got big and her face said *very funny*. "I don't think so."

He laughed at the incongruity.

The acts continued all day. One band consisted of three generations of the same family. Another featured a highly acclaimed Dobro player on lead. There were gospel groups in four part harmony, singers of all ages and more cloggers.

In the early evening, they found space at a crowded table in a shady area to eat a plate of barbeque and sides. Brax drained the last drop of iced tea from a Styrofoam cup and asked, "Are we having fun yet?"

"I'm hanging in there," Dae replied. "But you have to admit that last female singer was dreadful."

"That's the thing about bluegrass music—when it's bad it's *really* bad. I can run you home if you want to leave. I'll be back in time to see the Kruger Brothers."

"No. I need the cultural experience." She grinned.

By eight o'clock the night air had begun to cool, and Dae put on a light sweater as the emcee stepped to the microphone.

"Folks, sorry but we're gonna hafta make a change in the schedule. It looks like The River City Pickers won't be able to make it t'night. I was just told that their van has been in an ac-ci-dent out on Highway 36. Reports are that several vee-hicles are involved, but I'm told there're no serious injuries. I'll keep you posted on that soon as we have more information. Meanwhile, we're gonna take a break and see if we can get the Kruger Brothers set up a little ahead of schedule. We hope to get started again about eight-thirty."

A voice from the audience hollered, "Let Bob play."

Another man stood up and said, "Yeah, let's hear old Bob." He turned to the audience and said. "He can play good as anybody."

"That's for sure," a third voice yelled, and soon a chant swept through the crowd.

Brax grinned at Dae and joined the shouts. "We want Bob. We want Bob. We want Bob."

In less than a minute, two men escorted Banjo Bob down an aisle to the front of the stage while most of the audience stood and clapped.

"Okay," said the emcee. "I hear ya loud and clear." He waved for Bob to join him on the stage. "Come on up, Mr. Bob Atkins. These people wanna hear ya play yer banjer."

Brax turned to Dae and spoke into her ear over the noisy crowd. "That's the first time I've ever heard his last name."

Bob waved to the audience and strode to the center of the stage with his banjo strapped to his shoulder. The crowd settled down as he sat on a stool that a stagehand shoved to him. The emcee placed the microphone close to the banjo while Bob adjusted the strings and played a few warm-up notes. Then he began playing *Foggy Mountain Breakdown* at a fast tempo.

"That's a classic banjo piece," Brax said. "But it's not easy to play at that speed."

"I think he's really good," Dae said.

"Better than anyone we've heard so far," Brax agreed.

When the tune ended, Bob got a huge ovation. He thanked the crowd and played two more songs. Then he began plunking a few notes of *Rocky Top*. He stopped playing and spoke to the audience. "I love all you people of Rocky Ridge and this is just for you."

Bob began singing as he played the banjo. But he sang different lyrics to the well-known tune, using rhymes with words of local reference. When he reached the familiar refrain, he sang:

Rocky Ridge is where I'll be
It's the only place for me
Good old Rocky Ridge
On the lake called Gansag-ee.

The big tent erupted with cheers, whistles, and fists in the air. Several people left their seats and moved into the open area in front of the stage to buck dance.

Bob continued with more verses and each time he came to the chorus, everyone joined in with *Rocky Ridge* in a thunderous boom.

When Bob finished the song, the ovation continued as he waved to the crowd before ambling off the stage.

"Well, that was a real foot stomper," said the emcee. "I think we need to ask ole Bob to come back next year."

The comment was greeted with wild shouts of agreement from the crowd.

Brax kept his eyes on Bob as the banjo man made his way to the back of the tent, stopping to shake hands and exchange remarks with people in the aisle. Several rows behind him, Brax spotted Ty, still wearing his red and white clogging outfit. The man beside Ty began sidling toward the aisle with the boy right behind him. They met up with Bob and walked out of the tent with him.

"That's the no-good…" Brax said, holding his tongue.

"Who?" asked Dae.

"Ty's dad. It has to be."

"Well, don't pay any attention to him. And *don't* start anything."

"Hey, I'm here to listen to the music." He grabbed a handful of boiled peanuts from a bag. Leaning down, he cracked open a shell and let the salty juice drip onto the ground between his feet. As he ate the peanuts, the image of a chunky man with dark bushy hair stuck in Brax's mind: Tom Benefield.

The crowd settled down for a few minutes after Bob left. Another round of applause began as the Kruger Brothers made their way to the stage.

An hour later, the clapping and yelling died down after the Kruger Brothers last song and the tent began to empty.

"They were great," said Dae. "They weren't like the others."

"You mean they're not redneck," Brax said.

"I didn't say that." She yawned. "I'm tired. It's almost ten o'clock."

"Yeah, it's going to take a while to get out of here with this mob."

They left the big tent and weaved through the crowd toward the exit. Just before the gate, they came upon a small group huddled around Banjo Bob. Near him stood Ty and the man whom Brax assumed to be his father.

"I want to say something to Bob." Brax walked up to the group and wedged in between two men. Reaching out a hand, he said, "Good job, Mr. Banjo."

Bob shook Brax's hand. "Thank ya, kindly."

Brax stepped back from the crowd and raised a hand of acknowledgment toward Ty. Then he clasped Dae's arm and began to walk away.

"Hey," a voice from behind said.

Brax turned to see the man who had been standing next to Ty walking quickly toward him. He stopped and looked at the man without responding.

"Are you the fella who wanders in the woods around the hollow at Bent Creek?" the man asked.

Brax felt his blood pressure rise. "Who the hell are you?"

"I'm Tom Benefield and that's my son." He glanced back at Ty. "I know you've talked to Ty and I want you stay away from him."

"I hardly know your son. And I've never been anything other than *away* from him."

Dae tugged at Brax's arm. "Let's go."

Brax stared at Benefield with laser-like eyes, then began to turn away.

"I'll talk to the Sheriff if you bother him again," Benefield said.

That stoked the fire burning inside Brax. "You've already done that and it didn't work. I'll walk in those woods any time I please and if you don't like it, that's too damn bad."

The men stared at each other as some in the passing crowd stopped to observe the confrontation.

"Brax, come on." Dae pulled at him harder.

Keeping his eyes on Benefield, Brax tilted his head back with a sneer, then turned to Dae. They walked away and headed toward the gate.

"Did you see that dipshit? He looked like a furry turd."

"Just forget about it," she said.

After leaving the fenced area, they maneuvered through the throng of vehicles leaving the field. By the time they reached the car, he had cooled off a bit.

"Did you have a good time?" he asked, trying to put a hint of cheer in his voice.

"I really did. I'm glad I came."

Her comment brought him back to the moment. "I'm glad you did, too. You're a good sport." He pulled into the line of traffic and began quietly singing Banjo Bob's version of Rocky Top.

"Rocky Ridge is where I'll be…"

She interrupted. "Don't forget the other part of our bargain—The Nutcracker at the Fox."

He *had* forgotten about their agreement and it struck him as funny.

"Hillbilly music and ballet—that's quite a combination isn't it?"

"Yes, just like us."

Brax smiled. Being with her had made the music even more enjoyable. He tried to forget his unpleasant encounter with Tom Benefield. Yet, he couldn't help wondering about the apparent connection between Benefield and Banjo Bob. He knew that question would stick in his mind long after the music faded away.

15

ON MONDAY AFTER THE BLUEGRASS FESTIVAL, BRAX AND DAE circled the track with Charlie Kramer. A dark rain cloud hung overhead.

"I can bring Sunny to your house in the morning." Brax said.

"That'll be okay. I'll be up by eight."

With the move from Rocky Ridge settled upon, Brax had decided that he wouldn't bring Sunny along to Seaside. He knew that Dae didn't want a pet living in her new house, and she hadn't protested the decision. So he made arrangements to give the dog to Charlie who planned to give the friendly yellow Lab to his grandchildren.

Giving up Sunny had been a hard decision for Brax, and he'd gnawed on it like a tough steak. The dreary morning added to the aura of finality that clung to him like a shroud.

Shaking the mood, he asked Charlie, "So you're going to buy that house in Lakehaven?"

"I think so. We finally got a decent offer for ours."

"That's great. I hear it's a tough market these days."

The two men walked briskly to keep up with Dae. A few seconds later Brax said, "I didn't see you at the festival on Saturday."

"I was there Friday," Charlie replied. "That was enough for me."

"Were those young cloggers there? The ones called Apple something."

"Apple Cider? Yeah, they were. A bunch of local kids—I've seen them before."

"Did you notice Ty Benefield in the group?"

"No."

"Well, he was there Saturday night and so was his dad. We had a little meeting."

Dae gave Brax a cold stare. "Don't start that," she said.

"You met Tom Benefield?" Charlie asked.

"Yeah. He's a real nice guy. Good looking, too," Brax said, his voice thick with sarcasm. He glanced at Dae with a sly look.

Charlie looked at him with a squint. "I'm not sure what you have against him."

"Nothing. I said he's a nice guy."

Dae nudged Brax. "Let it go."

Charlie didn't respond and the trio continued to walk without speaking as rain began to fall. When they reached the side of the track near the parking lot, Dae veered off.

She turned back and asked, "Are you going to keep walking?"

"Sure," Brax replied. "We've only got two more laps."

"I'll wait in the car," she said.

"So you two are leaving tomorrow?" asked Charlie, as the two men kept their pace.

"Yeah," Brax replied. "Right after we drop off Sunny."

"How long will you be gone?"

"Forever."

"Sorry I asked."

Brax walked another five steps. "I don't know. Like I told you,

Dae's not comfortable up here. She needs to be in an *active community*. I'll keep the house here and we'll be back from time to time."

"I hate to see you leave."

"I have mixed feelings," Brax said. "But it's for the best."

The rain stopped, and the conversation faded for a minute before Brax spoke again.

"Banjo Bob sat in for a group that didn't show up Saturday night. He played his own version of *Rocky Top* with different lyrics. He called it *Rocky Ridge* and the crowd ate it up."

"I'll bet. The old coot has a lot of talent."

"He does," Brax agreed. "Ty and his dad hung around Bob after the show. Is there any connection between him and the Benefields?"

"Not really. You know how people are around here—they kind of take care of Bob."

"Hmpf," Brax grunted.

"Now that I think about it though," Charlie said, "I remember something that happened maybe a couple of years ago when I worked in the pharmacy at Walgreens. Tom came in one day and picked up prescription drugs for Bob and paid for them with his credit card."

"What kind of drugs?"

"Pain killers—pretty potent stuff. A doctor in North Carolina prescribed them, but I checked it out. It was legit. He came back another time and I told him I couldn't let him have somebody else's prescriptions. He didn't argue about it but later I saw him in Bob's truck when he came to the pick-up window. I'm pretty sure he handed Bob the money. I think he was just trying to help the guy."

Yeah, sure, Brax thought. Or bribe him for some dirty work.

Thunder boomed in the distance, and the two men picked up their pace as they finished the last lap.

"Brax," Charlie said, as they headed for their cars, "you're always bringing up Tom Benefield and his son. It's like you're hung up on them. What's the deal?"

Brax raised his T-shirt from his waist and wiped his face. "Sometimes things aren't always like they seem."

"What does *that* mean?"

"Nothing, really. I'm just a crazy old loon. Maybe it's best I'm leaving town."

"No, you're not crazy. An old loon maybe, but not crazy. And don't take this wrong, but maybe it *is* best you're leaving the Ridge. You've got a good thing going with Dae, and you need to be wherever she wants to be. Forget this crap about things that aren't always like they seem."

Brax looked at Charlie with a fake smile. "Well, thank you, Mr. Life Coach."

He returned to the car and found Dae in the passenger seat, preoccupied with her smartphone. The rain burst from the sky and the wind surged, pelting the car with a staccato clatter. He settled behind the wheel and looked at her without putting the key in the ignition.

"I think I mentioned to you that Charlie was a druggist until he retired last year. He just told me that Tom Benefield used to buy prescription drugs for Banjo Bob."

She put the phone in her lap. "I want you to forget about that man. We're moving to Seaside, and you can't get tangled up with whatever is going on up here. Officer Johnson said he was going to handle it and I believe he will."

"Dae, this is about children being abused, maybe right here in

Rocky Ridge. Or *up here,* as you call it. I can't just forget about it."

She slumped in her seat and closed her eyes. "I know," she said. "I'm sorry."

"Charlie said something else, too. He said…I need to be wherever you are."

Opening her eyes, she leaned to him and put her hand on his leg. "I'm right here."

He patted her hand, and then started the ignition as she sat back in her seat. Recalling Charlie's advice, he tried to forget about things that weren't like they seemed. He pulled out of the parking lot and turned in the opposite direction of home.

"You want to see the neighborhood where Charlie's buying his new house?" he asked. "It's in a part of town you haven't seen before."

"It's raining hard."

"We'll just drive through and you can see what it looks like. It's on the other side of the lake from where the festival was."

"Okay, if you really want to. But we can't take long. We have to get packed to leave in the morning."

He drove through the heart of town and five miles beyond. The rain slacked off to a light drizzle. The shoreline of Lake Gansagi appeared as he approached the entrance to a subdivision. An artificial waterfall splashed down from huge stacked stones next to *Lakehaven* lettered on a granite wall.

"What a beautiful entrance," Dae said.

The cedar shake guard shack was unoccupied and the gates were open. Brax followed the main road up a hill and wound through a neighborhood of modest-sized homes nestled on wooded lots.

"This development is pretty new," he said. "The road was already here, and they were clearing the lots when I moved up. They did it right. A lot of retirees live here."

"Imagine that." Her tone was flippant as if dismissing the not-so-subtle hint.

He stopped in the driveway of a new home with a For Sale sign in the yard.

"It's probably locked, but we can look in the windows," he said.

"It's still raining," she said.

"It's barely coming down. We have an umbrella in the trunk."

"I don't want to get out."

Brax got out of the car, walked to the front porch and looked through the sidelight. Wide-plank hardwood floors in the foyer continued into the great room. Stepping carefully on the wet grass, he walked around to the small patio in back. Through the rear windows he could see most of the great room, kitchen, and master bedroom. Then he turned back to study the wooded area behind the house. On one side a sliver of the lake gleamed in the distance.

He returned to the car, took a towel from the trunk and placed it on the floorboard for his wet shoes. Looking back at the house, he said, "It doesn't have a basement but it's pretty good sized." Bigger than the ones in Seaside, he started to say, but held the thought.

"I like the lot and the landscaping," Dae said.

"Charlie said he was tired of keeping up an old house."

Brax backed out of the driveway and onto the road that circled the neighborhood.

"Is this where you'd like to live?" she asked. "Is that why you wanted me to see it?"

"No, we've decided that."

"You're the one who said we should live in Seaside. If you've changed your mind, you need to say so. I don't want you to go just for me."

"No, I said it's decided and I'm good with that. And, what do you mean—just for you? Wherever we live will be right for both of us. But I wanted you to see there *are* signs of civilization around here. Not everyone lives like a countrified hermit."

"That's unfair. I've never said that."

"Yeah, I didn't mean...I don't know what the hell I meant."

Brax drove slowly, meandering through the development. Dae made an occasional remark about a home she liked and the setting around the lake. By the time he passed the guard shack on the way out, the rain had stopped. He thought that his little excursion might have opened her eyes to a new possibility. Something else weighed on his mind though, and he didn't know how to say it tactfully. But the time had come, so he took a deep breath and just spit it out.

"How does your family feel about your getting married so soon after John's death?"

"They're fine with it. How do you feel about it?" The words flew from her mouth like darts.

"I want to be married to you. I just don't want your kids and grandkids to hate me like I was a vulture that hung around waiting for John to die."

"They don't think that. They like you and they're happy for me." She turned in her seat to him. "Why are you bringing this up now? It's all set." Her voice quivered.

He slowed down, then moved to the shoulder of the road and stopped the car. He pulled her to him with her head on his chest and her still damp hair against his face.

"Everything will be fine," he said, stroking her back. "We're together. That's all that matters."

Dae raised her head. "I want us to always be together." She took a tissue from her purse and wiped the moisture from her eyes.

"We will be. I promise."

Driving home, Brax turned the windshield wipers on slow speed. *Swoosh, Swoosh.* The pulsating sound repeated with the regularity of a metronome. Like two people with their hearts in unison.

~

After lunch Brax sat in a rocker on the back porch, sipping on a stiff drink of scotch while Dae took a nap. The sky was clear and the land glowed with a fresh coat of spring color. He finished the drink, then went inside and poured another. Back on the porch, he rocked mindlessly as he downed the second drink. Gazing at the scenery, he felt a part of all that was around him as if he were Thoreau and this was his Walden Pond retreat. The scotch numbed him with a melancholy warmth and he felt the call of a farewell stroll.

"This'll be the last time," he said to Sunny, sitting at his feet.

He returned inside, wrote a note, and stuck it on the back door.

Took a walk in the woods. Back in a few minutes.

Walking down the steep path behind the house, he felt light-headed yet exhilarated as if being greeted by the nature around him. Sunny was only a few steps ahead. At a steep pitch, Brax teetered forward, bracing himself against a tree trunk.

"Whoa," he said, as Sunny scooted aside.

When he reached the creek, he found the water running swiftly from the morning rain. He sat on a bent sapling and, mesmerized by the sweet, gushing sound, lost all sense of time and place. Then, stirring from the trance, he stood and slowly began walking in the direction of the fire pit. On the path, he snagged his foot on a vine and fell. Drained of energy but compelled by an inexplicable urge, he pulled himself up and continued walking. As he neared the clearing where he had first seen Ty, Brax was exhausted. He sank to his knees before settling face down in the wet foliage.

"Sunny," he said. But his voice was weak and the dog didn't respond.

Rolling to his back, he looked up. Everything was out of focus. The treetops and clouds appeared jumbled like a kaleidoscope. He felt a rush of anxiety and turned on his side as the last ounce of energy drained from his body.

Then the world went dark.

16

BRAX WAS AWAKENED BY A TOUCH ON HIS SHOULDER. HE LIFTED his head and looked through narrow slits in his eyes at a blur leaning over him.

"Are you hurt?" a voice said.

His eyes began to focus as he stared up at Ty with Sunny beside him. *Why am I lying here? Am I dreaming?*

"No," he replied out of impulse. "I was just resting."

He reached up and put his hand on the back of Sunny's head as the dog nuzzled his face. After sucking in a breath of fresh air, he slowly raised himself to his feet. His head throbbed and his body trembled with the sudden rush of blood. Steadying himself from the lingering effect of alcohol, he brushed the damp debris from his clothes.

"What are you doing here?" he asked Ty. Though still a little foggy, he knew it was an odd question, considering his own situation.

"Just playing over there." Ty pointed behind him. "Sunny barked at me and I followed him."

Brax looked down at Sunny standing beside him. Gradually, the jumbled fragments of his memory started to fit together. Two glasses of scotch on the deck; a walk on the path beside the creek. One last trek into in the woods before leaving Rocky Ridge was all he had wanted, but maybe it wasn't a good idea to get pie-faced beforehand. It was a painful reminder that he couldn't handle the booze like he once could.

With his bearings clearer, Brax looked at Ty and realized that standing in front of him was the reason he hated to leave Rocky Ridge. There was no time to wait for things to develop. He had to know what the boy knew.

"Were those pictures your daddy's?" he blurted out.

Ty's face lit up as if he had touched a live wire. "No." He began to back away.

"Yes—I know they are," Brax said. "I want to help you."

"No they're not," Ty insisted, then turned and ran away.

Dae's voice came from the woods in the opposite direction. "Brax," she called.

He started to follow the boy, but his body would hardly move. "Where did you get them?" he yelled. "Whose pictures are they?"

Ty slowed down. "I showed you," he shouted, his head turned halfway around. "Make it bigger." He began running faster and disappearing into the woods.

Dae appeared from the path and approached Brax.

"Why are you here?" he asked, his mind still a little jumbled.

"Why do you think? I was worried about you. Are you all right? You've been gone a long time."

"I'm okay."

"Who were you talking to?"

Brax flicked a leaf from his hair. "You won't believe it. I was just sitting here and Ty showed up."

"What do mean—you were just sitting here? Your eyes are red and you look a mess."

"I guess I got a little too friendly with Mr. Johnny Walker." He straightened his back, arched his shoulders with a grunt, and teetered to one side with a half step.

"You passed out, didn't you?"

He moaned and rubbed his head.

"You know you're not supposed to drink alcohol with those pills you take."

"Ah hell, I've done it before. I guess I overdid it this time."

"You sure did and you could have hurt yourself."

"Damn, I've already given up cigars. There's only so much healthy living I can handle. It seems like living is almost as worrisome as dying."

"Come on, let's go home. You need to get some rest."

On the way home Brax trudged along with Sunny at his side and Dae slightly ahead.

"I know I'm a dumbass for getting snockered," he said," but I found out something from Ty that blows my mind. He said those pictures didn't belong to his dad."

"He might be covering up," she replied, turning her head. "Or maybe he doesn't know who they belong to. He's just a child."

"Yeah, but he knows. And he said something else. He said that he '*showed* me.' Then he said, 'Make it bigger.'"

"It sounds like a riddle." Impatience rang in Dae's voice. "You need to quit listening to what that boy says. I told you to let Lance Johnson handle it."

"I don't have any choice since we're leaving."

Dae stopped abruptly and Brax almost bumped into her.

"Yes, we are leaving," she said. "I don't want to feel guilty about that. We're getting married in three weeks, and our lives will be back like they were when we first met."

He took her hand. "I don't want you to feel guilty about anything."

"Good."

"I'll be glad when we're married." He tightened his grip and forced a smile. "And I can almost smell the ocean from here."

She tilted her head down, then looked up and sighed. He could see in her eyes a reflective look he'd seen before and he knew what it meant: a stroke of softness. A change in her heart.

"You're such a romantic," she said. "That's what I love about you."

"Oh hell—that's almost enough to make my head stop hurting."

He released her hand and they started walking again.

At the base of the big hill behind the house Brax stopped and put his hands on his knees.

"Whew, looks like Mount Everest." Still bent at the waist, he reached and patted Sunny on his flank.

"Maybe," Dae said, "you'll remember that the next time you come down here after drinking."

The water in the creek gurgled over the rocks and shafts of sunlight lit the damp forest in a blaze of emerald green. But now the beauty around him wasn't as inviting to Brax as the prospect of getting home. He couldn't wait to lie down on the couch. He wondered if Thoreau had ever found himself in that condition at Walden Pond. Then he started up the hill with a grunt.

∼

Brax awoke to find himself on the sofa and Dae sitting in his favorite recliner with a book in her hand.

"How do you feel now?" she asked.

"Like road kill from an eighteen-wheeler."

"You need to take some antacid." She went into the kitchen and returned with a glass of water and two tablets. She dropped the tablets into the glass and handed it to him.

Brax forced down the fizzy liquid as it spritzed in his face. "Thanks, nurse," he said as she sat back down in the recliner. He walked to the rear window and stared out at the trees, still gleaming with the freshness of a spring rain. "Seriously, I feel a lot better."

He turned back to her. "I have to call Johnson."

"What will you tell him?"

"That I've been wrong." He sat down on the sofa. "That the pictures didn't come from Tom Benefield. And that Ty not only knows where they came from but said he had *showed* me."

Dae tilted the chair forward. "He means the picture he left on the deck."

Brax nodded. "There's something in that picture. We've got to look at it again."

"It's being held as evidence in the Sheriff's office," Dae said.

"That's who needs to look at it." She paused with a glazed look in her eyes. "Ty said to make it bigger, didn't he?"

Brax knew where she was heading. "Yeah, enlarge it."

Neither spoke for a while as the mystery of the missing clue in the picture lingered. The thought of leaving town with so many things unresolved weighed heavily on Brax.

Dae broke the silence. She got up from the recliner and sat beside him on the sofa. "We can't leave tomorrow," she said.

He felt a quick jolt of adrenalin. "What are you saying?"

"Something horrible has happened and we can't ignore it."

"But you have your heart set on getting back to Seaside. We're all packed."

"We can unpack. As long as we get there a few days before the wedding, I'll be okay."

"Are you sure?"

"Yes. I know what this means to you." She shook her head. "I'm sorry I've been so selfish."

He moved to Dae and put his arms around her. "No, you're not selfish. And I swear I won't let this interfere with our wedding." A gentle squeeze and he stepped back.

"I'll make the call now," he said.

Brax grabbed his cell phone and called Lance Johnson's office. As the phone rang, he checked his watch. "It's almost six-thirty. He's probably gone by now."

On the fifth ring, a recorder answered and he left a message. "Lance, this is Brax Donovan. I have some important information about the pictures I gave you. Please call me at this number as soon as you can."

He put the phone in his pocket and looked at Dae with a sense of relief. "Thanks for understanding."

"I try." She smiled and her eyes seemed to sparkle in the evening light.

A few minutes later, Brax made another call.

"Charlie, we've had a change of plans. Dae and I won't be leaving tomorrow. Uh…would it be a problem if I don't bring Sunny tomorrow?"

"When *are* you leaving?"

"We're not sure. Something has come up and everything is on hold for right now. I know it's asking a lot, but I'd like to keep Sunny a little while longer if it doesn't upset your grandkids too much."

"They don't know anything about it. It was going to be a surprise." Charlie's deep exhale was audible over the phone. "He's your dog, Brax, and I know you're attached to him. Just keep me in mind once you know what your plans are."

"Thanks." Brax ended the call and gave a thumbs up signal to Dae.

Looking at Sunny across the room, he said, "You're staying for a while."

~

The next morning, Brax got up early with mixed feelings of reprieve and regret. He was relieved to know that he had a few more days in Rocky Ridge and Sunny would be there with him. Yet he felt bad about his bull-headed insistence that Tom Benefield was a pedophile. Though nothing had resulted from his accusation, the loss of credibility felt like a knife stabbing at his pride.

After a shower, he left Dae half asleep in bed and went downstairs. The coffee brewed quickly, and after pouring a cup, he sat down at the kitchen table with a crossword puzzle. He expected a call from Lance Johnson but it was barely after seven o'clock. So he tried to concentrate on the brain-twisting New York Times puzzle to fill the early morning vacuum.

An hour later, Dae came down and joined him at the table. "Are you going to call Lance again?"

"Not yet. I'll wait an hour or so. I don't want to pester him."

Dae set her smartphone beside her and began scrolling through the screens.

Brax looked up from his puzzle. "I screwed up big time about Tom Benefield." He leaned back in his chair. "I went off half-cocked."

She looked up from the phone. "You haven't done any harm."

"I believe I have. I made an accusation against him to the police. And I had no real evidence—just my brilliant intuition."

"You know they're not going to take action on what you said. They won't arrest anyone unless they have evidence."

Her comment didn't lessen his feeling of responsibility. "Ah hell, Lance won't believe anything I say now. But I've got to clear the man's name."

Brax left the table, poured a fresh cup of coffee and started for the deck. "And we have to figure out who the bastard is that Ty says is in the picture."

He had just stepped outside when his phone rang. Dae walked onto the deck as Brax pulled the phone from his pocket. But the call wasn't from Lance Johnson. Instead, the voice on the other end was that of Charlie Kramer.

"Hey, Charlie. You know I was going to bring Sunny—" Brax started, thinking Charlie was having second thoughts about not getting Sunny for his grandchildren.

"Don't worry," Charlie said. "I'm not calling you about Sunny. It's about Tom Benefield. Have you heard?"

"Heard what?"

"He's in jail. I don't know what's going on but two Sheriff's deputies marched him out of the school this morning."

Brax looked at Dae in puzzlement. "Really?"

"Yeah. I thought you probably knew since you obviously know something I don't."

"No, I'm just as surprised as you are." Brax thought quickly to cover himself. "My problem with Benefield is simply—you know—a clash of personalities."

"Brax, I'm not buying that. I remember what you said about things not always being like they seem. And there's gotta be something about Tom that's not like it seems."

"Charlie, I was just blowing smoke. I really don't know what's happening." There was enough truth to his comment that Brax didn't think it to be a blatant lie.

"I'll take your word for it, but the timing sure is bad. School will be out next week. Wonder why they couldn't wait a few more days without stirring up the kids."

"I don't know."

Despite Charlie's assurance, Brax sensed the doubt in his friend's voice. That made him even more conflicted about circumventing the truth of his involvement. However, of more concern was to make sense of Benefield's arrest in light of Ty's profession of his father's innocence.

"Anyhow," Charlie continued, "I saw Jose Rojas at Chik-fil-A the other day and he told me he did some painting for you. You're going to stay in the Ridge for a while, aren't you?"

"Yeah, like I told you, we haven't decided exactly when we're leaving."

"Okay, I'll find out pretty soon what the deal is. I know a lot of people around here, and you can't keep something like this under wraps in a little town like Rocky Ridge."

"I'm sure you're right."

"You can bet your ass I am. I'll let you know as soon as I get the word."

"Thanks."

"You want to walk in the morning?"

"I don't know. I'll call you later."

"What did he say?" Dae asked, as Brax put the phone in his pocket.

"It wasn't Lance. It was Charlie." He shook his head. "Tom Benefield's in jail. They arrested him at his school."

She looked at him with her mouth agape.

Brax raised the coffee cup and took a sip. It tasted bitter.

17

BY TEN O'CLOCK, BRAX STILL HADN'T HEARD FROM LANCE JOHNson. He sat in his recliner, legs crossed, a propped foot wiggling, on the verge of calling the Lieutenant again. When his phone rang, he grabbed for it from the side table, fumbling as if it were a live grenade.

"Brax, this is Lance Johnson. I'm returning your call."

"Yeah, thanks for calling me back. I just heard that Tom Benefield has been arrested. What happened?" He silently mouthed "Lance" to Dae as she walked into the room.

"I can only tell you what's been released to the public. He's been charged with possession of child pornography. I can't give any details to individuals." He paused a beat. "You said you had some new information about the pictures."

"Yeah. Ty told me some things you need to know."

"Why were you speaking to him? I told you we would handle this."

"I didn't seek him out. We ran into each other in the woods."

"That seems to happen a lot with you and him."

"I know it sounds hard to believe, but it's true. He told me that the pictures didn't come from his father." Brax sat up in the chair. "You might have the wrong person."

"No. We have the right person and the evidence to prove it. And I'm sure there are others involved. We'll find out who they are."

"I know you will." Brax looked at Dae with a squint, then turned back to Johnson. "But you remember that last picture I brought you—the one that wasn't torn?"

"Yes."

"Ty said we need to look at it again. 'Make it bigger,' he said. I think he meant for us to enlarge it. Look at it closer."

"That's interesting but…you know, he's a kid. He might be playing games or just confused."

"I don't think so. Besides, it won't hurt to check it out. Can I come down and see it again?"

"I keep telling you this is an official investigation by the Sheriff's Department." Johnson's voice simmered with impatience. "I can't have private citizens handling the evidence."

"Lance, the last thing I want to do is screw things up. You can tell your people I'm a witness, or someone with a lead, or…whatever. We can look at the picture together. Maybe I'll see something you don't."

"Dang, you're persistent." The phone was quiet for a moment. Then Johnson said, "Okay, come on down and we'll look at it in my office. But don't say a word to anyone about this. We're being overrun with reporters from newspapers and TV stations. If I find out that you've leaked information, I'll come down on you like a ton of bricks."

"Don't worry, you can trust me."

Brax kept his eyes on Dae as he asked Johnson, "Could we get together in about an hour, say…eleven o'clock, to look at the picture?"

"Sooner if you're coming. Things are about to get crazy around here."

"Be right there." Brax put his phone away.

"He wants me to come right now," he said to Dae.

"Do you want me to go, too?"

He thought for a second. "I don't think so. Lance seems a little uptight about the possible appearance of outside involvement. And—"

"You don't have to explain. I don't want to go."

Fifteen minutes later, Brax was on his way to the courthouse.

Johnson met Brax in the front office and led him directly into a small room containing only a table and three chairs. "We'll have more privacy here."

The officer laid a manila folder on the table, and the two men pulled up chairs next to each other. Johnson opened the folder to reveal the picture inside.

Brax put on his reading glasses. "I'm not sure what we're looking for." But with his glasses on, he noticed something he hadn't seen before. He pointed to one of the figures.

"I want to look at this guy. That spot on his shoulder—I think it's a tattoo."

"Yeah, I believe you're right," Johnson said. "But it's hard to make out."

"Can you enlarge it on a copier?"

"Let's try using a magnifier. I'll be right back." Johnson left the room, closing the door behind him.

Brax spied a camera in the ceiling and wondered if he was being recorded. There was nothing for him to hide, but he felt uneasy as if someone were looking over his shoulder. He lifted the picture and looked at it again. His eyes focused on a naked man with his back to the camera. The photo was in black-and-white but the man appeared to have pale skin and, though he wasn't fat, his flesh hung loosely. His head was turned slightly to the side, revealing a glimpse of a white beard. On his shoulder was the blurry dark spot of what looked like a tattoo.

Johnson returned with a large magnifying glass in his hand and sat down beside Brax. He lowered the instrument to the spot on the man's shoulder. Peering down with his eyes next to the glass, he mumbled to himself. Then he handed the instrument to Brax.

Brax leaned over and looked closely. In the larger view, the fancy scalloped flourishes of the design revealed the distinctive outline of a banjo. Less clear, even when enlarged, were the two letters on the banjo. The magnifying glass began to tremble in Brax's hand and he set it down.

"I think the letters are BB," he said, looking at Johnson.

The officer nodded.

"Banjo Bob," Brax said.

"Maybe," Johnson said. "But a lot of people play the banjo or like that kind of music. And BB? Bob's last name is Atkins. Who uses their nickname for initials?"

"It's his musical moniker," Brax said, sensing that the officer was simply playing devil's advocate. "You know, like a stage name. This is what Ty wanted us to see."

Johnson placed the picture in the manila folder and leaned back in his chair. "I'll follow-up on this. Old Bob is well liked in this town. And he's never caused any trouble even when he's drinking. But you might be right and, if you are, it will blow this town wide open."

"Well, don't take this wrong, but arresting the school principal has already done a good job of that." Brax arched his brows. "Bob and Tom Benefield are big buddies. I saw them together at the bluegrass festival last weekend. Ty was there, too, and the three of them were as tight as ticks."

Johnson stared straight ahead without responding.

"I'm in it deep now," Brax continued. "Whether you want me to be or not. I remember you said you had a plan to solve this case. What led you to arrest Ty's dad?"

"Well, first of all, I don't consider this case solved by any stretch. And secondly, I didn't think your suspicion—and mine—about Tom was sufficient for a warrant. But his computer at school is public property, and I didn't need a warrant to search it. The guy was dumb enough to have some pictures in one of his personal files. Not a lot, but enough."

Johnson stood up. "Remember what I said—don't say a word about this to anybody. Not even your lady friend. Like I told you, things are about to get crazy around here. Maybe crazier than I realized."

Brax left the Sherriff's office with the strong suspicion that the man in the photograph was, in fact, Banjo Bob. But, having already jumped to a conclusion about Tom Benefield, he didn't want to repeat that same mistake. He would let Lance Johnson take it from here.

From the courthouse, he walked past the bench where he had often seen Banjo Bob wearing a big smile as he played his instrument. Approaching the square he saw a white panel truck emblazoned with the lettering of an Atlanta television station. It was a stark reminder of the dramatic events unfolding around him. Yet, even though he was an integral part of those happenings, he felt a surreal disconnect, as though he were watching from a distance.

In a semi-daze, Brax couldn't remember where he had parked the car. He paced the street for a couple of minutes with no luck. Then he realized he was on the wrong side of the courthouse. Feeling relieved but foolish, he quickly located the car and started for home with the confusing reality of the day's events thrashing about in his head.

"How did it go?" Dae asked, as Brax walked through the door.

He drew a breath and looked at her stone-faced. "It's unbelievable. Banjo Bob was in the picture," he said, completely ignoring Johnson's instructions and his own self-avowal to avoid a rush to judgment.

"Banjo Bob?" She squinted as if to comprehend the words.

Brax nodded and began walking toward the main room. "Johnson and I looked at the picture with a magnifying glass, and we saw a tattoo on one of the guys. It was a banjo with the initials BB."

"Could you see his face?" she asked as Brax sat down in the recliner.

"No, but it was him. I know it was. That's why Ty left the picture—don't you see? He and his dad were with Bob at the festival. There's a connection somehow."

"What about Ty's father? Do you really think he's involved?"

"He must be. Lance said they searched his computer at school and found pictures like the ones we saw."

Dae dropped to the sofa with a stunned look on her face. "How disgusting."

Brax tilted the recliner back and stared across the room at the blank television screen.

"What are you going to do?" Dae asked.

"Nothing, right now. I don't know how solid the picture is as evidence. Lance will put the pieces together." Brax tilted the chair forward and stood up. "This will hit Rocky Ridge like a bomb."

He got up and headed for the kitchen. "Want a Coke?"

"I have one." She reached to the end table and grabbed a glass he had been too preoccupied to notice.

Brax returned with his drink and stood with his back to the window. "Can you imagine—the school principal and the harmless town drunk caught up in the most heinous of crimes? It's like Silence of the Lambs comes to Mayberry."

"There's no telling how long this has been going on," Dae said. "Or exactly how much Ty understands. But he's a smart little boy, bless his heart. I hope when things are made public he's not traumatized more than he already is."

Brax turned to gaze out the window and looked at Sunny lying on the deck. He took a swig of Coke and stared into the forest. His mind turned back sixty years, and a scene appeared like he was in a movie.

He was roaming the woods with his dog as a young boy, carrying a BB gun to shoot tin cans and stick-men. It was a different world when he was alone in the woods; one free of the cruel demands of his father and the cold detachment of his mother. A world in which he could shed his loneliness in the comforting solitude of nature. Then he saw Ty walking toward him with a BB gun. They stared at each other shyly. Soon the reticence disappeared and they spoke with ease. The two boys joined to walk among the hills and hollows while the dog named Sunny scampered about them. Occasionally they stopped to compete in shooting contests with their air rifles, acting out war games and cowboy shoot-outs. At the creek they raced stick-boats that floated lazily down the stream before rushing through rocky rapids. They walked a log across a creek. In the late afternoon sun, they lay on a blanket of leaves and argued who would win a fight between Lash Larue and the Cisco Kid. They were buddies.

Then the vision disappeared, and Brax was jolted back to the present. He was reminded that Ty was not a character in a dream but rather a small boy caught up in a very grim reality.

He turned back to Dae. "I need to do whatever I can to help that boy."

She stood up and moved beside him, crooking her arm in his. A beam of light from the window put an amber glow on her face.

"*We* need to do whatever *we* can," she said.

∽

Brax filled in the spaces to complete the last words of the crossword puzzle and scooted the chair from the kitchen table. It was almost eleven o'clock and Dae was in bed. His mind churned and there was no use trying to sleep. In the main room he turned on the television to watch the late news on an Atlanta station.

Halfway through the program, a "breaking news" flash appeared. He jerked to attention as the anchor led off the special report.

"*A Georgia elementary school principal has been arrested and charged with possession of child pornography. For that story we go to Ramona Chavez.*"

The screen switched to a female reporter standing in front of the Pate County courthouse. A sidebar showed a map indicating the location of Rocky Ridge in relation to Atlanta. "*I'm here in Rocky Ridge, about seventy-five miles north of Atlanta, where this morning Tom Benefield, the principal of Seqouyah Elementary, was arrested at his school and taken to the county jail.*"

The camera panned back to include a uniformed officer standing beside the reporter. "*This is Pate County Sheriff Billy Wainright. Sheriff, can you tell us what happened?*"

"*A search of Mr. Benefield's school-owned computer revealed images of sexual relations with minors,*" the Sheriff replied. "*He has been charged with possession of child pornography, child endanger-*

ment, and improper use of school property. Further charges are under investigation."

"What led to the search of Mr. Benefield's computer?"

"We received a tip from a source with information that appeared credible. After checking it out further, we decided to search the computer for evidence."

"Are there others parties that might be involved in this activity?"

"We're looking into that possibility. We'd like to find out where these images came from."

"Thank you, Sheriff." The camera isolated on the reporter whom the anchor in Atlanta addressed.

"Ramona, what do we know about the principal?"

"Chris, Tom Benefield is forty-two years old and has been the principal of Sequoyah Elementary for three years. He has been a teacher in the Pate County school system for twelve years and, according to school officials, has an outstanding reputation. To say that the people in Rocky Ridge are stunned would be an understatement. Everyone I have spoken to here is in total disbelief. Chris, we'll keep our viewers posted on any new developments on this story. Live from Rocky Ridge, this is Ramona Chavez, Total 10 News."

The screen returned to the anchor in the studio. "Thanks, Ramona. What a shocking story."

Brax turned off the television and the lights. He lay down on the sofa and stared into the darkness. He knew it was just the beginning. When people found out about Banjo Bob, the ripple in the calm waters of Rocky Ridge would turn into a tidal wave.

18

BRAX OPENED HIS EYES TO THE SOFT GLEAM OF DAYLIGHT PEEKING through the window. Lying under an afghan on the sofa, he was still fully clothed and groggy from a restless night. When he heard Dae's footsteps coming down from the bedroom, he sat up and pulled the cover aside.

"Did you have too much to drink again?" she asked.

He ignored the sardonic edge in her voice. "No, but I wanted to. I watched the late news, and Channel 10 had a story on Tom Benefield's arrest. They even had a live report from up here. That pretty reporter with the long black hair interviewed the Sheriff in front of the courthouse."

"Oh for God's sake." Dae grabbed the afghan and folded it. "It's just the kind of thing to make the whole town look bad."

"Yeah. You know how the media jumps all over stuff like this. Child sexual abuse may be sickening, but it's sensational and gets a lot of attention. Especially when someone like a school principal is involved."

"I'm afraid you're too wrapped up in this. I know it's a terrible situation, but you can't let it consume you to the point you can't sleep."

Dae was right, of course. But Brax couldn't clear his mind of the responsibility he felt for starting a criminal investigation that seemed to be mushrooming by the day.

"I'll be all right," he said, unconvinced in his own mind.

"I'll get the coffee started." Dae set the afghan on the back of the sofa, then walked into the kitchen. She spoke from the doorway. "Are we going to walk this morning?"

"I told Charlie we would. I'm sure he saw the news or at least heard about it. He knows everything that happens around here. And he'll bug the hell out of me. He knows I haven't leveled with him."

"You couldn't tell him anything. Lance Johnson warned you about that."

"I'll have to keep fudging about what I know. Especially the bombshell about Banjo Bob," he said, entering the kitchen. "Hey, that reminds me—Lance told me to not say a word to anyone about Bob. And he said that includes you, so *play dumb*." He grinned at her.

"Don't you *dare* say it."

"Just a figure of speech."

As they ate breakfast, Dae questioned the relationship between Tom Benefield and Banjo Bob.

"They seemed pretty friendly when we saw them at the festival," she said.

"It does scare me, knowing what Bob has been involved in," Brax said. "I'm really concerned about the environment that Ty might have been exposed to. Remember what I told you he said the first time I met him? He said, 'My daddy's mean.' So, I think his father has some complicity."

Brax stared down at his plate while his mind drifted back to his own tormented childhood. His father was cruel at times and rarely showed emotion other than anger or cynicism. Yet, Brax looked at him with a confusion of love and hate. Martin Donovan had given him the breath of life, and nothing would ever change that. For many years Brax had longed to hear the words, "*I love you, son.*" But he never heard them. He could only hope they were trapped inside an aging casket in Athy.

～

Brax tried to act as if everything was normal when he and Dae met Charlie at the high school track for their morning walk. But Charlie was clearly hyped up.

"That was quite a scene on Channel 10 last night wasn't it?" Charlie said, talking louder and faster than usual. "Rocky Ridge makes the big time."

"Not exactly the way we'd like to," said Brax.

"I guess you don't have to worry about your *personality clash* with Tom anymore. Like you said, things aren't always as they seem. That's pretty obvious now." Charlie took three steps and then asked, "What did you mean by that. You don't have ESP, do you?"

"No." Brax looked at Dae and they continued for a few more paces. "Look, Charlie, all I can tell you is that there is a criminal investigation, and I have some involvement as an incidental witness. I'm not trying to be evasive, but the Sheriff's department has me under wraps. I can't say any more without getting myself in trouble."

"So, you know what's going on?"

"I said I'm a witness but it was by accident. And I only know bits and pieces of the whole story."

"You've talked about Ty a lot. That's how you got involved, isn't it?"

"I really can't talk. Trust me, I would tell you what I know if I could."

Charlie relented for a few minutes, then spoke to Dae. "Do you know what's going on?"

"No." She lied without hesitation and then glanced at Brax who mouthed, *"It's okay."*

"Not really," she added. "I've heard a little."

"She's not involved," Brax said.

"What do you think will happen to Tom?" Charlie asked. "Child pornography is a serious charge. Especially for somebody who works with children."

"I'm not sure what the penalties are," Brax replied, "but I think they're pretty severe."

"I hope that all he's done is look at some pictures," Charlie said. "My grandkids go to that school. If I find out something has happened to them, I won't wait to see what the law does."

"It'll all come out in time," Brax said.

"Well, I'll be at the Rotary luncheon today and tongues'll be wagging about this mess."

Wait till they find out about Banjo Bob, Brax thought. *Those tongues will go into overdrive.*

～

After the walk, the lack of sleep caught up with Brax and he took a long nap. When he stirred from the sofa it was past noon.

"Feeling better?" Dae asked.

He sat up and stretched. "Yeah, a lot better."

"You have a call on your phone. I set it on vibrate so it wouldn't wake you. It's from the Sheriff's office."

"Ah heck, I wish you had woken me up." He rubbed his eyes.

"I was about to. It was only fifteen minutes ago."

Brax took his phone from the side table and pressed the number to return the call.

Lance Johnson answered. "Brax, there are some questions about the case we're working on that you might be able to help us with. Can you come down?"

"You bet. I can be there in less than an hour."

Brax looked at Dae as he set the phone down. "Lance wants to talk to me about *the case I'm helping them with*. Maybe he'll give me a badge. Ha!"

He took a quick shower, changed clothes, and fifteen minutes later hustled out the door.

As he got into the car, Dae shouted, "Good luck, Sherlock."

At the Sheriff's office, Lance Johnson ushered Brax into his office. Captain Hembree sat at the adjacent desk. Brax sat down in front of Johnson.

"Brax," Johnson began, "I appreciate your help in this investigation."

"You're a good citizen," Hembree added.

"Thanks," Brax replied. "Just doing my civic duty." His pride swelled and he fought back a smile.

"Does anyone besides your lady friend know of your involvement?" Johnson asked.

Brax felt the eyes of Hembree and Johnson bearing down on him. "No," he replied.

"Good," Johnson said, and looked at Hembree with a slight nod.

Then Brax thought of his walks with Charlie Kramer. "Well, not exactly. There *is* a guy we walk with in the mornings that knows a little. I opened my big mouth a few weeks ago, but I didn't say anything about finding the pictures."

"What did you tell him?" Johnson asked.

"Nothing really. I asked him if he knew Tom Benefield and he said he did. I also asked him about Ty. He figured out that I didn't like Tom but he didn't know why. I told him it was just a personality clash."

Hembree fiddled with a pen and made some marks on a note pad, apparently content to let the junior officer do the talking.

"What's your friend's name?"

"Charlie Kramer. He's a retired druggist from here in Rocky Ridge."

"I know Charlie. Are you sure you didn't mention anything about the pictures to him?"

"Yes, I'm sure."

Johnson thrummed his fingers on his desk. "What did he say after he learned of Mr. Benefield's arrest?"

"He kept grilling me about my involvement. I had to admit that I knew something, but I couldn't tell him what."

"That's not a problem," Johnson said. "You haven't done anything wrong. We just want to know what information is out there. The main thing I need to determine is if anyone else knows that Banjo Bob might be involved?"

"I don't think so. But, after the bluegrass festival, I asked Charlie what connection there was between Bob and Tom Benefield. At first he said he didn't know of any, but then he told me about Tom coming to Walgreens a few times and picking up prescription drugs for Bob."

"So he knows that Tom bought drugs for Bob?"

"Yeah, that's what he said."

"When's the last time you talked to Charlie?"

Feeling his mouth go dry, Brax licked his lips. "This morning. Dae and I walked with him at the high school track."

Hembree lurched from his desk. "We've got to put a search out with the GBI." He left the room quickly.

"What's going on?" Brax wondered what would cause the Georgia Bureau of Investigation to become involved.

"Like I told you," Johnson said, "you've been a big help in this case. In fact, you're the one who got it started. So I'm going to tell you what the deal is." Johnson took a breath. "Banjo Bob lives in a rundown trailer off a dirt road fifteen miles from town. We obtained a search warrant based on his likeness in the picture that you and I looked at. We found more pictures and quite a few drugs in the trailer. We've had a stakeout there since last night. Bob hasn't been seen in a couple of days. Maybe somebody tipped him off. But he probably left the area after Tom got arrested."

"You think the two of them are in it together?" Brax asked.

"I'm sure they are." Johnson paused with his eyes fixed on Brax. "We found some Social Security papers in Bob's trailer and his last name is not Atkins. His real name is Bower Benefield."

"Benefield?" Brax pictured the cozy trio of Bob, Tom, and Ty at the bluegrass festival. He hissed through his teeth, then said, "They're related."

"Bob is Tom's father."

Brax slouched down in the chair. "Damn."

∼

Dae picked up the empty dinner plates and walked to the sink. "It's all so bizarre," she said.

Brax opened the back door and set some scraps in a bowl on the deck for Sunny. He returned to the table and cleared the other dishes. "That's what this screwed up world is coming to." As he rinsed the plates and set them in the dishwater, his phone rang.

"Brax, this is Lance. Bob is dead." The officer's words ran together as he spoke quickly. "The Sheriff will be on Channel 10 at eleven with the story and you'll find out all about it. I'm real busy now. I gotta go." The phone went silent.

"Thanks for the heads up," Brax muttered to the dial tone.

He turned to Dae with a dazed look. "Banjo Bob is dead." He grabbed a wet dishtowel and yelled, "Hell fire!" as he threw it hard at the sink. Silverware and soapy water splattered onto the counter.

~

At ten o'clock a "breaking news" scroll appeared before the start of the regular program. The camera focused on the news anchor in the studio.

"*A well-known man from Rocky Ridge suspected of child pornography and child abuse has taken his own life.*"

An aerial view of a wooded area and several cars on a dirt road appeared on the screen.

"*This is the scene from earlier today near the location where the body of the man known locally as Banjo Bob was found. This story and how it may connect to yesterday's arrest of a local school principal are all coming up on Total 10 News at eleven.*"

Brax turned off the TV and stared at the blank screen. "This is unreal."

"It's really hard to understand," said Dae. "He seemed so happy and carefree. How could he be that evil and destroy so many lives—those poor girls he abused as well as his own family?"

"There was a part of himself he couldn't control," Brax said. "He was sick."

"You don't feel sorry for him, do you?"

"No. I hate people like him because they know what they're doing is wrong. But they keep doing it."

"Do you think Tom is like him?"

"I doubt it. But I can't figure why he had those pictures on his computer. I think he was an enabler though. He could have stopped it."

Dae got up from the sofa. "I think the only way would have been to get his father out of society," she said. "Probably in some sort of mental facility or even jail."

"He wouldn't fit anywhere—that's the problem. It's better that he's dead."

Brax felt guilty for saying it, but his words revealed his true feelings. Dae didn't respond and made her way to the kitchen for a glass of water.

The lead story on the eleven o'clock news focused on Banjo Bob's death. The anchor introduced the same reporter as from the day before. She held a microphone in the glare of bright lights for the cameras and a floodlight illuminated the lettering of The Pate County Courthouse in the background. Next to the reporter was a concrete bench.

"I'm standing next to a bench which was often occupied by a man known as Banjo Bob. He could be seen playing his banjo on the lawn of the courthouse here in Rocky Ridge almost every day. He was an iconic figure in this town and, from all we can gather, was not only liked but, some would say, doted upon by many of the local citizens. But today Banjo Bob is dead after taking his own life. And in a real shocker, his true identity has been revealed. For the second day in a row this town is reeling from charges of sexual crimes involving children leveled against two of its most well known citizens. And what we have found out about the connection between these two men is even more stunning."

A taped report from earlier in the day began with the aerial view shown on the breaking news flash. The camera then turned to the reporter on the side of the dirt road. Behind her were two cars with Pate County Sheriff markings, an EMT vehicle, and a pick-up truck.

"This wooded area is where officers from the Pate County Sheriff's Department caught up with Bob Atkins, better known as Banjo Bob. Earlier, the officers had searched the suspect's trailer a few miles from here and found evidence of child pornography. They also discovered documents that revealed the real identity of Mr. Atkins. More about that later. When the suspect arrived at his home, he saw the police cars and made a quick getaway. The officers followed and a chase ensued. Sheriff Wainwright, can you tell us what happened after that?"

The camera shifted to the Sheriff.

"The suspect abandoned his truck—you can see it over there—and fled into the woods. The officers followed and, shortly after that, they heard a single gunshot. Concerned about a possible exchange of fire, they approached cautiously. A few minutes later, they found the body of the suspect with a gunshot wound to his head. At that time he was dead."

"Sheriff, what led to the search of Mr. Atkins' trailer?"

"We received information from a local citizen regarding suspected child sexual abuse by Mr. Atkins. The evidence was strong enough to authorize a search warrant of his premises. There we found an abundance of drugs as well as evidence of child pornography and sexual abuse."

"I understand," the reporter said, "that Bob Atkins was an assumed name."

"That's correct. His real name is Bower Benefield."

"And he is thought to be the father of Tom Benefield, the school *principal who was arrested just yesterday. The man who now sits in the county jail charged with possession of child pornography. Is that correct?"* the reporter asked.

"There appears to be a relation, but we haven't confirmed that at this point."

The picture returned to the reporter live at the courthouse.

"The more we learn about this story, the more difficult it is to comprehend. Events of this nature are unheard of in this part of Georgia. Pate County, including its largest town, Rocky Ridge, is justly proud of a very low crime rate. Yet to be determined is the extent of the sexual abuse of children suggested by the evidence against these two men and the impact on this community. Live from Rocky Ridge, this is Ramona Chavez, Total 10 News."

Brax turned off the television and sat frozen with the remote in his lap. He felt nauseous.

"They would have never been caught if weren't for you," Dae said.

"Sooner or later they would have," he replied. "I didn't want to be a part of something like this. I just wanted to take a walk in the woods."

"It's a good thing they were caught."

"There's more to it. We don't know the extent of Tom Benefield's involvement or what Ty has been exposed to." Brax leaned his head back and stared at the ceiling. "The main thing we don't know about is the girls. Who are they…what happens to them?"

"At least they'll be safe now."

"I hope so. But they'll never be the same again." Brax knew the emotional trauma would continue to fester long after the physical abuse. "Now they have their lives to live."

"You're right. It's not over." She sighed and stood up. "Let's go to bed."

"Living, that's the hard part," he said as he stood up. He knew about that.

Brax snapped his fingers and pointed to the back door for Sunny. "Go do your business."

The Lab moseyed to the back door and Brax let him out.

Following Dae upstairs, Brax was pleased with the solid feel of the stairs under his feet. He had ignored the creaky steps for a long time, but they bugged Dae, so he had drilled new screws into the treads to eliminate the annoyance. He was good at repairing *some* things.

As he lay in bed, Brax's mind roiled with the hellish revelations of the last two days. All of his thoughts revolved around Ty. The boy was a hero in his mind. But now, with his father in jail and his grandfather dead, there were a lot of missing parts to Ty's life.

And he wondered how you go about repairing the life of an eight-year-old boy.

19

AT HOME AFTER THEIR MORNING WALK, DAE UNZIPPED HER warm-up top and sat down in her chair on the deck. "I'm glad you told Charlie everything. I think he understands now why you couldn't say anything before."

"Yeah, I feel better about that," Brax said. "But there's still a lot we don't know about Tom Benefield. Not to mention the young girls in the pictures."

He leaned forward in the slat-back rocker and pulled off his sweatshirt. "I'm afraid Ty will be questioned by the authorities. This whole situation has to be confusing to a kid."

"I know you care about him, but let's not think about all that right now. It's such a beautiful day and that breeze feels good. I love the cool mornings."

They settled back in their chairs to absorb the blush of a bright spring day. A potpourri of sweet woodland scents filled the springtime air. Before them the land was alive with the white blossoms of dogwood trees and patches of pink mountain laurel amidst the dappled green palette of the forest.

"It's supposed to get to seventy today," Brax said.

However, his mind wasn't on the weather. He hadn't spoken

to Dae about the wedding or their living arrangement in a while. But he hadn't forgotten his promise regarding their future.

Brax looked at her out of the corner an eye. "Are you ready to go to Seaside?"

She stopped rocking. "Are you?"

"It's probably time." He was afraid he sounded unenthused, but she didn't seem to take it that way. He figured she had heard what she wanted to hear.

"Yes. The wedding is only two weeks away, you know."

"That's why I brought it up."

"What about everything that's happening around here? Lance may need you as a witness." She looked at the dog sitting next to him. "And is Charlie still willing to take Sunny? Are you ready for that?"

He was tempted by her comments, but he couldn't disappoint her now. "This whole case could drag on for months. We can't stop our lives. I'll give Charlie a call. If he's still willing to take Sunny, we can leave the day after tomorrow if you want."

Dae stood up and the smile on her face told him he had said the right thing. "Oh, I'm excited. I'm going to call Sally." She went inside.

Brax knew that Dae wanted to return to Seaside but he had to be the first to bring it up. It was his duty and suggesting it was his way of saying he would do anything to please her. When she said she was excited he wasn't sure if she was referring to the wedding or about returning to Seaside. Probably both, he guessed.

He stepped off the deck, picked up a broken limb and threw it into the woods where it landed among the thick ground cover. Sunny rooted it out and bought it back. Brax gave him a pat on the head and surveyed the scene around him. Everything in sight belonged to him—the trees, the land, the wild plants—and he felt a mystical sense of oneness with his domain of seven acres. It was an infinitesimal speck of the planet that had been there from the beginning of time and would be there until the end. He drew strength from knowing he was tied to something permanent, a piece of nature that grows and changes with the seasons, but never dies. Yet, the more he thought about it, the more he realized that the land belonged not to him but to God. His earthly days were numbered just as they were for those who had once occupied the land; prehistoric beasts, Cherokee Indians, European settlers, and, lastly, people like him who sought refuge from the clamor of urban living. Though the land had taken hold of him, he realized his hold on it was only passing.

He turned around and viewed the house in perspective. It was a comfortable home but he knew it wasn't ideal for an aging couple. With the desirable lot and the improvements he had made, he could get a decent price for the property. Enough, he thought, to buy a new place like the one he and Dae had seen in *Lakehaven*. It was a more suitable size yet still in the midst of a natural setting. Maybe after the excitement of the wedding died down, he would mention it to her.

∼

Brax laid the garment bag on the bed and placed his dress clothes for the wedding inside it. Then he opened a drawer from the chest and pondered how much casual wear to pack.

"Charlie said he would take Sunny. When do you think we'll be back?" he asked Dae.

"I don't know," she replied from the bathroom. "I'm taking all my summer things."

Brax walked from the bedroom and approached her as she put her toiletries and make-up in a bag.

"We need to have a plan," he said. "Are we *ever* coming back?"

She put the bag down and looked at him. "We need to see how we like living at Seaside again. I don't hate living here, but I'm drawn to the ocean and all the friends I have there."

"That's fine. It's not like we're moving to a foreign country. I can get back here in a few hours if something happens." He tried to look nonchalant.

Dae stared at him for a moment. "You don't want to go." She tilted her head. "It's about Ty, isn't it?"

Brax eyed himself in the vanity mirror before looking back at her. "It's about thinking of someone other than myself."

She stared at him. "The wedding is all set. We can come right back after that." Her eyes opened wider. "I guess I won't need all these summer things after all."

"We can live in both places," he said. "We agreed to that. It's just not convenient to be gone for a long time right now." Keeping his eyes on hers, he bridged the distance between them and embraced her. "I like Seaside, too. We'll spend a lot of time there once things are settled here."

"I'll feel better about everything once we're married," she said.

He kissed her on the cheek and whispered in her ear, "Love you."

She returned his kiss and snuggled to his chest. "That's all I need."

Brax returned to the bedroom and continued packing. His phone rang and when he pulled it from his pocket, Lance Johnson's number appeared on the display.

"Brax, Tom Benefield would like to talk to you."

Caught off guard, he hesitated. "Right now—on the phone?"

"No, in person. He asked me to see if you would be willing to come to the jail and spend a few minutes with him."

Again, Brax took a second to respond. "I can't imagine what he wants to talk about. Dae and I are leaving town tomorrow."

"You're not obligated to come. I'm just passing along the request of a man who's in our custody. Frankly, it's not normal protocol, and I'm taking a risk in even allowing it."

Unable to resist the pull of curiosity, Brax looked at his watch and weighed the chance of upsetting Dae. "I can come this evening. It's five o'clock now. I could be there about six."

"I'll set it up for then. Come to my office and I'll escort you."

"So, you'll be there?" he asked, looking at Dae as she walked in from the bathroom.

"I'll be nearby, but it will be a private conversation between you and him."

After the call, Brax kept his eyes on Dae and shrugged his shoulders. "I need to leave for a while. Tom Benefield wants to talk to me for some reason. Don't ask me why."

She sighed. "Don't get angry with him." She turned and opened a drawer from the dresser.

"I won't." He felt her mood shift, as if the warm kiss of a minute earlier had evaporated and she had turned cold.

"We're still leaving tomorrow," he assured her.

"We have a few days to spare," she said with her back to him.

From behind, Brax put his hands on her shoulders. "We'll be in Seaside by tomorrow afternoon."

Dae turned around with an unconvincing smile. "We'll be there soon enough."

Lieutenant Johnson met Brax at the front office and drove him to the county jail several blocks away. They made their way down a hall and through a door that led outside to a small yard encircled by a high security fence. Tom Benefield sat at a metal table shaded from the evening sun by the brick wall of the building. An armed officer in uniform stood nearby.

Johnson led Brax to the table. "This is Mr. Donovan," he said to Benefield.

"Hello," Benefield said, showing no emotion. He remained seated, looking up at Brax.

As he returned the greeting, Brax was surprised by Benefield's appearance. Wearing a polo shirt with jeans and his hair neatly combed, he looked much sharper than when Brax had seen him at the bluegrass festival.

"I'll let you men talk in private." Johnson walked away and took a seat beside the security guard at another table out of hearing range.

Brax sat down across from Benefield. He pushed the chair away from the table, leaned back and folded his arms across his chest.

"I'm glad you came," Benefield said. His voice was soft, and he fidgeted with his hands. "My lawyer would go ballistic if he knew about this."

Brax shifted his weight and unfolded his arms. "I'm not sure why I'm here."

"You found some pictures, didn't you?" Benefield asked.

"They were just there. I wasn't looking for anything."

"I tried to hide everything from Ty, but he found the pictures and recognized Bob. I believe you thought they came from me."

Brax thought it strange that Benefield referred to his father as "Bob." He supposed that Bower Benefield's true identity had been hidden for so long that his own son had gotten used to calling him by his assumed name.

"I've made accusations against you," Brax said. "I may have been wrong about some things."

"Yes, you were." Appearing more relaxed, Benefield's voice was stronger. "I'm not a pedophile."

"You don't have to convince me of anything. I'm just a private citizen." Brax paused to consider the curious position he found himself in. "How did you know I found the pictures?"

"Charlie Kramer told me you had met my son. He said you asked a lot of questions about Ty and me. I just put two and two together. We teachers are good at basic arithmetic." Benefield's lip curled with the hint of slyness. "At first I was suspicious of your interest in Ty. You can probably understand why."

"Your dad," Brax said.

Benefield leaned back, looked aside and shook his head. "Some things make no sense. What he could have been," he mused as he turned back to Brax. "He adopted me as a young child, and he was always good to me. I never knew my real parents. Ty doesn't know that. He thinks Bob was his Uncle."

He sat forward again. "I shouldn't have had those pictures on my computer. Legally, there's no defense for that and I'll pay for it. But I had to keep tabs on my father and confront him about things I had seen. I discovered some pictures he had downloaded on his computer and thought I had them in a secure file. I was going to turn him in. I swear I was."

"Why are you telling me all of this? I'm not a judge or jury."

"Because I know what's going to happen. At the very least, they'll find me guilty of sheltering a predator. People will think the worst of me since I work with young people. I'll wind up in prison for a long time."

"You don't expect sympathy from me, do you?"

"No, not for me, but for my son." Benefield closed his eyes and took a deep breath. "My wife can't take care of him. She's not a strong person—emotionally or physically." He paused. "Right now, she's very distraught."

Brax kept his eyes on Benefield's face, trying to read the man's sincerity. "I can understand that. But I still don't understand how Ty got hold of the pictures."

"He found them in a box in Bob's truck. He showed them to his mother, and she became hysterical. When I found out about it, I asked him what he had done with them. He said he burned them up. I whipped him and told him never to say anything to anyone about what he had seen."

"You whipped him, eh?"

"I took out my frustration on him. Hit him too hard."

Brax recalled Ty's words etched in his memory; *My daddy's mean.*

The two men shifted their eyes from each other.

When they reconnected, Brax asked, "Do you have relatives nearby?"

"A few. None that I'm close to." Benefield rubbed his chin and looked down. Raising his head, he said, "Look, what I want you to know is that no matter what happens to me, I want Ty to be taken care of. I don't know a thing about you except what Lance Johnson has told me. But Ty has spoken of you and, for some reason, he likes you. And this may be my only chance to talk to you in private. So, regardless of what you think of me, I'm asking for your help. I want you to look out for him."

Brax's mind raced ahead. The thought of becoming involved in Ty's life was tempting. "Ty seems like a nice kid." He sat straight with his hands gripping the arms of the chair. "You're right—you don't know a thing about me. But I know a lot more about you now and…ah."

Brax gritted his teeth. Then he growled, "For some stupid reason, I trust you." In a softer voice, he said, "Understand though, I don't owe you a thing, and I think you're a rotten excuse of a father for not looking out for your son. That said, I don't know what I can do but I'll help Ty as much as I can."

Benefield lened forward. "That's all I'm asking."

Brax stood up and started to leave, then stopped. "I'll be out of town for a few days but I'll be back."

"Don't forget about Ty."

Brax felt the words cling to him like a child tugging at his leg. He walked across the yard to join Johnson. The two men rode back to the courthouse sharing only a few words.

"He knows I helped expose him," Brax said.

"He's worried about the boy, isn't he?"

"Yeah, did he tell you?"

"He didn't have to," Johnson replied.

Approaching Brax's car, Johnson said, "I'll call you if there are any questions about your statement."

"I'll be giving another testimony soon," Brax said. "The next time you see me, I'll be a married man." He laughed, and the solemn mood lightened for a moment.

On his way home, Brax couldn't shake the burden of his own words to Tom Benefield. *"I'll help Ty as much as I can."* It wasn't a magnanimous gesture to a man he hardly knew. Rather, it was a commitment to a boy in whom he saw his own likeness.

He was already packed for the trip, and he knew there was no way to talk Dae into postponing the wedding. She had said she would come right back to Rocky Ridge afterward, though. That was the day he was waiting for. He had a promise to keep.

Dae said little as Brax recounted his conversation with Tom Benefield at dinner. When he finished she asked, "What do you think he meant when he asked you to *look out* for Ty?"

"I don't really know."

"It doesn't make sense," she continued. "You've only met him once before. And I remember he told you at the bluegrass festival to stay away from his son. Why does he now want you to take care of the boy?"

Brax raised his brows without responding.

"He wants you to be responsible for Ty. That's what this is all about, you know. You're old enough to be his grandfather, for God's sake."

Brax swirled the ice in his glass and nursed the last drop of tea. "When Tom and I first met we had preconceived ideas about each other. We see each other differently now. He's no candidate for father-of-the-year, but he's looking out for his son's best interest. I think he's trying to do the right thing. The boy needs someone." He kept his eyes directly on Dae.

"Okay. I trust your judgment. But, please don't try to do more than you can handle." She stood up and stacked the plates and tableware. "And what about the young girls in the pictures? Don't forget about them."

The girls? How could he have been so callous as to ignore their wellbeing? "No, we can't forget them."

"We need to try to find out who they are. They're the real victims, you know." She turned to take the dishes to the sink.

When Dae said "we," Brax knew he was committed to helping more people than Ty.

"I agree," he said. "I think we make a good team. Maybe we should get married." His chest heaved as he let out a chuckle.

"Maybe so, she said."

He caught her smile as she leaned over to rinse a plate.

~

There was little traffic on the way to Charlie Kramer's house. Brax let the window down on the passenger side, and Sunny stuck his head out. The wind roared through the open window and Brax turned up the volume on the Kruger Brothers CD. He bobbed his head in rhythm to the up-tempo bluegrass song.

"That's good music, isn't it boy?" He figured it was probably the kind of music a country dog would like.

Sunny kept his head out the window.

The CD ended and Brax replaced it with another. The music had barely started again when he pulled onto the driveway at Charlie's house. As he let Sunny out of the car, Charlie walked from the front door to meet them.

Sunny was calm and friendly when Charlie patted him on the head.

Brax pulled a sheet of paper out of his shirt pocket. "Here's a list of things about Sunny that might help you, including what he likes to eat. He's a good dog. Your grandkids will like him."

"I'm sure they will," Charlie agreed. "You want to come inside. Liz isn't here—she's at the beauty parlor.

"No thanks. I need to get back and help clean up the house."

"You're not selling it are you?" Charlie asked.

"No. I'm going to hang onto it."

"I didn't really think you meant it when you said you'd be

leaving *forever* the other day. I know it's none of my business, but are you sure that you and Dae are on the same page?"

"Yeah, we're on the same page. We're getting married."

"Now, you know that getting married and being on the same page are two entirely different things." Charlie laughed.

Brax laughed too, but he was a little edgy about Charlie's perceptiveness. He walked a few paces and shooed Sunny away from digging in a flowerbed. He turned back to Charlie. "We'll come back up here after the wedding. I'll have to hang around for a while depending on what happens with Tom Benefield."

"Yeah, that's a helluva situation. I think it's gonna be rough on his wife and son. You like that boy, don't you?"

"He and I get along."

Charlie bent down, pulled a dandelion out of the grass and tossed it aside. "Look Brax…I know how attached you are to that dog, and I know you're torn about leaving the Ridge. Why don't you just let me keep Sunny at my place for a while and see what happens. I've talked to Liz, and she says it's all right with her."

Brax felt a surge of optimism. "What about your grandkids?"

"They come over here a lot. They can play with the dog and not have to take care of him. My daughter will like that."

"You don't have to do this, Charlie. I don't know exactly how long I'll be gone, or what my plans are when I return."

"Yeah, we've already gone over that. And I know I don't have to do it. But I need a new walking partner and I figure Sunny will fit that bill just fine." A smile formed on Charlie's face as he reached out to shake Brax's hand. "Now, leave my dog with me, and get the hell gone from here."

When Brax shook Charlie's hand, the reality of the moment sunk in. Now he could leave Sunny and not have a sinking feeling of abandonment. "Thanks, Charlie."

Brax whistled Sunny to him. He took the Lab by the collar and led him to Charlie. After Charlie took the collar, Brax stepped away and looked down at Sunny. "He'll take good care of you."

Brax walked to the car and waved good-bye to Charlie. As he turned the key, the CD started back up where it had left off. He sang along with the Kruger Brothers to a bluegrass version of *People Get Ready*.

He was ready to go to Seaside.

20

THE MOUNTAINS AND HARDWOOD FORESTS OF NORTH GEORGIA disappeared from view early the next day. Passing through the flat, piney landscape in South Georgia, they arrived in Brunswick in the early afternoon.

Brax followed the causeway over the marshes, then onto a long suspension bridge. Arching over the backwaters with tall cables that pointed upward like wings, the bridge had the graceful appearance of a giant heron in flight. At the peak, there was a clear view of the island and the glistling Atlantic Ocean on either side.

"Isn't this beautiful?" Dae asked. "It's almost mystical."

"Uh huh," Brax mumbled. "But the developers will screw it up."

She didn't respond, and he felt guilty for sounding negative. "I mean it really *is* beautiful."

"Nice try," she said, without turning from the window.

The sky was blue-gray and the temperature in the eighties, ten degrees warmer than in Rocky Ridge.

"You know I love this place," Brax said. "I lived here for four years and enjoyed every minute." He had a second thought. "Well, except for that day when you kicked me to the curb."

"Oh, hush," she said.

He glanced at Dae with a grin and the afternoon light framed her smile in a soft glow.

On the drive across the island, he made no mention of the signs of new construction that littered the roadside. He had fought the battle against development and lost. The island would never be the way it was when he first moved there seven years before. But he regretted opening his big mouth earlier and decided that nothing was going to dampen his spirits this day.

Though it had only been three weeks since his last visit, when he passed through the entrance gate of Seaside Village, Brax felt a wave of nostalgia slap him like a breaking white cap. His heart began to stir with memories of old friends and good times, as though he were arriving at a family reunion.

"Welcome home," he said as he drove into Dae's garage.

She sighed and said, "It feels good."

He parked her sedan beside his pick-up truck he had left there. After grabbing the luggage from the trunk, he followed Dae inside. When he closed the door behind him, he felt like he had stepped into another world. Thoughts of the tragic events in Rocky Ridge and the futures of Tom Benefield and Ty were tucked away in the recesses of his mind. He placed their bags in the bedroom, then stepped outside to join Dae on the patio.

"I can smell the ocean," she said, looking starry-eyed as if the oleanders and live oaks in front of her were invisible. "And I can hear it, can't you?"

"Yes."

It was true. Even though the sea was too far away for them to actually hear it, the sound was present in their minds. It was a good sound and a good smell. Everything felt right in a way that had been missing for a while. He was glad they had returned to the very place where they had first met. It was a fine place for a wedding.

~

A week later, Brax pulled the laundry tag from the gray pinstriped pants and sucked in his belly as he buckled his belt. He couldn't remember the last time he had worn a suit but it had been a few pounds ago. Dae turned from the dresser mirror, and he pinned a white orchid on her navy blue dress.

"You look fetching, m'dear," he said, as he put on his coat.

"And you're so dashing. Are you ready?"

"I've been ready for three years." He kissed her on the neck, careful not to muss up her hair or makeup. Taking her hand, they walked into the living room.

Brax's oldest son, Mason, and Dae's daughter, Julie, rose from their seats to greet them.

"Mom, you look beautiful," Julie said. "And Brax, you're a handsome groom."

"Yeah," said Mason, "Y'all make a sharp couple."

The comment wasn't taken lightly by Brax. He was always conscious of the fact that Dae was uncommonly attractive for a woman her age, and he was never comfortable with his own looks. Yet, she made him feel handsome.

He tucked Dae's arm in his. "The carriage has arrived."

Outside, the couple got into the back of Mason's SUV. Julie sat up front for the short drive to the clubhouse.

"Give us a minute to get to our seats before you come in," Mason said as he parked.

"Let's wait out here and let them wonder if we've changed our minds," Brax joked.

"No, you can't back out now."

Out of the car, Brax crooked his elbow once again. Dae took his arm, and they entered the main room of the clubhouse. As they walked down an aisle between the tables occupied by the guests, the silvery voice of a soprano singing *The Prayer* spilled from speakers. Slowly passing by the thirty or so people in the intimate setting, he smiled and kept his eyes forward.

An unexpected feeling of closure settled over Brax. For the second time in his life, he would be wedded to another person for every minute of every day until parted by death. He loved Dae—there was no doubt in his mind of that—but he knew it meant sacrificing a bit of himself. Though he was sometimes lonely, he had grown used to his independence; the freedom from catering to another's needs. He felt a selfish sense of nobility in making that sacrifice even though he realized that she might feel the same way.

They stopped in front of Horace Hassell, a Seaside resident and retired Methodist minister. From the speakers the recorded voice of a baritone—deep, yet soft like lead—joined that of the soprano. The duet sang the final lyrics of the song with a powerful crescendo that sounded like a chorus raining down from heaven.

Brax squeezed Dae's hand and felt as if he could feel her heart beat. The preacher, a small man with a sharp, hawk-like face, spoke in a clipped, nasally voice. He was mercifully brief with his remarks.

Feeling oddly detached, Brax was in a daze for most of the ceremony. But when he responded to the preacher with, "I do," he regained his bearings and felt good about the finality of his commitment.

"So I now pronounce you, Braxton and Daedre, husband and wife," the preacher said.

Brax kissed his bride and caught a whiff of her perfume with the scent of gardenia. "You smell delicious," he whispered.

"I feel delicious," she whispered back. Then she turned to the onlookers with a big smile and said, "I'm Mrs. Donovan."

Brax led Dae to the dance floor. He motioned to Mason who turned on the sound system again, filling the room with the smooth sound of a trumpet playing *When I Fall in Love*.

"Does that sound familiar?" he asked, as he took her in his arms.

"Yes." She closed her eyes as they began to dance. "It expresses exactly how I feel."

"Good. That's why we're here."

The audience remained in their seats while the couple danced to a recording Brax had made more than thirty years before.

When the song ended, Brax spoke over the applause, "It's time to celebrate."

Mason pulled a bottle of champagne from a bucket of ice. "Cheers," he said as he popped the cork and it flew across the table. The party was on.

Around the room, champagne bubbled into goblets. Loud conversations broke out, drowning out the recorded piano music that tinkled in the background. The guests began filling their plates from the spreads of food set on tables against one wall.

Julie and her husband, Ben, had driven from Charlotte with their two young daughters. Mason, Brax' oldest son, had flown in from Dallas with his wife and two daughters. Dylan, the youngest son, had driven from Atlanta with his wife and two teenagers.

Among those absent were Dae's son, Justin, who was stationed with his Army unit in Germany with his wife and daughter. Brax's other son, Logan, a bachelor, had sent a card and flowers but did not attend the ceremony at his father's urging. "No need," Brax had said, "I'll plead insanity right off the bat and it'll be over in no time. We'll come visit you after the sentencing."

For the next half hour, the newlyweds made their way around the room sharing hugs and handshakes. Brax's friend, Jim Hawkins, was among the first to greet them.

"You're as pretty as ever," Jim said, hugging Dae. Then he reached a hand to Brax for a shake. "And you still look like a flop-earred hound but you're lucky as hell. Congratulations, you old scoundrel."

Sally Blankenship, Jim's companion for the evening, stepped forward and hugged Dae, then Brax. "I'm so happy for both of you. It couldn't happen to two nicer people."

"Yeah, it's a marriage made in AARP heaven," Jim said.

"Oh," Dae said, "You're only as old as you feel and I don't feel old at all."

Brax looked at Jim and grinned. "Just spittin' and gettin'." He looked at Sally and back to Jim. "It's never too late, you know."

Jim wrinkled his brow and eyed one of the food tables. "Nice spread." Turning to Sally, he said, "Let's eat," and started for the buffet line.

Dae's eyes caught sight of something behind Brax and scrunched her face. "My God, the devil."

Brax turned to see a heavyset man standing in the doorway. The man wore a short sleeve shirt draped on the outside of his pants. The man stared directly at Brax.

"That's John's brother," she said.

"The one that sent you the nasty e-mail? Frank?"

"Yes. I can't believe he's here. I can assure you he wasn't invited."

"I'll talk to him," Brax said.

"No. I don't want to spoil the party."

"Well, he's already here. I don't think he came to give us his best wishes." Brax took a couple of steps before Dae grabbed him by the arm.

"Don't say anything to him. He's just looking to start something."

"Relax. I can handle it."

Dae appeared doubtful. "I'm going to get Dylan. He needs to be with you."

"No need for him to get involved. We'll handle this peacefully."

Brax walked to the doorway and approached the man. "I'm Brax Donovan. We haven't met but Dae tells me you're Frank Whitehead."

"That's right." He looked at Brax with beady eyes and a sneer curled to one side of his upper lip. "I'm her ex-brother-in-law." He put a sarcastic emphasis on "ex."

A couple from the main room edged past the two men, walked through the doorway and down the hall toward the restrooms.

"Let's get out of the way," Brax said. He moved to a quiet spot in the clubhouse foyer. Frank followed him with slow, measured steps as if pulled against his will.

Brax noticed Dylan walk into the foyer and motioned for him to stay back. Dylan stopped but remained standing conspicuously nearby. At six-four, 280 pounds, he made an imposing and obvious bodyguard.

"I met your brother," Brax said to Frank. "He was a good man, a patriot."

"You don't know *shit* about him." Frank spit out the epithet like it was venom.

Brax inched closer to Frank and braced himself for straight talk.

"I know shit about you, though. I know you're a convicted felon. And I know you're still on parole. And I know that if you start harassing or threatening people, they'll put your ass back in that little six-by-eight condo behind a razor wire fence."

Frank began breathing heavily and his face turned puffy pink as if he were about to explode. "I haven't done anything. I hate your damn guts and that bitch in there you just married but that ain't against the law."

Brax held his temper over the bitch comment. "I have something that the parole board might not look kindly on if I showed it to them. It's just a piece of paper, a print-out of an e-mail." He paused and let the thought sink in. "Remember that one you sent to Dae when you found out she was getting married?" He paused again and Frank didn't reply. "The one where you called her a nasty name," he continued.

"That was no threat. They can't lock me up for that."

"Maybe, maybe not. But, I know this—if you say or do anything else that remotely resembles harassment, that'll show a pattern. So I suggest that you leave us the hell alone, and don't interrupt our wedding party."

"Screw you and your goddamn wedding party," Frank spewed.

Dylan took a few steps closer into hearing range.

Brax and Frank stood facing each other with neither making a move.

After several seconds, Brax said, "Dae loved your brother. She's told me that many times and I know it's true. She was faithful to her wedding vows. You need to accept that."

A uniformed security guard entered the front door and approached Frank. "Sir, this is a private party. I'll have to ask you to leave."

Frank clenched his jaws and looked aside. He turned back and made a quick tug at the waist of his pants. "Go to hell," he said and walked directly out of the clubhouse with the security guard right behind him.

Brax started toward the main room. He stopped and spoke to Dylan. "That's the last we'll see of that guy."

"You think so?' Dylan asked. "He didn't look too happy to me."

"Yeah, I'm sure he's not. But he doesn't want to go back to jail."

Dylan gave his father a way-to-go tap on the shoulder.

Brax really wasn't sure of anything. But he had a wedding reception waiting for him.

"How did you know he was on parole?" Dae asked, after Brax recounted his conversation with Frank Whitehead.

"I've got sources." He took a bite of wedding cake. "This is delicious."

"Sources like who?"

"Like Lance Johnson. He gave me all the skinny about our friend, Frank."

"How did Lance know?"

He took a sip of coffee. "Beats me," he said, deadpanned.

She sat back from the table. "You asked him to find out about Frank's record, didn't you?"

Brax pulled his head back and gave her fish eyes.

"And I suppose," Dae continued, "Lance has friends in high places who told him about the parole."

"Okay, Agatha Christie, you got me."

She looked at him with a gleam in her eyes. "Sometimes you amaze me."

"You'll get used to it," he said with a smug grin.

Then he had a suspicious thought. "Where did that security guard come from?"

"Hmm," Dae said, "I wonder." She speared a chocolate covered strawberry with her fork and smiled as she stuck it in her mouth.

~

That evening they strolled the beach. Under a full moon and pewter gray sky, the air hung heavy with the threat of rain.

"I've been thinking," Dae said.

"About?" Brax asked.

"About those girls. Will we ever know who they are?"

"Sure. Lance will find them. I know him and he'll do all he can to identify the victims. That's his job."

"But then what happens? I think they'll need help in coping with what they've been through."

"I'm sure they will. But we might just be pulling a string from a big ball of yarn."

"What do you mean?"

"I mean we may be dealing with something a lot bigger than a few girls. They found a lot of pictures in Bob's trailer. And there were other men in the pictures. He wasn't acting alone."

She seemed to weigh his words and didn't respond.

Brax took her hand and they walked to the edge of the water. Tiny waves pushed foamy surf ashore, then ebbed before reaching their feet.

"I worked with young people when I was a teacher," Dae said. "And I have a daughter and two granddaughters, so I know a thing or two about girls. I want to do what I can to help those dear things who were abused."

Feeling the passion in her voice, he stopped walking. "Does that mean—?"

"Yes. We'll go back to Rocky Ridge soon."

"Only if you're sure you want to."

"I am."

Brax knew Jim Hawkins was right. He was lucky; she was a good wife.

He pulled Dae to him. They stood silently as the sea churned in rhythm and the moon drifted behind a cloud. Afterward, the soft sand squished beneath their shoes as they walked through the dunes on their way home. Yes, it was a fine place for a wedding.

~

"There's only so much we can do," Brax said as he stripped to his shorts, preparing for bed. "I promised to take care of Ty, you know."

"I want to help the girls," Dae said from the bathroom. "They're the ones that are hurt the most."

She didn't understand. It was more complicated than just saying, "*I want to help.*" What kind of help could she give? What if the girls were druggies or mentally challenged? He knew Dae's heart was in the right place, but others were better prepared to take care of them; people that had training and experience in that sort of thing. Besides, he needed her to help him take care of Ty. Once they got back to Rocky Ridge, he would convince her of that.

Dae came into the bedroom, turned off the bedside lamp and snuggled close to him under the covers. He tasted her neck and smelled the faintest scent of gardenia perfume. At least, he imagined he did. Just as he imagined that one day she would say, "*Yes, we can take him in for a while.*"

In the morning, Brax leaned over a crossword puzzle at the breakfast table, a cup of coffee in one hand and pen in the other. Across from him, Dae sat in her robe with a glass of orange juice, reading a magazine. When her phone rang on the counter nearby she got up to answer it.

"Hi," she said. "No, we haven't turned on the TV...Yes, we know him—not that well but we've met him."

"Who are you talking to?" Brax asked.

"Sally," Dae said, holding the phone away. She put the phone back to her ear and said, "He claims he wasn't involved." A moment later she sighed, "O-o-h."

Brax set the crossword puzzle aside. "What—?"

Dae lifted a finger and formed a silent "ssh" with her mouth. "This is such a shock, but thanks for letting us know...I'm not sure. I'll call you back in a few minutes." Looking stunned, she set the phone down.

"What's going on?"

"Tom Benefield is dead. They found him in his jail cell this morning. He hanged himself."

21

AFTER HEARING OF TOM BENEFIELD'S DEATH, BRAX GOT UP AND walked to the back door. His mind in a fog, he stared through the glass panel of the track door into the outside.

"How did Sally find out?" he asked.

"She got a news alert on her phone."

Brax thought about something Benefield had said at their meeting outside the county jail. *"No matter what happens to me, I want Ty to be taken care of."*

"I should have known," he said. "He planned it all along."

"No one could have known that," Dae said, as she walked over to him. "This story is all over the news. A lot of people see Tom and his father as monsters."

She walked away; he kept his eyes out the back door. He heard her rinsing plates in the sink behind him.

When the water stopped running, she asked, "Are we going for our walk with Sally?"

"No, you go. I don't feel like it right now."

After Dae left, Brax sat in a chair on the patio and looked up at the sky. He couldn't smell the salt air or hear the ocean. But he could see Banjo Bob sitting on a bench in front of the courthouse, plucking his five-string; Tom Benefield sitting at a table in a jailhouse courtyard; Ty with a big smile on his face as he walked on a log across the creek. Everything had changed in a matter of days. Now that the wedding was over, he felt like he was in the wrong place. It was time to go home.

～

By one o'clock, they had their bags packed for the return trip to Rocky Ridge. This time they took both vehicles, Brax in his truck following close behind Dae in her car.

When they stopped at the main road in front of the entrance to Seaside, Brax called her on his cell phone.

"I think I saw Jim's car in Sally's driveway."

"He's been there for the last two nights," Dae said. "He walked with us on the beach this morning."

"I'll be damned. How 'bout that?" Brax smiled to himself. "Let's get going. I'll be right behind, so don't drive like an old lady." He laughed and ended the call before she could retort.

Six hours later, they joined up at a Cracker Barrel for dinner.

"I should have realized how desperate Tom was," Brax said as they waited for their order. "His personal humiliation had to be hard to deal with. Then everyone found out that Bob was his own father and a pedophile. It sent him over the edge. He had already decided what he was going to do before we met."

"You can't know what's in someone's mind," Dae said.

"Why else would he ask me—someone he hardly knew—to look after his son?" He gazed to the side. "I wish I had talked to him again. Gotten to know him better."

"None of this is your fault. The abuse of the young girls—those *children*—is a terrible thing, and I'm proud of you for getting involved and exposing it. You've done all you could. So don't feel sorry for Tom Benefield—he'll answer to God for what he did."

Brax absorbed her comment for a moment. He decided she was right. It wasn't his place to judge. "Yeah, he'll answer alright. We all will in the end."

The waitress set their food down, and the mood lightened for a few minutes before Dae restarted the conversation.

"What we need to think about now is what we can do to help the real victims of all of this—the girls."

"Yeah, but we don't know when those pictures were made. Those girls may be grown by now and scattered to the wind."

Dae seemed to be jarred by the comment, as if she hadn't considered that possibility. "It doesn't matter." she said, sounding less confident. "We know how they were treated."

"I made a promise to look after *Ty*," Brax said.

She set her glass of tea down. "What do you plan to do?"

"I'm not sure." He spread some butter on a piece of cornbread. "I'll start by talking to his mother and see what the family situation is. I need to get to know the boy a little better, too."

"Don't get carried away. It takes a lot of energy to be a full time babysitter. We're too old for that."

"Ty's not a baby."

"Lots of boys grow up without a father. He'll survive."

Brax put his hands on the table and looked directly at Dae. "That's not the issue."

She didn't respond and he left it at that.

∼

The next morning, Brax and Dae rose early in Rocky Ridge. They met Charlie Kramer for a walk on the track at Pate County High School as if nothing had interrupted their daily routine.

"I thought y'all might stay away on your honeymoon." Charlie laughed. "Couldn't blame you what with all that's gone on around here lately. Rocky Ridge is not exactly Sleepy Town USA anymore."

"It's the same place it's always been," Brax said.

"Nah, it'll never be the same again," Charlie rebutted. "We'll always have this stigma of redneck child abusers."

"It can happen anywhere," Dae said. "I think the town will get a lot of credit for the way they handled the problem."

"I hope so." Charlie turned to Brax. "You got all of this started, didn't you? I don't mean the bad stuff," he quickly added. "I mean finding out about it and reporting it."

"It would have come out eventually," Brax said.

"No, it wouldn't have," Dae said. "You're right, Charlie—the whole town should be thankful to Brax for exposing these men."

Charlie looked at Brax and nodded. "Yeah, in one sense it gives us a black eye but it had to be stopped. It's hard to think about what that son-of-a bitch Banjo Bob and his bastard son did."

"Tom wasn't like Bob," Brax said.

"He was a party to everything," Dae insisted.

Her brashness surprised Brax, but he thought better of responding for the time being.

"Both of the sorry cowards took the easy way out," Charlie said. "But their asses will burn in Hell."

They walked for a couple of minutes before Brax spoke again. "Have you seen Tom's wife since all this happened?" he asked Charlie.

"No. I heard she's been pretty much out of it ever since he did us all a favor."

Brax looked at Dae with a wrinkled brow and then back to Charlie. "What's her name?"

"Gee…" Charlie took a few steps. "Connie? Yeah, that's it—Connie."

A runner approached from behind and the trio moved to the outside lanes of the track. Brax watched the tall teenage girl glide by in long, graceful strides. She looked fresh and innocent, a striking contrast to the girls in the pictures he had found.

"You hear anything about what's happened to Ty?" he continued.

"Far as I know, he's at home. I think there's a relative—an aunt maybe—that's staying with them."

After the walk, Brax hung back while Dae walked to the car. "How's Sunny?" he asked Charlie.

"He's doing just fine. The grandkids like him a lot. Do you want him back?"

"Not right now. I'm still not sure how long we'll be here." He tilted his head in Dae's direction. "I'm working on her."

"Let me know when."

"Will do."

When he got into the car, Brax turned to Dae. "You told Charlie that Tom was just as guilty as Bob. You know that's not true."

"No I don't. He had those pictures on his computer at school. And that story he gave you didn't make sense. I've read about pedophiles and they're always in denial. Besides, why would he allow it to continue after his own son knew about it? He even admitted beating Ty. Don't you see? He was just like his father."

Brax glared at Dae. "You think that's how it works, eh?" His voice rang with anger and his chest heaved. "Abusive father begets abusive son, right?"

Dae closed her eyes as he ranted and then looked at him. "I'm sorry—I didn't mean it like that." She reached and put a hand on his arm. "You know I don't think that of you."

His pulse began to slow down and she moved her hand to his.

"You're probably right about Tom," she said. "You always have good intuition about people."

Brax knew it was just a gesture of conciliation on her part. But maybe he *had* been wrong about Tom Benefield. And maybe he would never know the truth.

~

"I need to meet Connie Benefield," Brax said as they walked into the house.

"It's too soon," Dae said. "She's still in mourning. Charlie said she was having a hard time."

"Tom told me she wasn't mentally strong even under normal circumstances. That's why he asked me to help."

"So you're going to jump right in?"

"I'll wait a few days."

"I want to be with you when you meet her." She plopped down onto the sofa.

"Of course. We're a team." He tried to look serious. "And let no man put us asunder," he said, imitating the nasal twang of Horace Hassel at their wedding two days earlier.

Ty would be there, too, Brax thought. Dae had only seen the boy a couple of times, and it would be good for her to get to know him. Then he realized that he didn't know a great deal about Ty himself. But Dae was right; he always had good intuition about people.

Brax walked to the back bedroom on the main floor. He stood for a moment, looking around the room and at the woods beyond the window. It would be a good room for a boy.

∼

Every day, Brax roamed the woods behind his house. He walked the path alongside the creek and other trails that meandered through the hills and hollows in all directions. Occasionally he crossed paths with hikers or campers. Once he eyed a small person in the distance that he thought might be Ty, then that figure disappeared into the woods like a forest creature. Each day he visited the clearing where he had first met Ty, but he never saw the boy.

"You've been gone almost two hours," Dae said one evening. "It's getting dark."

"I lost track of time."

"I worried that you might be in trouble and no one would know where you were. You know your phone doesn't work in those woods."

"People around here got by for hundreds of years without cell phones." Dae didn't respond but he realized he sounded obstinate.

"It's my Thoreau time," he said. "My spiritual workout."

"I know what it is. You've been with Ty."

"No." He shook his head." I haven't seen him since we got back from Seaside. Why do you think I would keep that from you?"

"I'm sorry. That sounded like I don't trust you. I just know how you feel about him."

"That's all right—I know I have some crazy ways."

"While you were gone, I called Lance Johnson," she said, changing the subject. "I asked him if they had any clues about the identities of the girls in the pictures. He said that counselors had talked to all of the children who go to Sequoyah Elementary and their parents. It doesn't appear that any of them are victims. Children can be easily intimidated though."

"Yeah, but I'm sure they know that both Benefield men are dead. They wouldn't have any reason to fear them now. Anyhow, I never thought any of them were victims. I don't think Tom would have allowed that to happen."

Dae didn't challenge him but Brax knew she didn't agree with his assessment of Tom Benefield.

"With all the media attention," she said, "I thought someone would have come forward by now. One of the girls in the pictures or an adult that knows something."

"I'm sure there's a lot of shame involved for the girls. They probably don't want anyone to know. Besides, a lot of people don't pay attention to the real news." He sensed her frustration. "Lance will keep at it. He'll find out who the girls are."

"I hope so."

～

More than a week went by, and Brax still had seen no sign of Ty on his forays into the woods. He thought enough time had passed since Tom Benefield's death that it wouldn't be imprudent to contact his widow. Dae sat on the sofa while he called from his recliner.

"This is Connie," she answered.

Brax identified himself as an acquaintance of her deceased husband.

"Yes, I've heard him speak of you. I couldn't forget that name—Brax. I've been expecting to hear from you."

He was taken off guard and wasn't quite sure what to make of her comment. Still, it was reassuring to know that he wasn't a complete unknown.

"I would like to meet with you at your convenience," Brax said.

"I'm here all the time but I don't get stirring till about nine-thirty."

"Would tomorrow about two be okay?"

She agreed and gave Brax her address, which he didn't admit to knowing.

When he ended the call, Brax looked at Dae. "That's strange—she said she was expecting a call from me."

"She probably knew you and Tom had differences. There's no telling what he told her about you."

Brax recalled how he had once judged Tom Benefield before even meeting him. Now he wondered if Benefield's widow had passed judgment on him in the same way.

22

BRAX HAD BEEN TO THE BENEFIELD HOUSE ONCE BEFORE, BUT only for a curious drive-by. This time he had an invitation. Though the circumstances had changed dramatically, he was drawn by the same interest in a young boy.

When Connie Benefield opened the door, he smiled as he introduced himself and Dae.

"Come in," she said, her face and voice expressionless.

She led the couple into the living room and offered them seats on a bulky sofa with overstuffed accent pillows. She sat facing them in a high-back upholstered chair with heavy wooden arms.

A thin woman with gray skin, Connie Benefield looked like someone who avoided the sun as well as make-up. Her hair, pulled back in a bun, accentuated the gaunt look of her sunken cheeks and deep-set eyes.

"I'm sorry about your husband's death," Brax said.

"Thank you. I'm afraid most people aren't."

"I'm sorry about that, too." He shot an awkward glance at Dae.

Connie also shifted her eyes to Dae. "I understand you just got married recently."

Dae arched her brows and lifted her head slightly. "Yes, less than two weeks ago."

Connie didn't offer congratulations. Instead, she said, "I was thirty-five before I got married."

Brax sensed he was looking at a woman barren of female instincts. She seemed cold, not with grief, but by habit as if part of her very nature. Even the house looked lifeless inside, functionally arranged but charmless, like a setting in a discount furniture store. The odor of lemon-scented air freshener reminded Brax of a cheap hotel room.

"I only met your husband a couple of times." Brax paused. "And I've met your son Ty."

"Yes, I know. He's actually my step-son but I'm the only mother he's ever known."

"I understand," Brax said, out of courtesy rather than actual knowledge.

"I don't mean to be rude, but I doubt that you do. Tom and I were only married for six years. Ty's mother had mental problems and died from an overdose of sleeping pills when he was less than a year old. He doesn't remember her but he knows I'm not his birth mother."

She glanced at Dae. "I've been good to him," she sad firmly.

"I'm sure you have," Dae said, empathy ringing in her voice.

The room went quiet for a moment before Connie spoke to Brax again. "He calls you the man in the woods."

Brax smiled but he wasn't sure he liked that description. "We saw him and his father at the bluegrass festival at Lake Gansagi."

"You saw the devil play his banjo too, didn't you?" Connie asked, twisting her face in anger with the first sign of emotion from her.

"Yes," Brax replied.

"I know why you're here," Connie said. "It's about Ty."

Brax swallowed hard, considering how to begin.

Before he could respond, Connie spoke again. "I talked to Tom the day before he died. He was denied bail and said he might be going away for a long time. He worried about me and Ty and said he needed to make arrangements for us. I'm no fool—I knew what he was telling me."

"Miz Benefield—" Brax stopped when a heavyset woman appeared in a doorway to the side.

Connie spoke to the woman without introducing her. "Jessie, bring me a glass of water, please." The woman left and Connie turned back to Brax. "Go ahead."

Brax took his elbow off the arm of the couch, leaned forward with his hands clasped together. "I met with Tom when he was in jail. He had asked to speak to me. We didn't talk very long." He looked aside, reluctant to say what had brought him there. "He said he wanted me to look out for Ty."

The heavyset woman returned and handed Connie Benefield a glass of water.

Connie grasped the glass in both hands. "Thanks," she said as the woman left without speaking. The water sloshed almost over the rim when she shakily lifted it to her lips. She swallowed hard and set the glass down on a side table, her hands still trembling.

Brax looked at Dae and she nodded to him as if encouraging him to continue.

"Yes, I know what Tom asked of you," Connie said, ignoring the interruption. "That's very odd, don't you think?"

"I guess so," he replied.

"Do you know why he said that? Do you even know what you might be getting into?"

Brax put his arm back on the side of the sofa and leaned into a pillow. "No, I'm not entirely sure why he asked me." He let the second question dangle.

"Ty is different," she said. "He doesn't have friends. You're his friend."

The sight of Ty dancing at the bluegrass festival, wearing a bright outfit and a big smile on his face, came back to Brax. "What about his clogging group?"

"That's his only outlet. The other kids are older, and he doesn't see them except when they are dancing or practicing." She took another drink of water, her hands still unsteady. "Tom wasn't a bad father, but he couldn't relate to his own son. He had a temper and would lose his patience with Ty." She set the glass of water on an end table. "Ty's a loner. Takes after me, I 'spose."

"I was kinda like that as a kid," Brax said.

Connie looked at Dae again. "What do you think about all this? You think I'm a crazy woman?"

"No," Dae uttered. She turned to Brax before answering the first question in a stronger voice. "I know this has to be a terrible thing to go through. Maybe we can help in some way."

Connie's eyes shifted back and forth like she was looking for something. "My health is not very good. Jessie's my sister but she can't help much. She's never been married and doesn't know a thing about children. I don't have any other family, and Tom's people are all of *questionable* character. I don't trust them and, truth be told, he didn't either."

She leaned her head on the back of the chair and fixed her eyes on Brax. "I know a little about you," she said.

"How so?" he asked.

"I talked to Lance Johnson at the Sheriff's office. I think he's a straight shooter and he vouched for you. Said he trusted you."

Brax felt the blush of a smile on his face. "That's good to hear."

"Ty needs a father figure. Do you have a son?"

"I have three. They're all grown, of course."

"And they're all good boys?"

Brax imagined each of his sons looking back at him. "They're men now. Each one is different but, yes, I'm proud of them."

Connie raised her head and looked beyond Brax as if absorbed in thought. Then she returned her eyes to him. "I need somebody who can help my son be…normal. Do you think you can do that?"

Brax leaned forward again. "Look ma'am, I'm not anyone special. I didn't ask to get involved with Ty, and I'm not sure what your husband had in mind."

He looked into Connie's eyes and saw emptiness. A mother lacking maternal instincts, she was no more "normal" than her son, he thought. The room closed in around him as both women seemed to await an answer to the question.

"But I'm willing to do whatever I can. I like Ty and I think he likes me."

The eerie haze of uneasiness that had hovered over the conversation seemed to lift in the long silence that followed.

Then Connie spoke again. "It will take time. You need to get to know him better."

"I agree," Brax said.

"He's still my son. He'll answer to me and you're not to undermine me."

"You needn't worry about that." Brax imagined himself not as a father figure—he was too old for that—but more as a surrogate grandfather. "I'll try to be a good mentor."

"Ty's in the back yard. I told him to stay out there while we visited. I need to talk to him alone after you're gone." Connie rose from her chair.

Taking that as a signal that the meeting was over, Brax and Dae stood up.

Brax took a slip of paper from his shirt pocket. "Here's my number. Give me a call when it's okay for me to come back. Maybe I can take him somewhere, a park or something like that."

"Tomorrow," Connie said. "I'll call tomorrow."

Brax and Dae walked to their car without speaking.

"Boy, that was interesting," Dae said when they settled into their seats.

"Yes, it was," he said looking straight ahead.

Turning to her, he asked, "Are you okay with what I agreed to?"

"I'm not sure what you *did* agree to. Are you?"

He shook his head. "Hell no."

"Well, as long as you don't forget me, I'll be fine." A hint of playfulness colored her voice.

He reached and squeezed her hand. "I'll never do that."

Brax backed out of the driveway and as he started down the street, he looked in the rear view mirror. Ty stood near the back corner of the house looking toward the car.

~

After the visit to Connie Benefield, Brax felt a new sense of purpose. With Dae, he had found love again, a passion for life. Now, in Ty he saw a way to help someone in a manner that wasn't necessary with his own sons. They had been "normal," each in their own unique way. There was something intrinsically satisfying, yet intimidating, about the prospect of shaping a young boy's personality.

Those thoughts coursed through his mind while he stood on the deck, tending the grill and absorbing the last rays of sun on a long June day. He scooped the hamburger patties off the rack and joined Dae who had set the outdoor table.

They ate their food and chatted about what people do to pass time: the weather, books they were reading, political scandals. The orange glow of daylight edged toward the tree line and shadows spread over half the deck. The mood turned mellow and they avoided talking about Ty or Connie Benefield as if by mutual consent.

Dae lifted the last remains of a burger to her mouth. Before she could take a bite, she turned her head and sneezed. "Ooh, this pollen," she said. "It really gets to me."

"Yeah, it's bad this time of year up here. You don't get it on the coast."

Brax was reminded of the different environment Dae confronted in the mountains compared to the seashore. Even the house was a step back from what she was used to.

"Remember that neighborhood we went to on the other side of the lake?" he asked. "The one that Charlie's moving to—Lakehaven."

"Yes, it was pretty."

"We could check it out again. The houses are new, even nicer than Seaside. And there are people our age living there. It might be perfect for us."

"It's too far away," Dae said. "You heard what Ty's mother said—he's staying with her. And I agree that's best for him. But you need to be close by."

Her response surprised him. "Yeah, but I want what's best for you," he insisted. "I don't mind driving a few miles. Besides, things can change."

"I'm not sure what you mean by that, but we can think about it some more if you're really serious."

"When it comes to pleasing you, I'm always serious." With a silly grin, he stuck a potato chip in his mouth.

They finished the meal and began to clear the table. As Dae took the plates inside, Brax's attention was drawn to something moving on the pathway from the creek. He thought it might be a deer; but as it got closer, he realized it was a person. First the face appeared, then the whole body. It was Ty. He emerged from the path and stopped as he approached the house.

Brax stepped to the edge of the rail and stared at the boy. Dae walked from the house and moved beside Brax.

Ty spoke clearly with a trace of shyness in his voice. "Wanna have a boat race?"

23

"A boat race?" Dae asked. "What in the world is he talking about?"

"He means with sticks in the creek."

Brax raised his voice and called to Ty who stood at the edge of the woods, about fifty feet away.

"Come up here and we can talk about it."

Ty walked to the deck and up the steps.

"Ty, this is my wife, Dae."

"Hello," the boy said softly.

"Hi," Dae replied in her cheeriest voice.

"Dae made some chocolate chip cookies," Brax said. "They're really good. Would you like one?"

Ty grinned and nodded. "Yes."

Brax took a seat at the table as Dae went into the house. "Sit down," he said to Ty, extending a hand toward a chair.

"There's not much water in the creek today," he said as the boy sat down beside him.

"There's a little."

"Not enough for a boat race. We'll have to wait until we get some rain."

"Okay." Ty squirmed in the chair with his feet dangling above the deck floor.

Dae returned with a plate of cookies. "Do you want some milk?" she asked Ty.

"Yes, ma'am."

Dae set the plate on the table, went back inside, and returned with three glasses of milk on a tray.

"How have you been doing?" Brax asked the boy.

"Fine." Ty held a half-eaten cookie in one hand and took a drink of milk. "My daddy died," he said.

Brax looked at the boy. He didn't detect the painful sense of grief that one might experience from the loss of a parent. "I know. I'm sorry."

"Mama says he's in heaven with God." Ty's face slowly puckered and tears welled in his eyes.

Dae moved beside the boy, put her arms around his shoulders, and leaned down to hug him. "Yes, I'm sure your daddy is in heaven." She held the embrace as Ty buried his face in her chest. He sniffled but never cried out. She pulled back when he tugged at his tee shirt and wiped his face.

Brax stood up and put a hand on Ty's back. He nudged the plate of cookies toward him. "Have another one."

Ty grabbed a cookie and turned his attention to a bright yellow butterfly perched on a potted geranium nearby. He took a bite of cookie, and his eyes followed the butterfly as it fluttered into the air. The innocent look of a child returned to his face.

Brax tried to lighten the mood by telling Ty about his youth. Ty listened attentively and asked few questions. The boy looked puzzled when Brax told him that only a few people had a television when he was eight years old. Then he told him that "back in those days" all TV programs were in black-and-white and computers hadn't even been invented.

"But we played in the woods and had boat races in the creek. Just like you and I do now."

Ty smiled and looked at Dae as if Brax had revealed their secret game.

"It's getting late," Dae said. "We need to call your mother and tell her where you are."

"I can go now."

"No," Brax insisted. "I'll call her to tell her you're here, and then I'll take you home."

Brax phoned Connie Benefield and told her of Ty's whereabouts. "He'll be home in a few minutes."

"I thought he might be there."

Damn, Brax thought, *she sounds no more concerned than she might be for a pet dog.*

When he arrived at Ty's house, Connie was waiting at the front door.

"I appreciate your bringing him home." She appeared friendlier, more relaxed than the first time Brax had met her.

"No problem," he said. "We had a good time."

"They gave me some cookies," Ty said. "And milk, too."

"That was nice. Did you thank them?"

Ty turned to Brax, a guilty look on his face. "Thank you."

"You're welcome," Brax replied. Turning to Ty's mother, he asked, "May I speak to you for a minute?"

Looking at her son, Connie said, "Ty, go on in." She closed the door behind him as he went into the house.

"Has he ever been to the Ty Cobb Museum in Royston?" Brax asked.

"No. Tom said that he would take him but he never got around to it. Do you know Ty's full name?"

"Yes, he told me—Tyrus Raymond." Brax paused for a second. "I'd like him to know more about the man he was named after. Could I take him there tomorrow? We might be gone four or five hours."

Connie looked aside and appeared to be in deep thought. Then she turned back to Brax. "It will be okay. I told Ty about you. He's glad you want to be his friend."

"That's good to hear. I'll pick him up about ten in the morning." He began to walk away, then turned back.

"Don't tell him where we're going. Kids like secrets."

"I s'pose they do. I won't spoil it."

Brax drove home slowly, the road winding through countryside awash with the colors of spring. The scenery looked to him like a huge landscape painting veiled in the softness of dusk. His senses intensified and he felt a new vigor to life. And with a childlike feeling of anticipation, he pressed down on the accelerator.

~

Brax arrived at Ty's house a few minutes early. Before he reached the front door, Ty stepped outside dressed in tan cargo shorts and a camouflage tee shirt.

Connie followed him outside. She shared a "Good morning" with Brax with a little more animation than the day before.

Putting a hand on Ty's shoulder, she said, "Be good now."

"Ready?" Brax asked, looking at Ty. "Let's get going."

Ty followed Brax as they started for the car. He turned and waved. "Bye, Mom."

From the front stoop, Connie raised a hand in a silent "Bye."

In the car, Brax said, "We're going for a little drive."

"Where are we going?"

"To a neat place." He looked at Ty and wondered if the word

"neat" meant anything to a kid his age. Maybe so, he thought, when the boy's face lit up. "It's not too far away."

∼

An hour later they arrived in Royston, a small town in the rolling hills of Northeast Georgia. Nearing the city limits, Brax pulled off the road in front of a sign with the picture of an old-time baseball player.

"Here we are. Can you read the sign?' he asked Ty.

Ty sat up in his seat and read the words on the sign aloud in drawn out syllables.

"Wel-come to Roys-ton, home of base-ball's leg…leg…"

"Legendary," Brax said. "It means famous."

"Leg-en-dary," the boy continued, "Ty Cobb."

"That's the man you were named after," Brax said. "Do you like to play baseball?"

"Sometimes. I have a bat and a glove and three balls."

"Great. We can play catch one day. Are you on a team?"

"No. I'm not very good."

"It takes practice."

Brax knew it would take more than practice. The boy's lack of confidence was as evident as the blond hair on his head. That thought was still on his mind when, a few minutes later, he parked in front of the modest office building that housed the Ty Cobb Museum.

Inside the building, Brax purchased two tickets and led Ty into the first of three small rooms containing Cobb memorabilia. They were the only visitors in the museum, and Brax stood by patiently as the boy studied each display. With occasional help, Ty read every article that accompanied the pictures.

Tyrus Raymond (Ty) Cobb, often called "The Georgia Peach," was the first inductee into the Baseball Hall of Fame. By any measure, Cobb was one of the greatest players in the history of the game, yet he was not without detractors. Ill-tempered and fiercely competitive, he played the game to win at all costs. Though the hard statistics bore out the brilliance of Cobb's athletic feats, there was no hiding the darker sides of his personality. He was hated not only by his foes, but often by his own teammates with whom he sometimes fought. He remains to this day a controversial figure. But after his playing career he became a well-respected philanthropist with a fortune amassed through early investments in Coca Cola and General Motors.

In the next room they sat on the front row of a small theater and viewed a short film of Cobb's life.

The last room contained more pictures and focused on Ty Cobb as a hometown hero. One banner provided clues to the duality of the man. It described him as fierce and calculating; feared and revered; famous and infamous; benevolent and a gentleman. The latter description, smothered with hometown sympathy, referred to Cobb in his years after baseball when he expressed remorse for being combative and racist.

Brax knew all of this and much more about Ty Cobb. As a young boy, he had been a self-avowed baseball authority, pouring over statistics in *The Sporting News* and plastering his bedroom walls with pictures of major league gods in colorful uniforms.

After finishing the tour of exhibits, they stopped at the gift shop.

"I have some money," Ty said. "Mama gave me ten dollars."

"That's all right, you're my guest. Just pick out what you want."

Ty examined each souvenir as if he were selecting a treasure of great value. After a few minutes, he picked up a book titled *Busting 'Em* written by Ty Cobb and a co-author.

When Brax paid for the book, the clerk mentioned that Cobb was buried in the public cemetery only a mile away. "Thanks," he said, taking his change. The last thing he wanted to do was visit a cemetery and risk reminding Ty of his father's death. Instead, he handed the book to Ty and asked, "Are you ready for lunch?"

"Yes, sir."

Brax drove to McDonalds, arriving at the height of lunchtime. After sitting down with their order, he asked, "Did you like the museum?"

"Yes. Thank you for taking me." Ty ripped the cellophane wrap from the give-away toy, a plastic Transformer robot.

"You're welcome. Now put that down and eat your chicken nuggets." Brax took a sip of Coke.

After Ty ate a few bites, Brax asked, "What do you think about Ty Cobb?"

"He was really good." Ty paused for a second. "But sometimes he was bad."

Brax couldn't help but laugh. "Yeah, that's funny, isn't it?"

Then he said seriously, "You know, that's how most people are. They have their good side and their bad side."

Not being sure if Ty understood, he continued. "We should always be good to other people but sometimes our bad side comes out. The main thing is to treat people like we want them to treat us."

Ty took a swig from his juice cup. "Uncle Bob did bad things."

Uncle Bob? It was common knowledge at this point that Bob was Tom Benefield's father, making him Ty's grandfather. Brax wondered if that fact had been withheld from the boy. Or maybe Ty had thought of Bob as his uncle for so long that he couldn't make the connection. A good thing, probably, since it had to be hard enough to deal with the accusations against his father.

"Well, let's not think about that."

Ty stuck a couple of French fries in his mouth and fondled the miniature robot.

"People think my daddy did bad things, but he didn't."

Brax wasn't sure how to deal with Ty's feelings about his father. He wasn't even sure of his own feelings about Tom Benefield. But it was important for Ty not to feel shame for the actions of his father.

"No one should judge another person. Only God can do that. Your father may have made mistakes but he loved you very much. And you should always love him no matter what other people say."

Brax kept his eyes on Ty who stared straight back at him. "Do you understand?"

"Yes."

Brax gathered the trash and placed it on the tray. Then he handed the tray to Ty and walked with him to the disposal bin. Outside, he took Ty's hand before they crossed the crowded parking lot. He gently squeezed the small hand and felt the boy grip tighter in response.

In the car, Ty opened his new book in his lap. "I want to learn to play baseball," he said.

The boy's voice had a distinct ring of enthusiasm. It was a start, Brax thought.

Just a start.

∼

"How did it go?" Dae asked at dinner.

"Good," Brax replied. "I think Ty enjoyed the trip. He was

fascinated with all the stuff about Ty Cobb. And we seem to have *bonded* pretty well." He took a swig of tea. "He wants to learn how to play baseball."

"I suppose you are to be his teacher."

"There's no one else." He kept his eyes on Dae as she ate. "It looks like we're going to be here in Rocky Ridge for a while."

She stopped eating and looked at him. "I know you would like that. And when you feel good, I feel good."

He left his chair and gave her a hug. "You're a good wife," he whispered.

Brax released the embrace and returned to his chair. "There's something else I'd like to talk to you about."

"I'm listening."

"It's about Sunny. When I gave him to Charlie, he asked me what my plans were as far as living arrangements. I told him that we had planned to move back to the island when we got married. But then this situation with Tom Benefield made everything a little iffy. Charlie knows that I've become attached to Ty."

"You said this was about Sunny."

"Well, long story short, Charlie said he would keep Sunny temporarily until my plans were more firm. He didn't want to keep him for good if I was going to still be living here."

"I thought he was going to give Sunny to his grandchildren."

"He changed his mind." Brax paused with his eyes fixed on Dae. "Charlie will let me have Sunny back. That's what I want. Is that all right with you?"

Dae looked taken aback. "Brax, don't act as if I'm a prison warden. I'm not that disagreeable. Of course it's all right. I like Sunny, too."

"I'm sorry, I didn't mean for it to sound like that. I was just trying to consider your feelings."

She stood from her chair and hugged him. "You're a good husband." She smiled and lowered her voice to mimic his.

As soon as he finished eating, Brax called Charlie and the deal was made.

Sunny and Ty would make a great pair, he thought.

24

THE NEXT MORNING, BRAX AND DAE SAT IN HIS PICK-UP IN THE parking lot of the high school football stadium, awaiting Charlie's arrival. When Charlie's truck pulled up, Sunny's head was sticking out of the passenger window.

"There he is," said Brax, a smile on his face. He and Dae got out of the truck as Charlie parked nearby.

Sunny leapt from the truck as Charlie opened the passenger door.

"Sunny," Brax shouted, and the frisky Lab ran to him, sticking his nose in Brax's face.

"Hey, Sunny boy, remember me?" Dae asked. She bent down and petted the dog who responded by licking her hands.

A few minutes later, the trio, along with their four-legged companion, began their daily walk on the track around the football field. Sunny tagged along on Brax's leash as they circled the track counter-clockwise.

Brax talked to Charlie about his trip to Royston with Ty. "When we left the Ty Cobb Museum, he was fired up about baseball. I told him I'd help teach him how to play. I'm going to buy a glove today."

"That's a good thing you're doing," Charlie said. "The boy needs some kindness. Especially considering the grief he'll have to put up with, thanks to that no-good father of his."

"Yes," Dae said. "Brax is taking on a lot of responsibility. It's not something he has to do, but he has a big heart."

Brax felt a surge of pride, tempered by the fear that his good intentions may have gotten him into something he hadn't completely considered.

After the walk, Brax thanked Charlie for returning Sunny. He put the dog in the back seat, and drove away feeling a little more settled about the future.

"I'm glad you have Sunny back," Dae said. "I think Ty will be glad, too."

"Yeah. A boy needs a dog."

And a father. He didn't say it but he knew she was thinking it as well.

Brax drove to Taylor Sporting Goods, located in a strip mall near downtown Rocky Ridge. He left Sunny in the truck with a window cracked and led Dae into the store.

Most of the building was devoted to hunting and fishing gear and outdoor clothes. They made their way past displays of hand guns and rifles, rods and reels, boots and coolers, and camouflage clothing. In the section devoted to team sports, Brax tried on a baseball glove.

"This fits all right. It just needs to be broken in."

"Let me see," Dae said. She put the glove on her hand. "It's too big."

"Well, it fits me fine."

"I need a smaller one." She handed the glove back to Brax.

"Huh? You want a glove?"

"Of course. If you're going to throw the ball with Ty, I want to play, too. I was a good softball player."

Oh geez, Brax thought. *Now I have to toss with a seventy year-old woman as well as an eight year-old kid.*

Dae picked-up a glove from another shelf and put it on. "This fits better."

"That's it then." Brax took the youth glove from her hand.

He took the gloves along with a pack of four balls to the cash register. As Brax took his change and picked up the bag of merchandise, he noticed Lance Johnson enter the store with a boy in a baseball uniform. Lance wore coach's shorts and a white tee shirt emblazoned with *Yankees* in blue script.

"Hey, Lance," Brax said, moving away from the counter.

Johnson walked over and exchanged greetings with Brax and Dae. Putting his hand on the boy's shoulder, he said, "This is my son, Corey." The boy was outfitted in a youth league version of a New York Yankees uniform, including pin-striped pants

"Hi," Corey said. He looked to be about Ty's age, but bigger.

Looking at Johnson, Brax asked, "Are you a coach?"

"Yeah. We just stopped for a minute to get a batting glove for Corey. Sorry to run, but we've got to get to practice."

"Go ahead," Brax said. "I'll talk to you later."

Outside the store, Brax said, "Lance told me he had a daughter that went to Sequoyah Elementary. I think that's why he took such a personal interest in exposing Tom Benefield. But he never told me he had a son." He tossed the bag of merchandise in the back seat beside Sunny.

"He didn't have a reason to." Dae walked to the other side of the truck and into the passenger seat. "There are probably a lot of things he doesn't know about you," she said as Brax got behind the wheel.

Brax laughed. "I hope so."

Driving home, Brax had more thoughts about running into Lance Johnson at the sporting goods store. "Lance and I talked about football a lot. He played college ball at Georgia Southern. But neither of us ever mentioned baseball."

"I know what you're thinking," Dae said. "Ty needs to be on a team with boys his age. That's what his mother meant when she said she wanted you to help him be normal."

Brax inhaled deeply. "Yep, that's the goal. I guess we're on our way to first base." He glanced at Dae and she groaned at his pun.

~

When Brax and Dae pulled onto the Benefield's driveway that afternoon, Ty was standing on the front walk. The boy rushed to the truck with a baseball glove on his hand.

Connie stood on the stoop as the visitors got out of the car to greet her son. "Be safe," she yelled.

"We will," Dae replied.

Ty scooted into the back seat. "Hey, Sunny," he said to the dog beside him.

The two adults got into the truck and within a minute of their arrival, they were off to West Hills Park.

The park was alive with kids frolicking on playground equipment. Four men carried on a lively game of horseshoes nearby while a few adults lolled under the cover of a pavilion.

Brax led Dae and Ty to a grassy spot near a pine thicket away from the activity. Sunny followed, exploring the sights and smells of a new place. Brax stationed Ty about ten feet away and tossed the ball underhand. Gradually he motioned Ty further away and threw side-armed or overhand. Dae stood beside Brax and caught every second toss that Ty returned. Soon Ty was out of Dae's range and she sat down in one of the folding chairs they had brought along.

Ty dropped a few of the pitches but he was better than Brax had expected. Recalling Ty's lament—*I'm not very good*—he had feared the worst. The boy's arm was strong enough but his accuracy was poor. Sunny chased after the stray balls, and Brax lumbered behind to take the ball from the dog's mouth.

After thirty minutes, Ty's confidence improved and he begged for harder throws.

"Okay, here's a pop-up." Brax threw the ball into the air with a big arc.

Ty circled under the ball like an outfielder and tried to catch it with one hand.

"Use both hands," Brax shouted.

Ty missed the first two, then caught three in a row.

"Yea!" Dae cheered after each catch.

"Throw it higher," Ty said, beaming with enthusiasm.

It had been years since Brax had thrown a ball and his joints were stiff. With a loud grunt, he threw the ball as high as he could. "Aaah!" he shouted in pain and grabbed his arm.

Dae jumped up from the chair. "Are you all right?"

Ty back peddled to catch the ball and began to stumble. The ball descended fast and bounced off his forehead with a thud, knocking him onto his back.

Dae and Brax rushed to Ty and knelt down beside him. Sunny stood by with his nose at the boy's feet.

"Are you hurt, darling?" she asked.

Ty didn't answer at first. Then he blinked his eyes and sat up. "No."

With his right arm still throbbing in pain, Brax used his left to help Ty to his feet.

Dae looked at the red spot on Ty's forehead. "We need to put some ice on this."

"He'll be all right," Brax said. "He's a boy."

Dae glared at him with dagger-like eyes. "We're supposed to be taking care of him."

That settled it. They collected the folding chairs and walked back to the truck.

"How's your arm?" Dae asked Brax.

He winced and tossed the chairs in the truck bed. "I feel great, coach. I could have gone another nine innings."

Brax stopped at a convenience store to get a cup of ice and a small plastic bag.

Dae moved into the backseat and held the bag to Ty's forehead.

"I think we'd all feel better if we had some ice cream," Brax said, eyeing a Dairy Queen ahead. "Whattaya say?"

"Want some ice cream, sweetie?" Dae asked Ty.

The boy nodded.

Brax pulled into the Dairy Queen lot and parked. Leaving Sunny in the truck, he led Dae and Ty inside and ordered three cones. While waiting, he spoke in a low voice to Dae. "Don't talk to him like a baby."

"As long as he's with us," she replied sternly, "I'm the mother."

Brax raised an eyebrow and stepped forward to pay.

They each took a cone and sat down in a booth.

Dae lifted the ice pack from Ty's forehead. "It's not as red now." She put the ice back on his forehead.

"It doesn't hurt," Ty said.

Within a few minutes, the ice began to melt. Dae removed

the soggy bag from Ty's forehead and put it in a trash bin. "Good grief," she said, returning to the booth. "We told Connie we'd keep him safe and now look what we've done."

"It's nothing serious," said Brax. "You can't even see the redness." He touched Ty's forehead. "Does that hurt?"

"No."

Brax and Dae finished their cones while Ty continued to work on his. Dae leaned close to him.

"Ty, do you know any of those girls in the pictures that Brax found?"

Brax frowned at her and shook his head for her to back off.

"No," Ty said. "They're from Fipa ...Fipali ...Fipaline."

"Fipaline?" Dae asked. "Where's that?"

Ty shrugged his shoulders.

Fipaline. Brax pondered on the word. "You mean the Philippines?"

"I think so."

"How do you know they're from the Philippines?" Dae asked.

"I heard Uncle Bob on the telephone. He called them those Flipalino girls, or whatever. He didn't know I could hear him."

Brax looked at Dae with a blank gaze. "Wow," he said as if to himself.

~

That evening, Brax called Lance Johnson. "I need to talk to you about those pictures I gave to you."

"I'm listening."

"The girls in the pictures—they're Filipinos."

"Filipinos?" Johnson paused, as if rolling the word around in his head. "What makes you think that?"

"Ty told me. He said he heard Bob talking about them."

"That's very interesting. I'm glad you called. I need to check out something."

"What does it mean? Do you have any leads about Filipino girls?"

"Not really, but it might add up."

"How?"

"Don't ask so many questions right now. I've got some work to do. I'll let you know if anything comes of it. Thanks for the tip."

Standing nearby, Dae asked, "What did he say?"

"He was interested, but he wouldn't tell me why."

Brax sat up on the sofa and adjusted the heating pad on his shoulder.

"Will you be able to throw with Ty tomorrow?" Dae asked.

"Oh yeah." He reached for the glass on the end table and took a swig of scotch. "We might work a little on grounders."

∼

On the next five days Brax went to Ty's house for more practice sessions of pitch. Dae tagged along the first time, but after that, she stayed home. "I'll let the male bonding process take its course," she had said.

Ty got a little better each day but still lacked the coordination that comes with hours of repetition. One afternoon they went to the local youth league park and watched a game between boys of Ty's age. Watching as if spellbound, Ty commented on the uniforms, the coaches, the playing field, and the way everything was organized like he had seen with the big leaguers on television. At the same time, Brax realized that many of the players were barely more advanced than Ty.

Halfway through the game in progress, the teams began arriving for the next game. While waiting their turn, the players warmed up by playing pitch and hitting in a batting cage not far from the field.

It dawned on Brax that he had not worked with Ty on an important part of the game. Turning to Ty, he said, "We need to practice hitting, don't we?"

"I hit in my backyard," Ty said. "But the ball gets lost sometimes."

"Yeah, it's hard to practice hitting by yourself."

The next day they went back to the baseball park. With the field vacant, they had the batting cage to themselves. When Ty stepped to the plate, he choked up on the bat and spread his hands several inches apart.

"Put your hands together." Brax repositioned Ty's grip.

The boy put his hands back where they were. "This is how Ty Cobb did it."

"Well, you're not Ty Cobb and I'm the coach."

"Were you a good player?"

"Are you kidding?" The answer in Brax's head was, *"Not really,"* but he considered himself a good *student* of the game. "Here, put your hands like I showed you."

For an hour, Ty swung away, hitting about half of Brax's pitches.

"You did great," Brax said when the batting practice ended.

"I want to play on a team," Ty said.

"We'll work on that."

～

That afternoon, Brax found a parking spot not far from the courthouse, thinking he might catch Lance Johnson at work. Luck was with him, and he was directed to the lieutenant's office.

"Good to see you. What brings you here?" Lance asked from behind his desk.

Brax took a seat in front of Johnson. "I was just in the area and thought I'd stop by. I know you're probably busy but I wanted to ask you something. It's personal, not anything about the law."

"So, go ahead—ask me."

"You remember seeing me and Dae in Taylor's Sporting Goods?"

"Yeah."

"I bought a baseball glove so I could play pitch with Ty. I've been spending time with him. I think you know that."

"Yes, I do."

"Uh...well, I know you coach your son's team. And I was wondering if you had room for Ty on the team. He's just learning the game, but he's as good as some of the kids I've seen."

Johnson raised his brows as if caught off guard. "The season has already started and the rosters are set." He seemed to give it thought for a couple of few seconds. "I have room for one more player, but I'd have to get permission from the other coaches."

"Would you give it a shot?" Brax asked.

"Hmm," Johnson rocked in his chair. "Okay, I'll ask. But if he's a ringer, I'll catch all kinds of grief. These other coaches and parents can be real hard losers."

"He's not a ringer. I can assure you of that. But he might need a little help adjusting socially. That's why I'd like him to play for you."

"I'll take that as a compliment. I'm just a coach though, not a father figure."

"I know. That's my role for the time being." Brax got up to leave.

"Hey, while you're here, there's something I can tell *you*. It's also about Ty in a way. And it's inside info right now, so keep it to yourself."

"You know you can trust me." Brax sat back down.

Johnson had a pen in his hand and put it to his chin. "Ty told you that the girls in the pictures were Filipinos, didn't he?"

"Yeah, pretty much so. He couldn't pronounce the word, and I'm not sure he knows what it means."

"He probably doesn't. But he might have put us on to something. We found prescriptions for some pretty strong drugs in Bob's trailer. They were from a doctor in a little town in North Carolina called Mount Vaney. When we called the doctor, he denied having written them. We faxed a few to him, and they turned out to be forged by his receptionist. He fired her and she was arrested for prescription forgery, which can be a felony. I hadn't thought any more about it until you told me what Ty had said."

Brax listened attentively, wondering what Lance was getting at.

"The receptionist is an American citizen now, but she was born and raised in the Philippines."

Brax blew out a puff of air and sagged down like a deflated balloon. "It fits."

Johnson pulled a large envelope from his drawer. "Look at these again." He removed the pictures in question and set them on his desk in front of Brax. "Tell me what you think the girls look like."

Brax studied the pictures. "They're all dark headed…kind of dark skinned maybe." He looked up at Johnson. "Filipino?"

"Could be. It's hard to tell. I'm going to Mount Vaney tomorrow and talk to that receptionist. These pictures are my ace in the hole. One way or another I'll find out who those girls are. You can count on that."

"I know you will." Brax got up to leave.

"Don't forget," Johnson, said, "I'm telling you this in strictest confidence, so don't tell a soul."

"I won't."

Brax left the courthouse thinking that the mystery of the girls in the pictures would soon be solved. He knew Dae would be thrilled to know that.

25

DAE LOOKED UP FROM HER BOOK AS BRAX WALKED INTO THE MAIN room.

"I talked to Lance about getting Ty on his team," he said.

"Good," she replied.

"He told me the rosters are set and they've already played a couple of games. He'll have to get permission from the other coaches in the league."

"That's silly. What could it hurt?"

"The league wants the teams to be balanced." Brax sat down in the recliner. "The best players get drafted by different coaches. They don't want some hotshot kid coming in later that will give one team a competitive advantage."

"Good grief, Ty's just learning. He's never played before."

"I told Lance that. I'm sure the other kids know it, too." He tilted the chair back. "It'll probably work out."

"I hope so. Ty needs to be on a team." Dae picked up her book again.

Brax began looking at a magazine, then set it down. His mind was still on something else he and Lance had talked over. He waited until Dae put a bookmark between the pages and looked up.

"Lance showed me the pictures again. The more I looked at those girls, the more I believed they *could* be Filipino."

"I don't doubt that. I think Ty was right."

"That's a real important lead in identifying the girls," Brax said. "Lance will find out who they are."

"I hope so." She set the book on the oversized ottoman and picked up a glass of water from the end table.

Brax flipped through the pages of the magazine, his mind still preoccupied. He had promised Lance Johnson he would stay quiet about the Filipino receptionist. But he couldn't in clear conscious keep that fact from Dae.

"There's another connection," he finally said. "Bob had drugs prescribed by a doctor in North Carolina. Lance did some follow-up, and it turns out that the prescriptions were forged by the doctor's receptionist. She's a Filipino."

Dae raised an eyebrow. "You weren't going to tell me about that?"

"Lance told me not to mention it to anyone or jump to a conclusion until he checked it out. It may not mean *anything*. It's just a hunch at this point. He's going to North Carolina tomorrow to question the receptionist."

"It can't be merely a coincidence," Dae said, sounding irritated. "A Filipino woman forging prescriptions for Bob and him engaging in sex with Filipino girls? You know darn well there's a connection."

She gave Brax a harsh look. "You know I have a personal interest in finding out about those girls. They are the real victims in all of this, so I don't want you to hold things from me."

"Don't be so testy. I wasn't trying to keep anything from you, I just—" Brax stopped short. More words would simply dig the hole deeper.

Dae set the glass of water down and picked up the book again. Brax set the magazine in his lap. It was time for dinner, and he wondered how long she was going to keep her nose in that damn book.

～

When Brax and Dae arrived at the high school stadium the next morning, Charlie was waiting beside his truck.

"We've got company this morning," Charlie said.

A group of fifteen or twenty teenage boys in shorts and T-shirts had gathered on the playing field. They began tossing footballs around as the trio started their usual morning walk.

"It's not football season," Dae said.

"Football camp is only a month away," said Charlie. "They told me they're getting a head start so they won't die in the heat. And they *need* to shape up after the year they had. The new coach might wear their butts out."

"That fat guy is not the coach anymore?" asked Brax.

"No. They made him Assistant Principal. That's a good thing—he wasn't worth a plug nickel as a coach."

"The season starts in a couple of months," Brax said. "And they still don't have a coach?"

"They hired a guy from a school near Augusta. But they found out a few days ago he had falsified his application and had to can him. One of the assistants is in charge for now. But I know some of the guys in the booster club, and they want a proven coach that can turn the program around. They haven't been to the playoffs in about ten years."

"Guys like that aren't easy to find," Brax said. "I have a son who coaches at a high school in Gwinnett County. He loves it, but there's a lot of pressure on winning."

"Gosh," Dae said, "it's only high school. You men make it sound like it's the Georgia Bulldogs."

Brax looked at Charlie and both men smiled.

The boys on the field began running wind sprints, grunting loudly as they pumped their arms and urged their legs along.

"I hated running wind sprints," Charlie said.

"Me, too," Brax agreed. "A lot of things have changed since you and I played, but that's a part of football that will never go away."

Brax felt a twinge of nostalgia as he looked around. On the home side of the stadium the concrete stands were set into a bank and topped with an elevated press box. A small section of metal bleachers stood across the way on the visitors' side. Beyond one end zone, a large scoreboard displayed *Home of the Panthers* across the top in large white letters against a green background.

Panthers: that was the name of Dylan's high school team. The scene reminded Brax of his youngest son's high school days. Of his three boys, Dylan was the biggest and most athletic. As an offensive lineman and defensive end, he was an All-County player with ambitions to play at a major college, preferably Georgia. But a serious knee injury cost him most of his senior year, and the scholarship offers dried up. While playing in junior college, he tore ligaments in his other leg and gave up the dream. After that, he set his sights on coaching and earned a degree in Physical Education at Georgia State.

Brax kept his eyes on the boys when they began a game of touch. Dylan could shape them up, he thought. He imagined his son as the savior of Pate County football. When Charlie spoke again, he snapped out of the trance.

"How's it going with Ty?"

"Everything's going well. We're still practicing, and he's getting better. I'm hoping to get him on a team."

"That's good. I hope you don't mind if I ask, but what do you think is going to happen with him and his mother?"

"Honestly, I don't know." Brax glanced at Dae, as if he were speaking to her as well as to Charlie.

"That's a good question," she said. "We're still trying to figure out who those poor girls are. They were abused and they need help, too."

"Yeah, I wonder how that investigation is going," Charlie said.

Brax felt uneasy with the conversation. "The Sheriff's office is working on it. I think they'll get to the bottom of it."

"They say they don't think any of the kids at Sequoyah were involved," Charlie said. "But the police found a lot of drugs in Bob's trailer. He could have baited some of these young girls. Heck, I see them going to school showing so much skin they look like little hookers."

Dae spoke up, her voice hard as steel. "Those girls in the pictures were *violated*. It's not their fault."

"I didn't mean it was their fault," Charlie said.

"Okay," Brax said. "Let's drop it."

Dae didn't acknowledge them and walked faster, striding ahead of the two men.

Brax looked at Charlie and shook his head.

After the walk, Dae got into the car before Brax. When he settled into the driver's seat, she seemed distant and didn't say anything. He thought she was still bristling over the comment Charlie made about the possibility that the girls in the pictures may have been students at Sequoia Elementary.

"I couldn't tell Charlie about the *Filipino* girls," he said.

"They are *girls*," Dae said huffily. "And it doesn't matter what they look like or where they came from. They are just as precious as my granddaughters. Yours, too. Just as precious in the eyes of God."

Brax wondered why she was so being so righteous. After all, she didn't know a thing about the girls in the pictures. They might not be as innocent as she assumed. But he didn't want to belabor the issue.

"You're right," he said.

They drove a mile or so before Dae spoke again. "I have my own demons," she said.

"Really? Do you want to tell me about it?"

She let her window down. "I need some fresh air. Let's stop at the lookout."

When they crested the hill, Brax pulled over and parked at the scenic overlook.

Dae got out of the car, walked to the low stonewall at the edge of the mountain and looked down at the valley below.

Brax followed, wondering what she was thinking.

They gazed at the landscape. The earth was awash in a blanket of green, the blue sky cloudless, and the air fresh with the scent of oak and cedar. A few cattle grazed in the meadow below and a series of heavily forested hills rose in the distance.

Dae stepped over the stonewall and sat down on the other side. Brax sat beside her.

"I made the cheerleader squad as a freshman in high school," she began, looking into the distance as if in a trance. "I had matured early physically and was very conscience of my body but I was clueless about sex. When a senior on the football team asked me for a date, I was thrilled. We went to a movie, and then he drove to a secluded place where we could make out. Remember, that was unheard of on first dates in those days. And I knew it was wrong. But I wanted desperately to please him."

She looked down and stared into the distance again. "We began with just normal petting—hugging and kissing—and it was exciting at first. But after a while his hands were all over me, and I was scared. I was at his mercy."

"You went all the way?" Brax asked.

"I told him no and screamed for him to stop."

Dae looked up at an eagle soaring over the treetops. Then she turned to face Brax. "He was too strong."

"He raped you," he said.

The look on her face confirmed it.

Brax didn't know a lot about Dae's past. Nor had he shared much of his with her prior to the trip to Athy. Now, after getting married, they had begun to share their deepest secrets. He wasn't sure he wanted to know more.

She continued. "It was late when I got home that night. My mother was still up, and she could tell something was wrong. I never told her everything, but she knew. Mothers always know. She wouldn't let me go on dates by myself for the rest of the year. And honestly, I didn't want to, so I double-dated a lot."

She rubbed a shoe on the ground. "Naturally, the jerk bragged about his *conquest* to his friends, and I heard things said about me behind my back. I felt ashamed, even guilty."

Dae stood up. "When someone takes something away from you—something you know you'll never get back—it's like a piece of your life is missing. I've never forgotten that feeling."

"I know," he said. "We have some things in common—you and me and Ty. And the girls."

"I'm sorry I snapped at you about the girls," she said. Her

mood seemed to change as though the confession had released the anger built up inside of her.

"Is that what it was? I didn't feel a snap. Anyway, you've been a good sport to go along with my commitment to help Ty. I love you for that." He pulled the words from his heart. "In fact, I love you for lots of reasons. And I always will."

Dae took his arm and put her head on his shoulder. "Don't make me cry."

26

"CHARLIE MENTIONED SOMETHING WE NEED TO DISCUSS," DAE said, as they drove home after the stop at the overlook.

"He asked what was going to happen to Ty and his mother."

"And we said we weren't sure," Brax said. "That's the truth."

"It's time we give it some serious thought, though. You've taken on a lot of responsibility with Ty, and he's becoming more and more attached to you."

"He needs somebody. We agreed on that."

"Yes, but who needs who?"

Brax turned to her with a scowl. "What kind of a question is that?"

"You know what I mean. You've become as attached to him as he has to you. And I don't mind. It's just something we have to face."

Keeping his eyes on the road, he didn't respond.

"Do you want to adopt Ty?" she asked.

"*Whoa*...you're jumping way ahead."

"So, what do you want to do?"

Brax knew the question had to come sooner or later, but he had refused to look beyond the present. He wasn't prepared for an answer. "I'm not sure what I want. But I can't decide it on my own. You have as much to say about it as I do."

"I need to know how you feel about it, though," Dae said. "Is adoption something you've thought about?"

He was afraid to admit it. "I've already raised one family and you have, too. The last thing I ever wanted in retirement was to start all over again." He turned onto the road leading to their house. "I think we're too old."

"Speak for yourself," she said. "I still have some good years left."

"Are you saying you're in favor of adopting him?"

"No. I'm saying I'm not too old to live a full life—whatever that requires."

"I need to talk to Connie, see what her plans are. We may not have an option."

"You know better than that. She's not really his mother, and I'm not sure she ever wanted to be. She's all but turned him over to you."

"Nah," Brax responded. "She was insistent that he remain with her. She just wants a full time babysitter."

"I don't think so."

"I'll talk to her," Brax said.

"About what?"

"Like I said, about her plans for Ty and herself."

"What if she says she wants you to adopt him?"

Brax sighed. "That's where we started this conversation isn't it?"

"Yes, it is."

A few minutes later, Brax pulled into the carport. He walked into the house behind Dae and let Sunny in behind her. When he closed the door, he had an eerie feeling that the shadow of Ty had followed him inside.

Later that evening, Brax sat alone in the living room. He had waited for Dae to retire to bed before calling Dylan, knowing his son was a night owl.

"How are things in Sodom?" Dylan asked.

"That's not funny."

"Sorry. Are things beginning to settle down? I haven't seen anything about Rocky Ridge on the news lately."

"It's pretty much back to normal. But I'm afraid there's more to come."

"Why? What's happening now?"

"Nothing new. They're just trying to locate the young girls that were involved. They think they have a good lead."

"Are you still spending time with that principal's kid?"

"Yeah. Dae and I are trying to help him and his mother cope." Brax cleared his throat. "Listen, I wanted to talk to you about something else."

"Okay."

"Well, first, let me ask—how are things going at school?"

"We're out right now, of course. But I'm still busy. I coach David's traveling baseball team, and Angie's playing softball. We've been doing some fishing and camping. I'm hanging loose till August when football starts back."

"I know you like coaching. Are you still the Assistant Head Coach?"

"Yeah, and Defensive Coordinator. What are you getting at?"

"There's an opening up here for a head coach at the county high school. It's not a big school, but the facilities are decent, and they need somebody right now. They're looking for someone who can make them competitive. It might be an opportunity."

"Dad, Rocky Ridge is not exactly a hotbed for football. It's different from metro Atlanta in a lot of other ways, too."

"I know, but it's a good place to live. Don't worry about what you read in the papers. That kind of stuff could happen anywhere. I'll bet we don't have a half as much crime as y'all do in that suburban jungle. And a lot less traffic." Brax laughed.

"I'm sure of that, but it's just a different world than what we're used to. I have to think about Jeanne and the kids."

"Maybe it's not for you. I just thought I'd let you know about it. Might be a chance to have a program of your own. Be a big fish in a little pond. Then again, if you failed, it would hurt your career."

"I *wouldn't* fail," Dylan shot back.

"It would be a challenge. They used to have good teams, but they've fallen on hard times lately. And this town needs something to rally around after all the crap we've gone through. Anyhow, I know you're comfortable where you are. Just thought I'd give you a heads up."

"Thanks. I'll, uh…give it some thought. Tell Dae I said hello."

After the call, Brax joined Dae in bed. She was still awake, propped on her pillow with the reading lamp on and a book in her hands.

"I called Dylan. He said to tell you hello."

"How are he and his family doing?"

"They're doing well. He said they might come visit us soon."

"That would be great." She laid the book on the table and turned off the lamp.

"I told Dylan he should look into that coaching job at Pate County." Brax had not planned to share that part of the conversation with Dae, but the words slipped out.

"You weren't serious, were you?"

"Oh, you know how I come up with these harebrained ideas."

Damn it, he thought, *I should have kept my mouth shut. Now she thinks I'm nuts just like Dylan does.*

Dae yawned, and her mind apparently shifted gears. She said, "I hope Lance finds those girls."

"He will."

Brax closed his eyes. Images of Ty and Filipino girls and Dylan swirled in his head like fish in a bowl. All of the images seem to be connected. And he thought that somehow they would shape the golden years for him and Dae in ways they had never imagined.

27

BRAX AND DAE SAT DOWN ON THE SOFA IN THE BENEFIELD LIVING room. Connie took a seat in a high-back chair. It was the exact setting as it had been the first time they met.

"Ty is with his clogging team," Connie said. "They're performing at the Golden Oaks senior center this afternoon." Her hair, no longer in a bun, fell over her shoulders and her hands were steady. She appeared more at ease than during their previous meeting.

"That's good," Brax said, "We wanted to talk to you about him."

"Is there a problem?"

"No, no," Dae said. "He's a sweet boy and he's as polite as can be. We love him to death, but…" She looked at Brax.

"We're not sure what our role is," he said. "At least, not in the long term."

He took his arm off the side cushion and sat up with his hands on his knees. "Let me get straight to the point. This may sound as if we're interfering in your affairs, but we would like to know what your plans are for the future. For you *and* for Ty. We have to understand where we're headed with this relationship between us and your son."

"I'm sorry he's been a burden to you. I had hoped it wouldn't turn into that."

Brax shook his head. "No, that's not it at all. In fact, it's just the opposite. I'm very attached to him." Looking at his wife, he added, "And Dae is also."

"Yes," Dae agreed.

"Mr. Donovan—"

"Brax," he insisted.

"Brax…my situation is not good. Financially, I'm up against it, and honestly, I don't have any plans for the future."

Brax shifted his weight, searching for a response. "I know Tom's death has to be hard on you."

An awkward silence filled the room. Though it was a sunny day, the drapes of the picture window were closed. With no lights on, the dimness seemed to match the somber mood.

"With Tom's salary," Connie continued, "we were able to make ends meet. But without it, I can't pay the bills. He had a life insurance policy, but it's tied up because of the circumstances of his death. Plus there are burial costs and some debts. On top of all that, I may not be able to keep my part-time job." She paused and looked down at her hands. "I learned just this week that I'm in the early stages of Parkinson's disease."

The enormity of the widow's situation began to sink in. Brax felt numb.

"I'll have to sell the house." Connie's lips began to quiver. "Excuse me," she said, and quickly left the room.

Brax leaned down and rubbed his forehead. Then he looked at Dae and exhaled a deep breath.

"That poor woman," Dae said. "She needs a lot of help."

"Yeah," Brax agreed. "And that's not what we came for. I'm not sure what the heck we do now."

Connie returned with a tissue in her hand and rheumy eyes. "I don't mean to dump my problems on you. I appreciate what you have done for Ty. I can already see a change in him."

Brax leaned back. "Do you need us to help more?"

"That's kind of you to ask. I know you are both retired and recently married. You have your own lives to live. But, as you can tell, I'm not in a position to refuse help from anyone." Connie dabbed her eyes. "It's so humiliating."

"Connie," Dae said, "Brax and I have talked about this, and we're both willing to do whatever is right for Ty. But what will *you* do?"

"Jessie has a home in Clayton and she said I could live with her. She's a nurse and she's very good to me. After all that's happened, it's probably best that I leave this town anyway. But I'm more concerned for my son than for myself."

Connie looked at Dae. "I love Ty just as much as if he had come from my own flesh."

Love. The word sounded strangely powerful coming from a woman whose emotions to this point had been fiercely guarded. For the first time, Connie's veneer of impassivity began to peel away.

"We know you do," Dae said.

"There's no doubt of that," Brax said.

"But you can take care of him better than I can," Connie said. Her words were shocking.

"You mean full time?" Brax asked. Then he looked at Dae.

Dae looked stunned.

Connie put the tissue to her nose. She appeared on the verge of crying again. "If you're willing.

"What will Ty think?" Brax asked.

Connie seemed to collect herself. "He'll be fine. Clayton isn't that far away and I'll see him as much as I can."

"Exactly what kind of arrangement do you have in mind? I mean, do you want us to be Ty's legal guardians…were you thinking of adoption…or what?"

"I don't believe we need anything legally binding at this point. I think everyone needs a period of adjustment to make sure it all works out."

Her words hung in the air as the three of them sat without speaking. Brax put his hand on Dae's shoulder and looked into her eyes. He sensed that she knew what he was thinking.

Finally, Brax said, "He can live with us." He turned to Connie. "But we'll make sure he understands that you're still his mother."

"We need a transition plan," Dae said.

"Yeah," Brax agreed. "I think we need a little time to think about it and get back with you. In the meantime you can talk to Ty and…we'll go from there."

"What if we come back in a couple of days—say Friday morning—with our suggestion?" Dae asked.

Connie stared aside vacantly. Then, looking at Brax, she said, "All right."

Brax stood up and the two women shared a hug.

"Keep your spirits up," Dae said. "Things will work out. We're here for you."

Connie closed her eyes. "Thank you."

When Brax gave Connie a polite hug, their bodies barely touched. Yet he felt as if their hearts had connected.

Back in the car, Brax and Dae sat silently for a moment.

"Are we crazy?" he asked.

"No doubt about it," she replied. "It's like a dream."

He started the car. "It feels good to help someone, doesn't it?"

∼

A **FOR SALE** sign stood in the front yard when Brax and Dae arrived at the Benefield house on Friday. Connie met them at the door, and they went inside to the living room.

"Dae and I talked it over," Brax said. "And we're all in."

"I'm glad to hear that," Connie said.

"We can start any time you think Ty is ready. Or, if you like, we can wait until you sell the house and have to move."

"No, I'm not going to wait for the house to sell. That could take months. Ty knows I'm sick, and I told him I need to be with Aunt Jessie. I let him know he might be staying with you, but I didn't say for how long. He likes the idea."

"That's comforting," said Dae. "What kind of timing do you have in mind?"

"There's something we haven't discussed," Connie said. "School starts back in a couple of months. What happens then?"

"He goes to school like he always has," Brax said. "We'll look after him and make sure he does well. Dae was a teacher, and I helped three knuckle-headed sons get through school."

"I don't want him to go back to Sequoyah," Connie said. "I'm afraid he will be constantly bullied about his father. There's a new elementary school—Lakeside—but it's on the other side of town."

"We'll check it out," said Brax. "If it looks like a good school, we'll enroll him there. I'll take him and pick him up."

"I can't imagine why you're offering to do so much for me and Ty. And I can't begin to tell you how grateful I am."

"As a mother, I know how hard this must be," said Dae. "But we're willing to start whenever you are."

"A week from now?" Connie asked. "Is that too soon?"

Brax looked at Dae and she affirmed with a nod. "No, that'll work for us," he said.

"Very well. Ty is in his room. Why don't I have him join us?"

"Yes, do," said Dae.

When Connie stood up, she tilted slightly to one side and braced herself on the arm of the bulky chair. She left the room and a couple of minutes later returned with her son.

"There's my buddy," Dae said.

"What's up, slugger?" Brax asked.

"Nothing." Ty grinned and sat down in a big chair that almost swallowed him.

"Ty, Mr. and Mrs. Donovan have said you can stay with them while I'm at Aunt Jessie's."

"Would you like that?" Dae asked.

Ty looked at his mother and then Brax. He nodded his head in approval.

"Yes," Connie said. "They're very nice and they will take good care of you."

"Okay," Ty said.

"Come give me a hug," Dae said.

Ty moved from the chair and Dae pulled him to her.

Brax got up from the sofa and gave Ty a handshake. "Glad you're coming to stay with us." He faked a serious look. "I need another man around the house. You know how these women are."

Ty grinned again.

"You can go to their house next Friday," Connie said.

"Can I take my glove?"

Brax laughed. "Yeah, you can take your glove. And we'll bring all your things to our house—your toys and clothes and stuff."

From the look on Ty's face, Brax wasn't sure if the boy realized he had just been traded to a new family.

28

After leaving Ty's house, Brax stopped at the main road before leaving the Eagle Bluff neighborhood.

"It's beginning to dawn on me," he said. "We'll be like parents to Ty, won't we?"

"I'm afraid so," Dae answered. "It's a lot of responsibility."

He wouldn't admit it, but the thought of "raising" Ty weighed heavily on him. Having made that commitment only a few minutes before, he now felt older. "Being a parent is a hard job," he said.

"It can be hard at times and it can be fun at times," she said. "But it's always a job—twenty-four-seven."

"Hmm, it's kind of like being married. I must be a glutton for punishment." Laughing at his own cleverness, he pulled onto the main road.

"You're so funny," Dae said dryly. "But for me it's like having another kid around the house to take care of."

Brax glanced from the road and saw the smug look on her face.

Soon the playful thoughts melted away and Brax was back to reality. He recalled Dae's blind faith encouragement to Connie—*Things will work out*—and he believed she was right.

Dark clouds hid the sun as Brax and Dae sat in their rocking chairs on the deck after lunch.

"Have you said anything to your sons about Ty?" she asked.

"Only that I had befriended him and met with his mother. Of course, they know about him from what they've seen and heard in the media. You know—all the nasty stuff about an eight-year-old boy discovering his father and grandfather's depravity. But I haven't mentioned that we might take him in."

"I talked to Julie," Dae said. "At first, she thought I was kidding, But as we talked, she warmed to the idea. She knows how much I love children and said she was all for it if that's what I want. When she asked about adoption, I told her it hadn't been discussed."

"I'm glad you talked to her. I'll let the boys know when things are settled, but we need to do what's right for us—and for Ty."

A few minutes later Brax received a call from Mason. Brax made light-hearted comments about readjusting to married life. Mason, a lawyer in Dallas, briefed him on the latest with his family. However, when Brax revealed his commitment to Ty, the conversation turned as ominous as the weather.

"Dad," Mason said, "you can't do that."

"Why not?"

"You have to have this arrangement documented and legalized. You'd be liable for all sorts of things without a written consent of guardianship from the boy's mother."

Brax had a sinking feeling and didn't respond.

"How long have you known this boy?"

"A few months." Brax grunted. "Aah…he's a good kid."

"That doesn't matter."

"Maybe it doesn't to a pinhead lawyer, but I know this boy and I know what I'm getting into."

"Look, he's been exposed to sexual abuse. He could have some deep psychological issues. For all you know, he may have been abused himself."

"What do you mean, 'for all you know'? Don't talk to me like I'm some old fool who doesn't know anything."

"I'm sorry it came out like that. Dad, you have a good heart and you want to do the right thing. I'm just trying to keep you from getting yourself into trouble."

As the conversation went on, Brax became angrier—not at his son, but at himself. He had let his idealism blind him to the legal implications of the agreement with Connie Benefield. Still, he was convinced he was doing the right thing.

"I can see you're dead set on it," Mason said. "And everything will probably work out if you'll let me help you. We have to cover all the bases."

"So, what do you want me to do?"

"I have a buddy in Atlanta that went to law school with me. He practices family law. I'll call him and get back with you."

When the call ended, Brax got up from the rocking chair, feeling flustered.

"I take it he didn't like the idea of Ty staying with us," she said.

"That's putting it mildly. He thinks we're off our rockers." He couldn't resist a chuckle. "I need a drink. You want me to bring you something?"

A boom of thunder sounded in the distance, and Sunny jumped to his feet from beside Brax.

"No. I'm going in. It's about to rain."

When Brax opened the door, Sunny scooted inside and Dae followed.

In the kitchen, Brax poured a glass of scotch. He walked to the back window as raindrops began to splatter on the deck.

Dae sat at the kitchen table, nursing a Coke and nibbling from a bowl of chips. "What did Mason say?"

"He said we need to go through a bunch of bureaucratic BS. And I hate to admit it, but he's right. It's a hell of a note when your own son has to keep you from being a royal screw up. He'll help us though. "

"So we can't take Ty now?"

Brax let out a deep breath. "I don't know."

A bolt of lightning flashed in the sky and the patter of rain on the metal roof became more intense.

Brax imagined the worst. *Legal Guardianship. They'll probably do a background check on me. Ask some real personal questions. What will I say if they ask me about any sexual abuse in my family? If I deny it, I'd put Dae in a position of knowing I lied to them. Worse yet, will they think I'm a predator, ready to take advantage of a boy I hardly know?*

"We'll do whatever we have to," Dae said. "Connie will give us her permission and Ty is excited about living with us. It's a perfect solution for everyone involved. When it quits raining, I'm going to the Blue Hen to buy a new bedspread and linens for his room. He'll be here in a week. "

Brax wasn't so sure about that anymore. Maybe things wouldn't work out after all.

He finished the scotch and sat down in the recliner. Soon he dozed off, tranquilized by the sound of the rain.

∼

When Brax awoke from the nap, the rain had stopped. On the

side table, a note from Dae said that she was at the Blue Hen. A few minutes later, he received a call from Lance Johnson.

"I got back from Mount Vaney last night," Lance said. "The sheriff there located the Filipino woman who used to work at the doctor's office. He got a search warrant for her house. She and her male companion had four Filipino girls—twelve to fourteen years old—living with them, basically in a state of captivity. They were being hired out as prostitutes. The couple is in jail now, facing a whole list of charges."

"That's unbelievable. What about the girls?"

"They're in state custody in Charlotte."

"Good. Dae will be glad to know that."

"Since they crossed state lines, the feds are handling the case. A bunch of reporters left my office a couple of hours ago. I'm sure the story will be on television later today and in the newspapers tomorrow. The media is calling it a case of child sex slavery."

Brax felt the warm sense of closure that he long hoped for. And something else: vindication.

"Lance, you've done a great job in tracking down these scumbags. A lot of people would have ignored an old guy with a couple of tattered pictures of child porn. But you trusted Ty and me and stuck with the investigation. I appreciate that."

"Well, it's caused the death of two people and a lot of bad publicity for Rocky Ridge. But it had to be done. And I had a lot of help. That tip you gave me about the girls being Filipino was the key to breaking this case."

"You know I got that bit of information from Ty," Brax said. "He was the one who exposed the sick goings-on in the first place."

"Yeah, he got the ball rolling. Oh—by the way—I received the go-ahead for Ty to join my team. You can bring him to practice Monday afternoon, and I'll make sure he feels welcomed."

"Thanks, that's super. He'll be tickled pink." Brax paused to gather his nerve. "There's something else I may need your help with."

"What is it?"

"I'm sure you know that Connie Benefield is in rough shape both financially and physically."

"Yeah, I gathered that."

"Well, Dae and I have agreed to take Ty under our wings."

"That's quite a gesture on your part. I'm sure she appreciates the help."

"Actually, it's more than that. He'll be moving in with us."

"*Wow.*" The officer sounded stunned.

"I know it may seem unusual but we think it's the right thing to do. We have a good understanding with Connie, but we haven't gone through any legal channels. One of my sons is a lawyer, and he says we need to have a document of legal guardianship to make sure everything is legit."

"I think he's right," said Johnson.

"Yes, but there's something else. There may be a complication."

Brax sucked in his feeling of guilt and told the Lieutenant about the abuse he suffered from his father.

"Was your father ever charged with child abuse?"

"No. I never told anyone."

"So, there's no record of it?"

"No. I guess I could lie about it if the question came up but—" Brax suddenly realized he was leaving something out. "Actually, I did tell someone. I told Dae, and I don't want her to get caught in the middle. Besides, I haven't done anything wrong."

"I agree. If you've never been a party to a criminal case, I wouldn't worry about it."

"Good." Brax exhaled a breath of relief. "My son also said that there may be an issue with the fact that Dae and I have only known Ty for a couple of months. The court might think we have some ulterior motive and that Connie just wants to rid herself of responsibility for Ty. She's not his birth mother, you know."

"I don't know how they look at those sorts of things. If I were you, I would just be honest. I think they will see you and Dae as good caretakers."

"I'm glad you feel that way. Would you mind if I use you as a character reference?"

"Not at all. I'd be happy to give you a good recommendation."

It made Brax proud the to have Johnson in his corner. And it didn't bother him, like he thought it would, to share his most intimate secret with a man whose respect he valued. He would never forget what had happened to him as a boy, but he had moved on with his life. It hadn't destroyed him. Realizing that fact was liberating, and sometimes he had to remind himself that he was a survivor.

∼

When Dae returned from shopping, Brax helped her unload two large packages from the car. In the bedroom designated for Ty, she pulled a bedspread from a clear plastic bag and laid it on the bed. Then she laid newly purchased sheets, pillowcases, and bath towels beside the spread.

"How do you like it?"

Brax looked at the forest green spread and tan linens. "It all looks good to me. Reminds me of the woods."

"I'm glad you said that. Look what else I have." Dae pulled several framed photographs from a bag.

Brax eyed the photos in amazement. "That's our woods. There's the creek...and the giant oak...a mountain laurel...the trail. Did you take these pictures?"

"Yeah."

"When?"

"Yesterday afternoon while you were taking a nap. I just got them framed and wanted to surprise you. But they're really for Ty. I want you to hang them right here." Dae pointed to a wall beside Ty's bed. "Now they will be his woods, too."

She looked pleased with herself. Maybe she was getting used to living in this house. Come to think of it, he realized he couldn't remember the last time he had heard her mention Seaside.

29

CONNIE BENEFIELD RODE WITH BRAX AND DAE TO A LAW OFFICE housed in a renovated historic home in downtown Rocky Ridge. Attorney Karen Olsen greeted them and led them into a spacious room wih Victorian style furniture. They sat down at a conference table made of heavy, dark wood.

Olsen, an attractive woman who looked to be less than forty, spread some papers on the table across from Brax. Dae and Connie sat to either side of him.

"Mr. Donovan, I work with John Covington in Atlanta on a referral basis. John is a good friend of your son, Mason, and he has asked me to represent you in a petition for guardianship."

The attorney then turned to Connie. "The child involved is your son, Mrs. Benefield. Is that correct?"

"Yes," Connie replied.

Olsen looked at her papers. "Your son, Tyrus Raymond Benefield, is eight years old. His father is deceased."

"He committed suicide," Connie said.

"Yes, that's well documented," Olsen said. "And please don't think I'm being insensitive, but it's not relevant. What we want to document is the agreement of both parties for the transfer of legal guardianship from the parents, or parent, to another person, or persons. In this case, Mrs. Benefield, you would relinquish your parental rights and responsibilities to Mr. and Mrs. Donovan. Is that what you want?"

"It's not what I want, but it's best for my son. My health is not good and my financial situation is very shaky."

"I have a daughter," Olsen said, "so I know this must be hard. But you have to testify that this is what you sincerely *want*."

"I understand. It *is* what I want."

The attorney turned her attention to Brax and Dae. "Are you fully aware of the responsibilities you are assuming for the welfare of this child?"

"We've both raised kids before," Brax said.

Olsen glared at him as if he were being sarcastic.

Dae spoke up. "Yes, we understand our responsibility. We've spent a lot of time with Ty and we know him very well."

"He likes Brax and Dae," Connie interjected. "He would be comfortable living with them. A woman from Family Services has visited with us and arranged for a psychological exam for Ty. But she said she wouldn't contest temporary guardianship at this time."

"I'm glad to see you've thought this through. It's a serious step. And it's my professional duty to provide proper legal counsel." Olsen looked directly at Brax. "In all honesty, Mr. Donovan, you and Ty are well-known figures. And not just in Rocky Ridge but around the country, thanks to the media coverage surrounding—" Olsen looked at Connie "—recent events." It appeared as if she was careful to avoid a reference to Tom Benefield or the child abuse scandal. "So, I'm confident your reputation will serve you well in this petition."

"I hope so," Brax said. "Here's something else that might help."

He handed Olsen a letter signed by Lance Johnson in support of the request for guardianship.

Olsen read the letter and then looked up. "This is excellent. Lance Johnson is a highly respected officer of the law, and his recommendation carries a lot of weight within the legal system around here. I think we have a solid case." She picked up the papers lying beside her. "If I could get each of you to sign these documents, I'll file them with the court clerk today."

"When will we hear something?" asked Brax.

"Probably forty-five days or so."

Brax looked at Dae and Connie. Both had a pained look. "We were hoping more like a couple of days."

Olsen laid the papers down and rested her pen on the table. "Is it that urgent?"

Brax looked at the other two ladies again. "Yeah."

The attorney seemed to ponder the request.

Then Connie spoke up. "Ty has gone through a lot. He's lost his father and the man he thought was his uncle. And he found those *disgusting* pictures. I want him to be in a home where he can have a normal childhood. I can't give him that but Brax and Dae can."

"Me and Ty are big buddies," Brax said.

Connie continued to state her case. "He needs time to get adjusted before school starts back. That won't be easy with all the bad things he's liable to hear about his father and grandfather."

"Okay," Olsen said. "You've convinced me. I can't promise anything but I'll try my best to speed up the process."

∼

Three days later, Brax, Dae, and Connie were back in the conference room of Karen Olsen's firm.

"I appreciate your getting this set up so quickly," Brax said.

The attorney smiled. "Thanks, I had some help."

Brax looked at her quizzically. "Oh?"

"Let's just say a certain officer in the Sheriff's Department is a good advocate."

Dae turned to Brax and said, "Lance."

"Is everything all set?" Connie asked. "Has it been approved?"

"The judge hasn't signed anything. We have to meet with him first."

"Some friends of mine know Judge Crowder," Connie said. "They say he's a fair man."

Olsen assumed her serious lawyer face. "We don't want to take anything for granted. In fact, let me just get to the heart of the matter." She scanned the faces in front of her. "We don't want to offer any information that the judge doesn't request. Be truthful in your statements but don't say anything that is not directly on point."

Brax addressed the attorney. "Will he ask us about our backgrounds? Try to determine if we're fit to be Ty's parents?"

"I doubt it. I've been before Judge Crowder many times. He's very down-to-earth. And like everyone in this town, he's completely familiar with the background of this situation. I believe he will be sympathetic to Mrs. Benefield and what she desires for her son. I'm sure the letter of recommendation from Lieutenant Johnson helps our cause."

"So," Dae asked, "do you think this will go smoothly?"

Olsen didn't respond directly. Instead, she spoke to the three as if they were one. "You all believe that this in the best interest of the child, correct?"

Brax answered first, followed by Connie and Dae. Each replied with a strong, "Yes."

"Then there is really no reason to deny the request. Remember though, it can be revoked at any time if there is reasonable cause that the boy's welfare is not being properly attended to."

Brax put a hand on Dae's knee and read the look of relief on her face.

Olsen's demeanor changed instantly, as if with the flip of a switch, and she smiled brightly. "Mr. and Mrs. Donovan, I know you will be wonderful guardians. It's my pleasure to help make this process as simple as possible."

Connie stared at the attorney stone-faced and then dropped her head.

The smile disappeared from Olsen's face. "Mrs. Benefield, are you all right?"

Brax looked at Connie, jolted by the thought that she might have changed her mind. Perhaps the finality of her decision had suddenly dawned on her.

Dae leaned to Connie and put an arm on her shoulder.

"Yes, I'm okay," Connie said, raising her head. She sighed deeply and her hands trembled as she raised them to cup her face. Then her hands stopped shaking and she appeared to regain her composure. "I want the best for Ty." She looked at those beside her. "And I'm grateful for all that Brax and Dae have done for him."

Dae pulled Connie to her. "You're still Ty's mother and he knows you love him. We'll do our best to be good guardians."

Brax got up and put a hand on Connie's back. Connie took his other hand in both of hers, held it firmly and looked up with a faint smile.

"We're good," Brax said, looking at the attorney.

Olsen straightened her papers. "Are you ready to speak to the judge?"

The three responded, "Yes," almost in unison.

∼

Brax, Dae, and Connie sat before Judge Oliver Crowder in his chambers. Karen Olsen occupied a chair to one side.

"I only want to ask you one thing," the judge said from behind his massive desk. "Are each of you *sure* you want to do this?" His beady eyes and double chin seemed to rise from his body without benefit of a neck and he spoke with a deep Southern accent. He looked and sounded like a bullfrog.

"Absolutely," said Brax.

"Yes, your honor," Dae agreed, "we're sure."

Connie added her assent with an unwavering, "Yes."

"That's good, because I have already signed and approved the consent for temporary guardianship. If all goes well, we'll review the situation in six months and consider permanent status at that time."

The papers were signed by all the parties and a round of handshakes followed. Within minutes, the attorney and her clients walked out of the courthouse.

Brax turned to Olsen as the four people stopped on the walkway. "Whew, I'm glad that's over. Thanks for your help."

"My pleasure."

"It's not over," Dae said. "It has just begun."

Brax looked at the other two women who had *she's right* written all over their faces.

On the way home, Brax began to think about the reality of what he had agreed to. The next day Ty would be moving into his house. Having lived alone for six years after his first wife's death, he was just getting used to living with Dae since they had renewed their relationship four months earlier. And it had been over twenty years since he had shared a home with two other people. He could only imagine what that would be like.

30

ON FRIDAY MORNING, BRAX STOOD IN THE FRONT YARD, SIPPING his coffee and admiring a freshly planted bed of vincas. The day had arrived to move Ty into his new home, and Brax felt a tingle of nervous anticipation. His thoughts were interrupted when his cell phone rang.

"Dad, you won't believe this," Dylan said. "I'm coming to Rocky Ridge tomorrow to interview for that Head Coach's job at Pate County."

"*Really?* That's quick. What changed your mind?"

"I got to thinking about it and decided it wouldn't hurt to check it out. I sent them my resume, and Coach Hartsell gave me a good recommendation. The Principal at Pate County called the next day. He said he wants to fill the position as soon as possible."

"That's super. I'm glad you gave it some thought." Brax kept a calm voice but pumped a fist in the air.

"Pate County is only Three-A and I've been in Six-A for a long time." Dylan paused for a moment as if rethinking the idea. Then he said, "But I'd really like to have my own program."

"It sounds like a good opportunity."

"Could be. It has to be a good fit both ways, though. They

may not think I'm the guy they need, or I may decide it's not a good move for me. I'm keeping an open mind."

"Why don't you come up Friday and spend the night with us?"

"I can't. Angie has a game that night. I'll just drive up Saturday morning. It's only an hour and a half from here, and the interview's not 'til ten o'clock."

"Okay, but come to the house afterward and have lunch."

"That's a deal. You know me—I never turn down a meal. I'll call when the interview is over. "

Brax hurried inside to tell Dae the news. She seemed as surprised as he was.

"I never imagined Dylan would seriously consider that job," she said.

"Ah, yeah," he said, feeling smug. "I figured he would jump on it."

"*Brax*," Dae exclaimed, "that's a big one. You told me there was no way Dylan would give a second thought to living in Rocky Ridge."

"I said that?" Brax grinned, and felt the satisfaction of knowing that, for once, Dylan had heeded a suggestion of his.

∼

A few hours later, Brax and Dae led Ty into the bedroom at the rear corner of the house. Sunny followed behind.

"This is your room," Brax said.

Ty set his backpack on the floor and walked around the room. He stopped in front of the framed photographs on one wall and silently studied them. Then he looked at Brax. "That's where we go."

"Yeah. Dae made them for you. She bought you some new things for your bed, too."

Dae stretched a hand toward the spread. "See? A new bedspread and pillow cases." She pulled back the spread. "And new sheets."

"Thank you, Dadie," Ty said with a smile.

Dae put her hand on the boy's back. "Do you like your room?" He looked up and the expression on his face said, "Yes," before he uttered the word.

"I have something else for you," Brax said. He went into the living room, returned with a sports bag and handed it to the boy.

Ty unzipped the bag and pulled out a shirt, pants, socks, and cap—a complete baseball uniform. The small shirt was imprinted with Yankees in navy blue across the front and number twelve on the back.

Ty's eyes lit up like it was Christmas morning. "Can I put it on?"

"Sure."

Ty began shedding his clothes. When he was in full uniform, he looked at himself in the dresser mirror, but couldn't see his whole body. "Pick me up," he pleaded.

Brax lifted the boy to the mirror with a grunt and held him a few seconds before setting him back to the floor. "Coach Johnson says you're doing great. You know your first game is tomorrow."

Ty reached down and stroked Sunny's back. "I like Sunny."

"He likes you, too," said Brax.

"My daddy said I was too young to have a dog."

"Well, we'll see about that. I'll teach you how to take care of him. You have to feed him and bathe him and give him medicine when he's sick."

"Okay."

Brax looked at Dae and back to Ty. "If you treat him right, he could be your dog some day."

"I will." Ty bent down and put his arms around the Lab.

Ty kept the baseball uniform on until bedtime when he spread it neatly on the floor in his new room. After his nighttime bath, he walked into the living room in his pajamas. "There's something under my bed," he announced.

Dae looked puzzled.

It dawned on Brax that he had stored his trumpet under the bed in what was now Ty's room. "It's my horn."

"Does it toot?"

Brax laughed. "Not by itself. There's a trumpet inside the case. I used to play in a band."

"He was very good," Dae commented.

"Why don't you play it anymore?" Ty asked.

Brax raised his brows. "That's a good question. You like to ask questions, don't you?"

Ty lowered his head as if he were being scolded.

"That's okay. Bring it here and I'll play you a tune."

Dae clapped her hands politely. "Yea."

Ty went to his room and returned with the black case.

Brax pulled out the trumpet, put on the mouthpiece, and fluttered the valves. Sitting up in his recliner, he moistened his lips, took three deep breaths, and put the horn to his mouth. A volley of discordant sounds came out.

Sunny rose from the floor, looked at Brax with his ears perked and yelped.

After a few false starts, Brax played seven notes of a simple tune and stopped.

"What song is that?" Ty asked.

"Shave and a haircut, two bits," said Brax.

"Play some more."

"Not tonight, it's late. Some other time."

When Brax placed the trumpet back in the case, Ty noticed something written on the outside. "B-B-D. What does that mean?"

"That's my initials. Braxton Bragg Donovan."

"You were named after some General, weren't you?"

"Yeah, Braxton Bragg was a famous General. But not a very good one." Brax laughed. "A long time ago his troops fought a big battle not far from here. Do you remember I told you that the first time we met?"

Ty nodded. "Uh huh."

Brax smiled and cut his eyes toward Dae. Looking back at Ty, he said, "Put the trumpet back under your bed. I'll play some more tomorrow."

"It's amazing that he remembered that," Dae said, as Ty took the case away.

"Yeah, he's a smart little booger. Don't you think so, *Dadie?*" he asked in a childlike voice.

She snickered. "I told him that's what my daddy called me."

Brax watched through the open door as Ty placed the trumpet case under the bed.

Dae walked to Ty's room and stood at the doorway. As she turned out the light, Brax heard Ty say, "Good night, Dadie." Then, just before she closed the door, he said in a louder voice, "Good night, Sunny. Good night, Braxton Bragg Donovan." The sound of a mischievous laugh followed.

Brax followed Dae to the bedroom upstairs. Later, as they lay in the dark, he said, "Everything feels different now, doesn't it?"

"Yes. Ty's a darling, but we'll have to get adjusted to living with him in the house. It's a big change."

Brax closed his eyes and thought of Ty asleep downstairs. *A big change? Boy, she's right about that.*

∼

Just before noon on Saturday, Dylan called again.

"Dad, I've been with these guys all morning, and now they want me to go to lunch with them."

"It must be going pretty well."

"I think so. I've talked to the principal, the acting head coach, and the president of the booster club. Now, we're meeting a few other guys at The Hungry Bear."

"All right. Call me when you get free. Dae and I want to see you before you leave."

Brax realized that Dylan had a serious interest in the job. His crazy idea might actually work out.

Dylan arrived at his father's house at half past two.

"Come on in, *Coach*," Brax said, opening the door with the dog at his side. "Remember Sunny?" he said, looking down.

"Hey, Sunny." Dylan patted the friendly Lab's head.

After the two men shook hands, Dae walked up and slipped into the open arms of her stepson. "Hello, Dylan. It's wonderful to see you again."

Dylan moved back and took her hands in his. "Gee, you look great."

"How did it go?" Brax asked, as they moved into the living room.

"It went—" Dylan stopped for a moment when he saw Ty sitting on the floor watching a baseball game—"well."

"Dylan, this is Ty," Brax said. "Ty turn off the TV. I want you meet my son, Dylan."

Ty grabbed the remote beside him, turned off the television and stood up. "Hi."

"Hello, Ty," Dylan replied.

"Ty is staying with us," Brax said.

Dylan looked at Dae, then back to Ty.

"Have a seat," Dae said. "Tell us all about your interviews. I'm anxious to hear what happened."

"It's all good." Dylan sat down on the other end of the sofa from Dae. "After I quit babbling, y'all can fill me in on what's new with you."

Brax sat down in his recliner and tilted it back. "Yeah, we'll do that."

"Can I put on my uniform now?" Ty asked Brax.

"Go ahead, but your game's not until six o'clock." Brax turned to Dylan. "Can you stay and go to the game with us?"

"It will be his first game," Dae said. "He's so excited."

Dylan kept his eyes on Ty as the boy disappeared into his bedroom. He didn't respond to his father or his stepmother. "I guess I'm not the youngest son anymore," he remarked with a hint of sarcasm in his voice.

Brax didn't feel the need to justify Ty's presence, so he resisted a smart comeback. "We're just taking care of him."

"He doesn't have anyone else," Dae added.

Brax and Dae explained the arrangements they had made for Ty. Yet it was apparent that their words could not capture the emotions that had evolved over time, leading them to such a bold decision.

"Some things can't be explained," Brax said. "They can only be experienced."

"Kind of like you and me, huh?" Dylan smiled but his tone thickened the air, and the room seemed to grow smaller.

Brax sparred back with his own rhetorical jab. "We had some real father-and-son times, didn't we?"

Dae shifted her eyes between the two men as if trying to determine how serious they were.

"I was an ass," Dylan said.

"You *were* that," Brax agreed. "And I was a lousy role model. You know, we were just alike—two hard heads butting against each other." He pulled his head back and chuckled. "You remember that Christmas when we got into a tussle? Knocked the tree down and fell all over the presents. It was bad enough that I was three sheets in the wind, but you had been drinking too and you were only seventeen."

Dylan shook his head in apparent bewilderment of the memory.

Dae offered the men drinks, but they were too busy recounting incidents from the past when Dylan was a headstrong hellion and Brax was an unyielding authoritarian. Time and perspective had clouded their memories, and each had his own version of long ago confrontations. She poured herself a Coke in the kitchen and stood in the doorway, an audience of one.

After several minutes, the stories ran their course and the conversation petered out as if retelling the past had washed it clean.

"I've mellowed over the years." Dylan said.

"Me, too. Hell, I've mellowed so much, I think I've become rotten."

The men had a good laugh, and a smile appeared on Dae's face.

Dylan's tone turned serious again. "I'm going to think about this job. I believe they're going to make me an offer, and they'll want an answer right away. It would be a good career move, and I like what I heard today. I was impressed with the school officials and the boosters."

Brax shrugged his shoulders. "So what's to think about?"

"If it wasn't for Jeanne and the kids I'd take it in a heartbeat. But the timing's not great. David will be a senior this year and Angie a sophomore. And it might take a good while to sell the house. Bottom line, I'd have to commute for at least a year. With the hours I'd have to put in, I'm not sure I could handle that. "

"Well, we have—" Brax started to suggest that he and Dae had another bedroom available. But he looked at her and her expression told him to shut up. "—hopes that it will work out," he said, feeling embarrassed.

"I don't know. Like I said, there're a lot of things I have to consider. It's a real longshot." Dylan stood up. "I need to get going. Sorry, but I can't make Ty's game. I'll catch one some other time."

Brax met his son in the middle of the room. They shook with firm hands and locked eyes.

"I'm proud of you, Dad," Dylan said. "The boy has a good home."

Brax felt his pulse surge. He wanted to tell his son he loved him so much it hurt. Instead, he said, "I hope he turns out as good a man as you."

When Dylan left, Brax closed the door and looked at Dae. His eyes glazed with moisture and he didn't say a word. He knew she understood.

Turning back to the living room, he saw a little boy in a baseball uniform staring back at him. He remembered that the Yankees had always been Dylan's favorite team.

～

Brax wore his baseball cap with the big Georgia "G" to shade his eyes. The sun was still a bright orange ball in the last hours of daylight. Next to him on the metal bleacher, Dae shielded herself with sunglasses and a visor. The air was dry, the temperature in the mid-eighties. A perfect day for baseball.

The Yankees took the field first. The starting players ran to their positions and, with a couple of boys absent, Ty was left alone on the bench with the coaches.

The other team, clad in green and yellow uniforms with "Athletics" lettered across their shirts, horsed around excitedly in their bench area until settled down by their coaches. The A's Head Coach then took his place in the pitcher's circle, ready to toss to his own players.

The young umpire behind the plate hollered, "Play ball," and the game was on.

Even the players on the bench were allowed to bat, so Ty came up in the bottom of the second inning. The score was tied at one-one with runners at first and third and two outs. After five tosses from Coach Johnson, Ty struck out on a pitch that was well outside the plate.

"My bad," Lance said. He placed a friendly hand on the oversized batting helmet atop Ty's head as the boy walked back to the bench.

"That wasn't Ty's fault," Brax said to Dae. "He can hit if he gets a good pitch."

"He's trying," she said.

"I know, he just has a real small strike zone, and Lance is trying not to throw it too hard."

In the third inning, Ty went out to play right field. One ground ball came his way, and he fumbled it. Then he threw it over a shouting infielder's head as two runners scored.

In the fourth inning, Ty was the first batter up after his team had scored the maximum five runs in the third. Lance gave him a good pitch to hit and Ty made contact. The ball dribbled back to the pitcher's circle where it was handled easily and tossed to the first baseman. Running as fast as he could, Ty was out by ten feet.

"Way to run, Ty," Brax shouted.

"Why didn't he drop it this time?" Dae said, referring to the previously butter-fingered kid at first base.

Ty came to bat one more time. It was the bottom of the fifth inning, two outs, and the bases were loaded. The Athletics held a one run lead, twelve to eleven, and the one-hour time limit had already expired. It would be the last bat of the game.

Brax stood up, along with the other cheering relatives and friends in the home team bleachers. "Let's go Ty—you can do it."

A chorus of noisy encouragement erupted from the fans, the players on the bench, and the coaches. "Come on one-two."… "Just need one, A's."…"Step on the bag, Josh."…"Go to second, Billy."

Dae clasped her hands and shook them in front of her. "Please let him get a hit." She spoke below the crowd noise, as if pleading to God.

After letting one pitch go by, Ty hit a fly ball to deep right field. Everyone in the stands, as well as the coaches on both sides, screamed at the players—"Yea!" ... "Run, Ty, run!"…"Catch it BJ!"…"Go, go, go!"…"You got it!"

The ball sliced toward the white chalk line and fell two feet into foul territory as the chubby outfielder fell down before he could reach it.

Brax groaned. "Aaah." He took his hat off with one hand and stroked his hair with the other.

Dae covered her face with her hands and then clasped them together again. She breathed out a big "Whew."

The runners returned to their bases and Ty hustled back to

the batter's box. On the next pitch, he tipped the ball behind home plate and the catcher scuffled for it, but it landed harmlessly against the wire backstop. He let one more wayward pitch go by, and then Lance threw one that was across the plate but a little high. Ty was late on his swing, and missed completely. Strike three, game over.

Ty turned and slowly headed for the Yankees bench as the Athletics ran from the field yelling in victory. In the stands, their parents high-fived each other and scrambled from their seats to join the celebration as if it were the seventh game of the World Series.

Coach Johnson met Ty before he made it off the field. Brax was close enough to hear Lance say, "You had a good swing. I threw it too high."

Ty lowered his head, and Lance pulled the boy into his midsection. Lance's son, Corey, the team's star player, gave Ty a pat on the back and walked beside him to the bench for the coaches' post-game pep talk.

Dae sighed. "I know he feels awful."

"He'll be all right," Brax said, but he knew better. "He was trying too hard. I think all the cheering and the whole atmosphere made him nervous."

Afterward, Brax and Dae tried to comfort Ty, but he was inconsolable. When they got into the car, he said, "I stink." He slammed his glove down in the backseat beside him. "I don't want to play baseball anymore."

"Yes, you do," Brax said. "You did fine." He tilted the rearview mirror and saw a tear trickle down the boy's cheek. He looked at Dae and knew she was thinking the same thing he was. *This is the hard part.*

They drove for five minutes in uncomfortable silence. Then Brax turned his head toward the back seat.

"Ty, when we get home do you want to take Sunny for a walk?"

Ty didn't reply at first. Then he asked, "Can we go to the creek?"

"If that's where you want to go. He's your dog now."

Dae looked back at Ty and then smiled at Brax.

He didn't have to look back to know what that meant.

31

TY DIDN'T QUIT. INSTEAD, HE RODE IN THE BACKSEAT OF BRAX'S truck with Sunny at his side to each game. The season ended all too soon.

At the awards celebration in June, Brax and Dae mingled with the adults in the noisy pizza restaurant while the kids jostled for position among the battery of arcade games. They were approached by Lance Johnson's father, a trimly built Baptist minister with short, white hair and high cheekbones that appeared to be cast in bronze.

"Ty really improved during the season," Reverend Johnson remarked.

"It was his first year to play," Brax said. "He tried hard."

"Brax worked with him a lot," Dae said. She looked at Brax as if to acknowledge his efforts.

Brax deflected the remark. "Corey is the best player on the team."

"He might be," the Reverend replied. "He has good genes. Lance was a good athlete."

"Yes, I know." Brax said.

"It's nice being a grandparent, isn't it?" the Reverend said with a smile. "You get to see the little imps grow up without all the headaches of being a parent."

Brax looked at Dae and wondered what to make of the comment. They were neither grandparents nor parents. What were they?

"We're just Ty's guardians," Dae said.

"We've taken him under our wing," Brax added. "We're not sure exactly where this leads. But," he said firmly, "Ty will be taken care of."

"He's in loving hands," Dae said.

"Oh, I'm sure. I know—"

"We understand," Brax said, interrupting. "And don't think we're being defensive. It's just that we're in kind of an unusual situation."

"Well, you've been a blessing from God to that young man," the Reverend said, leveling his attention on Brax. "He's seen his share of evilness, and I want you to know if there is anything I can do to help, don't hesitate to call on me." He turned his eyes to Dae. "My prayers are with you."

"Thank you," she replied. "Your family has been wonderful to Ty. Lance is great with all the kids—Ty loves him to death. And Corey has become his best friend."

A waitress began to set the pizzas on a long table, and Lance Johnson shouted over the din. "Okay, gather up, Yankees. It's time to eat."

A dozen eight and nine-year-old boys dressed in baseball shirts chattered like magpies as they scrambled to find a seat at the table. In short order, the pizzas were scarfed down. Then three of the mothers served slices of a big square cake. The name *Yankees* arched across the white frosting in blue decorative icing with each player's name and number inscribed in smaller letters around the edges.

One of the assistant coaches brought in a big box and set it on the floor at the head of the table. Lance Johnson stood in his coach's attire and thanked all the players, assistant coaches, and parents for their support. Then he began pulling trophies from the box and presenting them to the players in alphabetical order.

"Ty Benefield," Lance called loudly.

Ty stood up, wearing his number twelve jersey, and marched up to receive his trophy.

"Ty," the coach said, "You've done a great job this year. You played the game like it's supposed to be played. You always hustled, just like the player you were named after. The great Ty Cobb came from this part of Georgia, and he would've been proud to claim you as his namesake. Way to go."

Dae looked at Brax. "You told him to say that, didn't you?"

He replied with a sly, "*Who me?*" look.

Ty took his trophy with a sheepish grin and a handshake from his coach. He returned to his seat through a phalanx of high-fives and congratulations from the other players and adults. He sat down next to Corey Johnson who greeted him with a smile and a friendly poke in the arm.

Brax grabbed Dae's hand and gave it a squeeze. Then he lifted a bite of cake from the paper plate and licked the frosting from the plastic fork like an eight-year-old.

Back home, Brax and Dae repaired to the deck. Ty lay beside Sunny on the floor in the main room watching the Braves on television.

"Ty gets along with all the boys on the team," Brax said. "And all but a couple of them go to Sequoia."

Dae breathed deeply. "I know what you're thinking. It's about sending him to a new school. That's what Connie wanted."

"Yeah," he said. "It's going to be hard for him to leave his friends and start all over in a different setting."

She acknowledged with a slight nod. "Especially now that he's so close to Corey. Next to you, Corey's the best thing that's ever happened to him."

"It's hard to know how other kids will treat him at Sequoia. The older ones and the others who don't really know him might be tough." Brax paused for a moment. "And the main thing is—how will he feel? Do you think being there will be a constant reminder of his father?"

"I don't know. He could be bullied even if we send him to Lakeside. The kids there might even be more hateful to him. They all know who he is and what happened."

"School starts in a month, you know." Brax rose from his rocker. "I think we need to talk to him."

"I guess so. We have to at some point."

Brax went to the back door and called Ty outside.

Ty came out and sat on a wicker footstool with Sunny at his feet.

"Ty," Dae began, "we need to talk to you about school." She paused and he appeared anxiously attentive. "Your mother wants you to go to Lakeside Elementary this year. She thinks it would best if you were in a new environment."

"Lakeside?" he said with a frown. "No way." He looked at Brax.

"Do you think the other kids at Sequoia will tease you about anything?" Brax asked.

"You mean about my daddy? And Uncle Bob?"

"You might hear some hurtful comments," Dae said.

"I don't care. I want to be with Corey."

Brax was torn. Not thinking solely of Ty's best interest, he had another motive. Transferring Ty to the new school on the other side of Lake Gansagi would be the perfect opportunity for him to convince Dae of a move to the Lakehaven neighborhood. That might make her feel more comfortable in Rocky Ridge, a thought that had never left his mind. Yet he realized that changing schools wouldn't shield Ty from ostracism. Everyone in town had strong feelings about Tom Benefield and Banjo Bob. A move wouldn't salve that wound. And to separate Ty from Corey at this point was unthinkable.

He looked and Dae, then said, "Okay, you'll go back to Sequoia this year. But sometimes people can say stupid things... mean things...even lies. You need to let us know if that happens."

Ty leaned down and stroked Sunny's back. "I'll be in fourth grade," he said, his ninth birthday only a month away.

"Yes, you will," Dae replied. "You'll like fourth grade." She looked at Brax and sighed.

"Can I watch the game now?" Ty asked.

"Yeah," Brax said, "go ahead."

Ty went inside with Sunny right behind.

Brax rocked in his chair. "Fourth grade," he said, looking at the deck floor as he did the math. He would be eighty-three before Ty got out of high school. He turned to Dae and repeated louder, "*Fourth grade.*"

She leaned back in her chair and stared straight ahead as fireflies flickered in the shadowy woods.

After letting the thought digest for a minute, he said, "We could still look at a place in Lakehaven. I could drive him to Sequoia and pick him up in the afternoon."

"He likes it here," she said. "It's a perfect place for a boy and a dog."

A moment later Dae turned the conversation upside down. "I'm going to sell my house in Seaside. It doesn't make sense to keep paying the community fees. It's not practical as a part-time home."

Brax stood up and faced her. "Dae, you can't do that. I won't let you. You love that place."

"It's just a *place*." She rose and walked to the railing. "I love a lot of things. I love you and I love Ty." She looked out into the dark forest. "And this is my home now. This is what I love."

Brax moved beside her. "You can't sacrifice everything for me. I'm the one who brought you up here. And I'm the one who brought Ty into our lives. We're not retired anymore. We have a job now and it's an eight year-old boy. What the hell have I gotten us into?"

"Don't talk like that. I'm *not* sacrificing everything for you." She put a hand on his arm. "This is what I want. I never wanted to retire from *life*."

He lifted his arm and kissed her hand. Then he pulled her to him. Her cheek was cool against his and she smelled sweet, like a rose.

Or maybe he only thought she did.

∼

The rear tires eased into the shallow water as Brax backed the truck up at the boat launch. He pulled the canoe from the truck bed, put it in the water, and then tied it to a nearby post. Ty toted a small fishing rod and reel as they walked back after parking the truck. Brax placed his fishing gear in the canoe, then stood calf deep in the water, steadying the canoe while Ty made his way to the front seat. Sunny leapt aboard, soaking wet from a quick dip. Lake Gansagi was peacefully free of motorized watercraft on the warm weekday morning. They shoved off into the still depths with life vests snug to their t-shirts. Sunny stood upfront, his nose stuck high in the air like the bowsprit of a sailing vessel.

Ty paddled on one side and Brax, sitting in the rear, shifted from side-to-side, propelling the canoe slowly in the calm water. A vehicle passed over a bridge in the distance but it was too far away to be heard. For a few minutes, the only sounds were made by paddles slipping in and out of the water and birds chirping in the trees along the shoreline.

"I like to paddle," said Ty, breaking the silence.

"Good, you're doing great."

They didn't speak again for a couple of minutes and the quietness seemed to bind them in a spiritual way. Brax knew exactly how Ty felt at that moment and he felt the same way. *Maybe*, he thought, *this is what real joy feels like. Unspoken and unexplainable.* He wasn't a strongly religious person but it was at times like this—times when the most precious thing was simply the gift of life—when he felt the presence of God.

"We'll try over there, in the shade," Brax said. They approached a place where large oak trees cast shadows near the shoreline. He showed Ty how to put the plastic wiggler on his hook and cast his line about ten feet from the canoe.

They recast their lines in a new spot every few minutes as the canoe drifted randomly with occasional direction from Brax's paddle. Then he saw the bobber on Ty's line go under.

"Here, you've got a bite," Brax said. "Turn the reel...the other way," he said calmly when the line slackened.

Ty appeared to be in serious concentration as he cranked the reel slowly. Soon a small, silvery-gray fish came thrashing out of the water.

Brax tilted Ty's rod upward with one hand, grabbed the line

with the other, and pulled the fish to him. "Hey, you caught one," he said, beaming as if Ty had landed a five pound bass. "It's a crappie. You ever caught a fish before?"

"No," Ty said, with a grin as big as his face could hold.

"Well, we're going to throw him back in. But, we need to get a picture so you can show it to Dae and Corey and everybody else. Here, hold him up."

Ty held the line out to his side as the fish dangled in the air. Sunny tried to put his nose on the fish, but two flips from the crappie's tail shooed him away. Brax pulled his phone from his pocket and took a picture. Then he unhooked the fish and placed it in Ty's hands. Ty tossed the fish like it was a live hand grenade. It barely cleared the side of the canoe.

After forty-five minutes, they headed back without catching another fish. It didn't matter. They didn't need to.

Before they reached shore, Sunny jumped from the boat and swam the last twenty yards. Brax guided the canoe, pushing his paddle against the lake bottom with the final shove. He stepped into the water and pulled the front of the canoe onto the boat ramp, then took Ty's hand and helped him out. Sunny ran onto the concrete ramp and shook himself dry.

As Brax finished lifting the lightweight canoe onto the ramp, his phone rang. He flipped it open and Dylan's name appeared on the screen.

"Dad, I took that job at Pate County. Pretty crazy, eh? I'll be Head Coach."

"Oh, *man*," Brax exclaimed. "That's fantastic. Are you going to move up here?"

"No. Like I said before, I don't want to take David and Angie out of their schools. I'll have to commute. Maybe rent an apartment there if it gets to be too much."

"Don't be ridiculous—you can stay with us. Heck, we don't live far from the school and we've got room."

"Nah, I don't want y'all to have to put up with me. I know you're taking care of that kid."

"Ty's no trouble. And you wouldn't be either." In truth, he wasn't sure about the latter, but he was willing to give Dylan the benefit of the doubt.

"Well, let's not get into all that now. I'm coming up Monday with Jeanne and the kids to meet some people and get the ball rolling. I'll be busy as heck, but I'll give you a call and we can get together."

When the call ended, Brax felt his heart beat faster as if he, too, had just gotten a new job. "That was my son," he said to Ty. "You remember Dylan, don't you?"

"The big football man?"

"Yeah. How did you know about him and football?"

Ty hesitated before answering. "Dadie told me. She said he was going to be the high school coach and he might stay with us for a while."

"She did? Well she's quite a fortune teller."

Ty looked flush, as if he might have divulged a secret.

Brax grinned and began to take off his life jacket. "You'll like Dylan."

"Will he like Sunny?" Ty asked, now smiling.

"Oh yeah, he'll like Sunny."

Just one big, happy family, Brax thought, as his pulse settled down and his mind sped up.

32

TEN YEARS LATER

Living with Ty was sometimes a challenge for an older couple but more often a joy for Brax and Dae. When Dylan moved to Rocky Ridge with his family two years later, the Donovan families blended together as the years in Rocky Ridge turned into a decade.

~

Not far from the creek, Ty found a spot where the dirt was soft and loamy. He would do the job right, just as his adopted father had taught him. One thrust with his foot and the blade of the shovel buried into the ground. Within a few minutes, the pit was big enough for the body and deep enough to keep away keen-scented scavengers. Soon the grave was refilled with the freshly dug dirt and covered with a layer of leaves and pine needles.

He dug a round hole about two feet deep and drove the post of the pressure-treated marker into the bottom with a short-handled sledge. After dipping the bucket in the creek, he toted the water to the wheelbarrow where he mixed the concrete slurry with a flat-pan shovel. Then he tilted the wheelbarrow and dumped the thick concrete around the post. He straightened the marker with a level. The post steadied in the concrete after he held it for a minute or so, and he stepped away to admire his work. Then he ran his hands over the letters he had chiseled into the marker. The grooves were deep and the letters formed well from the template he had used. SUNNY.

He gathered his tools and placed them in the wheelbarrow to head up the steep hill behind his house. After a few feet, he stopped and set the wheelbarrow down. He turned back and looked at the marker. Moisture welled in his eyes and he took the work gloves off as the tears began. His heart rushed and his legs felt like they might collapse under his weight.

"Goodbye, Sunny boy," he whispered.

He started up the hill and with each step his sadness slowly dissipated. For ten years, the yellow Lab with a coat of hair that shone like the sun on a warm day had been a faithful companion. And, at thirteen-years-old, Sunny had lived a full canine life. Knowing that, Ty felt a contentment that comes when the joy of a lifetime of memories drown out the sorrow of death.

It was a lesson Ty would never forget. The once shy young boy was now eighteen-years- old and, at the top of the hill, manhood awaited.

~

Dae picked up the small frame from the side table and set it in her lap. She settled into the cushions of the white wicker chair and studied the photograph of her former house near the ocean. It was there where she had met Brax and fallen in love. And though she had once lost him to her conscience for three years, their love never died. The memories of that place were all that were left now. A high-rise condo development had been built on the land once occupied by Seaside Village.

Brax walked into the sunroom and looked over her shoulder. "Do you miss it?"

"Sometimes." She set the picture back on the table.

"I know." Brax laid his cane beside the matching wicker chair. He lowered himself down with a firm grip on its arms.

A sliver of sunlight beamed through the windows, casting a shine on the blue slate floor as if it were wet. Outside, a bluebird pecked seeds from a feeder under an oak tree and then flew away to be replaced by a tiny nuthatch.

"But I would miss this place more," Dae added.

For most of her life Dae had felt the lure of the seashore—the briny smell of the air, the calming sound of breaking waves, the warm softness of sand, and the unfathomable vastness of the ocean. But now she had learned to love a totally different part of the world. A land of hills and forests and changing seasons. A land that honors heartfelt tradition and simple ways. A land that becomes a part of you and you of it. This was her home now.

Maybe she wouldn't have felt the same had she not loved Brax so deeply. At first she merely tolerated the place because of his love for the land. Over time, she learned to overlook the clash of primitive ways against the tide of modernity and came to embrace the allure of small pleasures in a small town.

Brax tilted his head with a faraway look in his eyes. "Can you believe it's been ten years?"

"No. It seems like the time just flew by."

"I never could have guessed everything would turn out like this," he said.

"It's been quite an adventure. A good one." Dae remembered

the look on a young boy's face when he got his first baseball uniform. It had made her feel warm and, somehow, young again. "Ty's been such a blessing."

"I think it's worked both ways." Brax grabbed his cane from beside the chair and urged himself up. "I've got it," he said as Dae tried to help him. He arched his back and stood straight.

"Are you ready to go?" he asked.

"Yes."

Brax propped the cane against the garage wall and then wrestled himself into the passenger seat of the car.

"You left your walking stick," Dae said.

"I don't need that thing."

She opened her mouth to admonish him and then closed it without uttering a word. He didn't want anyone to see him with a cane, she thought. As if others couldn't see the condition he was in.

The garage door opened with a gargle of gears and chains. Minutes later Dae drove past the gates of their Lakehaven neighborhood.

When they arrived at the baseball field, the stands were full. More fans sat in folding chairs or spread on a grassy incline outside the chain link fence that surrounded the field. The green and white paint of the stadium, newly dedicated at the beginning of the year, sparkled in the bright sunshine.

Dylan met his parents at the entrance.

"Dad, I have a chair for you right behind home plate."

"Oh, hell no," Brax said, "I can sit in the stands like everybody else. I'm not a damn invalid."

Dylan looked at Dae and arched his brows. After leading his parents through the crowd, he walked behind Brax while his father labored up six flights of steps to a reserved section of bleachers.

The trio sat down in their seats next to Dylan's wife, Jeanne. On the other side of her were their adult children, twenty-six-year-old David and twenty-three-year-old Angie, who had driven up from Atlanta along with their spouses. The backrests of the green stadium seats had an image of a large white paw signifying the school's mascot, a panther. Brax wore a hat with the same design.

"I have to go down onto the field," Dylan said. "I'm throwing out the first pitch. I'll be back in a minute."

"*Ladies and gentlemen,*" the announcer said over the loud speaker, "*welcome to the third and final game of the Class Three-A Georgia State High School Baseball Championship featuring your Pate County Panthers and the Heatonville Warriors. Now please rise for the National Anthem.*"

The crowd rose to their feet while a recording of the Star Spangled Banner blared from the loud speakers. When the anthem ended, Brax and Dae remained standing with the other Pate County fans as Dylan walked to the pitcher's mound.

"*Throwing out the first pitch for today's game,*" the announcer said, "*is the Head Football Coach and Athletic Director of Pate County High School, Dylan Donovan.*"

The fans gave a hearty round of applause for the man who had led the school from the athletic doldrums to provide a much-needed infusion of civic pride into the community.

Dylan threw a looping pitch to the catcher, waved to the crowd, then headed back to the stands to rejoin his family.

When the home team took the field, the voice of John Fogerty singing *Centerfield* burst from the speakers.

Dae kept her eyes on Ty as he headed to centerfield as if the song were written especially for him. When she focused on the name "Donovan" arched across the number twelve on the back of his uniform, she felt a shiver of pride.

The pitcher, Corey Johnson, began his warm-up tosses and she felt a similar reaction. She noticed Corey's father, Lance Johnson, now the County Sheriff, sitting near the Panthers' dugout.

Ty reached his position in center and warmed-up with laser-like throws to his outfield teammates in left and right.

Dae turned to Brax and said, "Look at what a fine young man Ty has become. I'm so proud of him. This is all because of you."

Brax shook his head. "He learned how to play baseball from Lance and Dylan. Corey helped a lot, too. Those boys are inseparable. I didn't teach him anything."

She knew better. It all started with a visit to the Ty Cobb Museum and an empathetic man taking a personal interest in a shy young boy who had no one else to turn to. A man who taught that boy to believe in himself and not give up.

"I wasn't talking about baseball," she said.

Brax grunted as if downplaying her comment. "You did just as much for him as I did. It took a hell of a woman to marry an old coot like me, and then take in a boy you hardly knew." He looked back to the field. "*Damn*, Corey can put some smoke on that ball."

The game was well played and tightly contested. Corey hit a two-run homer and struck out ten batters with a fastball that cracked in the catcher's mitt like a gunshot. The crowd hung on every pitch with boisterous shouts or disappointed groans. The tension grew as the game reached the bottom of the seventh and final inning with the score tied at four runs each. Ty had gone hitless in three at-bats, including a strikeout, but was flawless in the field. And he had prevented the lead run from scoring by throwing out a runner at the plate. With the state championship at stake and the threat of extra innings, he came to bat with two outs and the bases empty. The fans of both schools ramped up the noise to max level, filling the air with an electric charge.

Dae tried unsuccessfully to stay calm as Brax and the others yelled encouragement to Ty at the top of their lungs.

Ty took the first pitch for a called strike. Wild shouts erupted from the players and fans of the visiting Warriors. Dae closed her eyes and Ty fouled off the next pitch. With the count at no balls and two strikes, everyone in the stadium stood on their feet screaming as the pitcher wound and threw a fastball. The umpire stood from his crouch and bellowed, "Ball." The crowd noise ebbed as Ty stepped from the batter's box to take a practice swing. He moved back to the plate and took his stance as the roar resumed. The ball flew from the pitcher's hand as if shot from a rifle. Ty swung hard, leaning his weight on his back foot. The metal bat met the ball with a sharp ping, like a blacksmith's hammer on an anvil.

Ty started quickly from the batter's box and then raised his hand triumphantly as the ball arced toward deep leftfield.

"It's gone!" Dylan shouted.

Brax looked wild-eyed and stood motionless as the leftfielder halfheartedly backed to the fence. The ball flew ten feet over his head.

Brax clinched both fists and raised them in the air. "Hot damn, thank you, ma'am!" he said to Dae. "How about that, Mama—a walk-off homer?"

"Oh, my lord," she gasped.

Dylan kissed Jeanne while she yelled and bounced on her toes. He gave Brax and David hard high-fives and then hustled through the frenzied crowd. When he reached the field, he was met by jubilant players as they untangled from the dogpile at home plate.

Ty was the last player to get up. His shirt hung from his pants and his batting helmet lay on the infield dirt where he had tossed it after rounding first base. He grabbed Dylan and the two stood hugging amid the chaos. Then Dylan put an arm on the shoulders of his adopted son and the two started off the field.

Dae gazed at Brax as he watched the scene. He looked calm but she knew he was churning inside. Though the chemo had weakened him physically, his mind was keen, his spirit strong. Joy, pride, love—she felt the same emotions. Yet she knew that no one could match the depth of Brax's feelings. And no one deserved them more.

She had never been happier for him.

~

Two hours of daylight remained when the family met for dinner at Dylan's home. They gathered in the house where Ty had grown up. The house with seven acres of woodland that Dylan had bought from his father eight years earlier as Ty's adoption was finalized. The house that was once a home to Brax and Dae.

Dylan spoke to Brax as they sat on the new, covered deck. "Dad, the Georgia Tech coach was at the game today. He said he's going to offer Ty a baseball scholarship."

"Are you kidding?"

"No. He'll send us the paperwork next week for our signature. They've already signed Corey."

"That's *wonderful*," Dae said.

"Ty," Brax called across the porch. "I would get up but I'm too lazy. Let David guzzle his beer and come over here."

Ty stepped away from his adopted brother and walked to Brax.

"Congratulations young man. I guess I can pull for a Yellow

Jacket." Brax tugged at the bill of his green hat with the white panther paw logo. "See, I didn't even wear my Georgia hat today." He gave Ty a firm handshake and smiled. "I'm just kidding. Tech's a great school."

"Thanks. I owe you and Dadie a lot."

"If we've helped you in any way, it's been our pleasure, son."

"It truly has been," said Dae. She had felt an odd twitch when Brax said "son." Yet the word seemed fitting and Dylan, looking on, appeared to take it in stride.

Dylan brought Brax a glass of tea. When they became wrapped in conversation, Ty pulled a chair next to Dae.

"I remember the exact day I moved into this house," Ty said. "It was June the second, almost ten years ago. You and Brax made me feel…" He took a swallow… "Loved. I still have those pictures on my wall—the ones you took of the woods where Granddad and I used to go."

"I'm glad you kept them," she said. "I remember that day, too."

Ty lowered his head and looked back up again. "It's funny—I feel like I've had three dads and three moms in my life. That's how I thought of you and Brax until Dylan brought me into his family." He turned his head to one side with a distant look. "There were times when I felt like a burden to everyone."

"No, Ty, don't ever think that. The two years that you lived with Brax and me were nothing but joy for us. And Brax will never tell you this, but he sees himself in you. There's no bloodline, but there's a deep connection that's hard for even me to fully understand." She leaned over and kissed him on the cheek. "You've never been a burden to anyone."

"I know how lucky I am. I'll always love my real dad and my step-mom, Connie. But since she passed away, I'm now a Donovan. I could never have better parents than Dylan and Jeanne, or grandparents than you and Brax. Dave and Angie have been great to me, too. They made me feel just as much a part of the family as they are."

Dae patted Ty's hand. "You've been loved."

Brax stopped talking to Dylan and turned back to look at Ty. "I saw that pretty young girl you kissed after the game," he said. "Tell me about her."

"Her name is Briana. Everyone calls her Bree." He shifted his weight as if he were being interviewed. "We go steady."

Dae sighed. "Oh, the beauty of young love."

"Young *hormones*," Brax said.

Ty grinned. "You'll meet her later. She had to work a short shift at Chick-fil-A. I'm going to pick her up at nine."

"When's the last time you went to the creek?" Brax asked.

"Today," Ty said. "I go every day, just like we used to."

"Let's do it."

"Brax," Dae said, "you can't walk to the creek. You'll never make it back up that hill."

"Yeah, I can. It might take a while, but I can do it."

Dae looked at Ty. "You can't let him go."

Dylan spoke up. "Ty, drive the Gator. Take the trail down to the flat ground. Y'all can follow the creek upstream."

A few minutes later, Ty backed from a shed driving an open-sided utility vehicle bearing a John Deere emblem. At the driveway he reached a hand out and helped Brax pull himself into the front seat.

Standing beside the vehicle, Dae asked, "How long will you be gone?"

"Maybe an hour," Brax said. "Longer if we run into old man Thoreau."

Ty drove away in the direction of a trail a half-mile away that led to the path beside the creek.

"I don't know what's so doggone special about going to that creek," Jeanne said, watching from the driveway.

"I know," Dae said. "I know exactly what's so special about it."

33

THE SNOW CAME EARLY. FOUR INCHES FELL OVERNIGHT IN THE second week of December. The ice followed, toppling trees and downing power lines in parts of Pate County. The lights blinked a couple of times during the night, but the electricity stayed on in Lakehaven.

In the morning, Dae stood at the bedroom window gazing out at the scenery. Snow clung to the limbs of trees, and the ground looked like a fluffy white blanket in the early light of day.

"So beautiful," she said, without turning around. "Maybe we'll have a white Christmas."

"Is it snowing?" Brax's voice was barely above a whisper.

"Not any more. I think the storm has passed."

"My horn," he murmured.

She pulled the trumpet from its case beside the bed and gently laid it beside him.

Brax turned his head toward the brass instrument and closed his eyes.

Dae sat down in a side chair. The room was quiet but she could hear music. The soothing notes of a trumpet playing *When I Fall in Love* floated into her head.

When they first met at Seaside, Brax had given her a CD as a Christmas present. On it were two songs he had recorded, *Star-*

dust and *When I Fall in Love*. The latter had become their love song and they had vowed to love each other forever. Now the tune came back to her and wonderful memories of her life with Brax scrolled through her mind like pages in a scrapbook.

~

It began the day after she moved into her new home at Seaside Village.

When Dae walked into the clubhouse that morning, she found it empty except for a lone man with short white hair sitting at one table.

He looked up from the newspaper in front of him. "Good morning," he said, and the distance between them seemed to vanish.

She returned the greeting and approached his table. "Don't let me interrupt you. I was just looking around."

"No, that's all right." He put down his pen and glasses. "You're new here, aren't you?"

"Yes, I just moved in a couple of days ago. My name is Dae Whitehead."

"Glad to meet you, Dae Whitehead. I'm Brax Donovan." He stood up and pulled a chair from the table. "Here, have a seat."

"Thank you."

Her eyes were drawn to the sharp features of his face, tanned by the sun and chiseled by the years. Wearing shorts and a T-shirt, he looked fitter than most men of his age. Seventyish, she guessed. *He's attractive.*

"Welcome to our little piece of heaven. I think you'll like it here."

"Yes, I love it already."

Raising a cup, he asked, "Would you like some coffee? I just made two fresh pots."

"No thanks, I'm not much of a coffee drinker. I just stopped by on my way to the beach."

"An early riser, eh? Me, too. I'm usually the first one here." He took a sip of coffee. "I saw you on the beach yesterday. I was with Jim Hawkins."

"Yes, I think I recall seeing you fellows. But I saw a lot of people, and I can't remember everybody's name right now."

"Well, that's kind of normal around here. If you have a good memory, you're not old enough to live in this place."

When he grinned, Dae knew she was hooked. *I want to know him.*

She glanced down at the table. "I see you're working on a crossword puzzle. I enjoy crosswords, myself." *Kind of.*

"Yeah, they're good for the brain cells. It's the first thing I do each morning. The paper doesn't come early around here, so I save the puzzle for the next day." He looked embarrassed as if he had babbled on with too much information. "Pretty fascinating stuff, eh?"

She smiled and felt the long dormant pull of attraction drawing her to this man with the interesting name.

"It looks like you're almost through. Don't let me keep you from finishing."

"I've got all day." He folded the paper and laid it in front of him. "Would you like to join me for your walk on the beach?"

"I would love to. Thank you for asking." *He's a flirt. I like it.*

On the walk, they came to a place where the shoreline narrowed. A pile of driftwood and debris stretched the width of the beach. He took her hand to steady her as they made their way through the jetsam. She stepped nimbly and held a firm grip as her hand was almost swallowed by his.

The masculine touch of his grip felt intoxicating. *I have to tell him. No, he'll feel sorry for me and lose interest.*

He clumsily snagged his foot and released her hand while staggering to avoid plopping face down into the sand.

"Are you okay?" she asked.

"Yeah, I was just practicing my pratfalls."

His humor was refreshing. It had been a while since she had been around someone who enjoyed a good laugh. *If I tell him, he won't laugh anymore.*

On the way back, they approached the flotsam on the beach again.

"Hey, watch this." He walked quickly through the debris, stepped over a knee-high piece of driftwood, and then made a three-hundred-sixty degree spin. When he reached the other side of the pile, he turned around and looked at her with his arms spread wide apart.

"*Voila,*" he shouted. "I'm the king of the driftwood!"

She laughed. "And sometimes you're the klutz of the driftwood." Then she started her way through the pile.

He grabbed her hand as she reached him and, with a flourish, bowed in front of her like a knight before royalty. Rising up, he extended an arm, bent at the elbow. "May I have the privilege, milady?"

She put her arm in his and for a few steps they walked, linked together, their beaming faces held high as if they were the King and Queen of the Island. *This is too good. I must be in a movie.*

She had never known a man of his age with such a spirit of abandonment. She felt an undeniable tug of attraction. It was a feeling she hadn't experienced in a long time and she wasn't used to it. But she felt trapped. *I can't tell him now—he'll drop me… No, I have to be faithful to John… What am I doing?*

That evening they had dinner at her house. After that, she knew where she was headed. And a name kept ringing in her head. *Brax.*

The first walk led to more, every day the hole of deception getting deeper. And then he learned the truth. Not from her, but from Jim Hawkins through one of his VFW buddies who served with John in Vietnam. *I'm a horrible person. But I'm in love and I don't want to lose that.*

She knew he was deeply hurt yet, after a long reflection, was willing to stay with her.

Over the Christmas holidays, they separated to visit their families in different cities. They had agreed that during the time apart, they would give serious thought to their future together. While attending a Christmas Eve service, she had a spiritual awakening and her conscience spoke clearly.

The morning after returning to Seaside, she met with him in the clubhouse. She took a seat in front of him and looked directly into his eyes.

He waited for her to speak.

It was hard and she didn't know how to say it. Finally, she simply said, "I can't."

He clenched his teeth and nodded.

She could see the pain on his face and buried her head in her hands. Then she looked up and said, "I'm sorry," as a tear rolled down her cheek.

He took a deep breath and the tension faded from his face. "No, it's for the best." His voice was strong and resolute.

She stood first and then he.

She stepped into his arms and buried her face in his chest, her cries muted by the soft cotton of his sweatshirt. Lifting her head, she started to speak. "I lo—"

"It's okay," he said, halting her words. "You don't have to say it. Neither do I. We'll always know."

She wanted him to hold her tighter and never let her go. Kiss her passionately like a young lover. Beg her to change her mind. She wanted him to do all of those things, but instead he wiped her tears with his fingers and released her.

"This is hard for both of us," he said. "But you've done what you had to and I respect you for that."

Struck by the finality of it all, her body began to quiver. *I've lost him.*

He took her hand and squeezed it gently. "Take care."

She sighed deeply and gazed into his eyes. When he let her hand go, she knew it was over. "Bye," she whispered.

She walked from the clubhouse, and drove away to the loneliness of an empty house. For days, she would burst into tears on the spur of the moment. *I hate myself.*

A month later he moved from Seaside Village.

Just as her wedding vows and her heart demanded, she was true to John until the end. But, with Brax, she had found love again.

And that love had never died.

～

Dae knew all the words to the song that played in her head and she sang them straight through. The lyrics of *When I Fall in Love* tell of a love that will live forever and that was the gift Brax had given her. When she stopped singing, faint noises stirred from within the house while the others moved about, talking in low voices. Outside, a gust of wind whistled past the window.

But the bedroom was quiet and she was now alone. She moved to the bed, laid down beside Brax and kissed him on the cheek.

34

TY RETURNED TO ROCKY RIDGE ON A HOT, SUNNY DAY IN LATE June. He had just finished his freshman year at Georgia Tech, and the baseball team ended its season with a trip to the College World Series in Omaha, Nebraska. On his way to Dae's house, he passed over the bridge at Lake Gansagi. It reminded him of the many hours he and Brax had shared while leisurely paddling a canoe on the lake with Sunny along in the boat.

When he arrived, Dae gave him a big hug. "I'm so proud of you. I watched all the games and you were great."

"Well, we didn't win, but it was a good season. Can't complain about finishing fourth in the nation."

"They mentioned Rocky Ridge on TV several times, and about you and Corey being from the same town. People around here are still talking about you boys making first string as freshmen."

"In baseball, it's called being a starter."

"They're going to have a day to honor both of you. Did you know that?"

The adulation made Ty uncomfortable considering the purpose of his visit. "Dadie, let's not talk about me anymore."

Dae poured each of them a glass of Coke and led Ty into the sunroom. After a few minutes of catch-up talk, she asked, "Are you sure Dylan and his brothers are okay with this?"

"Yeah. Dad spoke with Mason and Logan. When he told them it was what Granddad wanted, they agreed we could have a share. They had their farewell at the headstone they put next to their mother's grave. I can go by myself if it's too hard on you."

"No, I'm going."

Ty led his grandmother to his truck and drove from her Lakehaven neighborhood. He passed through Rocky Ridge, followed the road alongside the Saugoochie River and onto the mountain. Near the summit, he passed the turn-off to his father's house. A mile later, he left the blacktop and onto a lightly traveled dirt road until it became no more than a trail with two tire tracks worn into the grass. When the tracks gave out, he stopped and parked. Dae gave him the bag to carry, and they walked a short distance to a clearing close by a creek.

"This is where we met," Ty said. He pointed to a place a few feet away. "There used to be a fire pit right there."

"He found the pictures here, didn't he?" Dae asked.

"In the bushes somewhere around here. Do you still stay in contact with those girls?"

"Not as often as I used to. Ivelisse lives in Manila and I chat with her on Facebook every now and then. Val and Tamika and Angel are all married and live in different parts of the U.S. They each have children of their own and they've tried to put the past behind them. That group of female lawyers in Charlotte was a godsend to them."

"I'm glad they're able to get on with their lives."

As he spoke of the Filipino girls, Ty thought about his real grandfather. The man called Banjo Bob had seemed so harmless yet had inflicted pain on four young victims that would last a lifetime. And Ty's birth father had, at the least, acted as an enabler to that pain. What a difference they were from the man he had first met where he now stood. Brax had given him the promise of love, a promise that Ty would never forget.

"It's a good little hike from here," Ty said.

"I can handle it." Dae started toward the path that ran beside the creek. "At least we'll be in the shade most of the way."

Though shielded from the glare of direct sunlight, the path was uneven and overgrown in places. Not an easy trek for an eighty year-old woman. A half mile upstream, Dae stopped and wiped her brow with a handkerchief.

Ty pointed to a large fallen tree. "Let's sit down over here."

They sat on the tree that had cracked three feet from the bottom and sloped to the ground at a long incline. For a short while, they were silent and listened to the creek rippling over a bed of small stones.

Dae took a deep breath. "The honeysuckle smells wonderful." Then she asked, "Are you and Bree serious?"

Ty wasn't sure he wanted to answer the question. He ran his hand over the tree bark. "We're only nineteen."

"Yes, you're young. You have plenty of time to understand what love is really like."

He felt slighted by her words, but didn't respond.

"I'm sorry," she said a moment later. "I didn't mean you don't know about love. But living with someone for the rest of your life is more than that."

"I know." Ty looked into Dae's eyes. "I've had some good role models."

After resting, they continued upstream. In a short time, they arrived at a spot where the creek ran between two large rocks. "This is the place," Ty said. Behind them the land rose steeply and a footpath led to the house where Dae and Brax once lived.

They walked to a grave marker and stood silently for a moment, staring at the name *Sunny* carved into the wood.

"Hello, buddy," Ty said. Without looking at Dae, he said, "I remember the first time we took him to your house on the island. He loved playing in the ocean."

Ty put a hand on the marker and the hint of a smile formed on his face. "He loved a lot of things."

Then he turned away and led Dae to the creek bank. He pulled the cloth bag from the pocket of his shorts and walked into the water. Standing ankle deep in the creek and still in his sneakers, he emptied the bag into the water and watched the ashes float away before quickly disappearing.

There were no tears. The bitter days of mourning were past and now the future rested in the sweet fruit of a life well lived.

Ty stepped onto the bank and they began the journey back.

Before they had gone far, Dae stopped.

"Can you feel his presence?" she asked.

Ty gazed at the natural world around him—the trees, the undergrowth foliage, the creatures rustling among the leaves, the pure mountain water.

"Yes," he said.

"He's still with us," Dae said. "He always will be. That's the promise of his love. You'll grow up and there will be a part of him in you. And you'll leave a part of yourself in those you love."

Ty knew she was right. Yes, Brax was still there.

And his promise would live forever.

ABOUT THE AUTHOR

 MICHAEL K. BROWN'S NOVELS EXPLORE the universal human condition with a Southern accent. He is the author of two previously published books, *Somewhere a River*—for which he was named 2015 Georgia Author of the Year—and *Promise of Silver*. The latter is the prequel to *Promise of the Hills*. Mike was born in Alabama, educated at the University of Alabama, and presently serves as President of the Atlanta Writers Club. A long-time resident of the Atlanta area, he now lives in Loganville, Georgia, with his wife Judy.

CPSIA information can be obtained at www.ICGtesting.com
Printed in the USA
LVOW11s0836270815

451749LV00002B/3/P